A Chapter of Accidents

Twenty-seven Rediscovered Stories

Written by
L. M. Montgomery

Selected & edited by
Carolyn Strom Collins

Nimbus
Publishing
nimbus.ca

Nimbus Publishing Limited
3660 Strawberry Hill Street, Halifax, NS, B3K 5A9
(902) 455-4286 nimbus.ca

Printed and bound in Canada

NB1783

Nimbus Publishing is based in Kjipuktuk, Mi'kma'ki, the traditional territory of the Mi'kmaq People.

Editor: Marianne Ward
Editor for the press: Claire Bennet
Design: Jenn Embree

The L. M. Montgomery Institute (lmmontgomery.ca) promotes research into, and informed celebration of, the life, works, culture, and influence of the Prince Edward Island-born acclaimed Canadian writer, L. M. Montgomery.

L. M. Montgomery is a trademark of Heirs of L. M. Montgomery Inc.

Library and Archives Canada Cataloguing in Publication

Title: A chapter of accidents : twenty-seven rediscovered stories / written by L.M. Montgomery ; selected & edited by Carolyn Strom Collins.
Names: Montgomery, L. M. (Lucy Maud), 1874-1942, author | Collins, Carolyn Strom, editor
Identifiers: Canadiana (print) 20250191822 | Canadiana (ebook) 20250191970 | ISBN 9781774714546 (softcover) | ISBN 9781774714553 (EPUB)
Subjects: LCGFT: Short stories.
Classification: LCC PS8526.O55 C35 2025 | DDC C813/.52—dc23

Canada NOVA SCOTIA Canada Council for the Arts Conseil des arts du Canada

Nimbus Publishing acknowledges the financial support for its publishing activities from the Government of Canada, the Canada Council for the Arts, and from the Province of Nova Scotia. We are pleased to work in partnership with the Province of Nova Scotia to develop and promote our creative industries for the benefit of all Nova Scotians.

FSC www.fsc.org MIX Paper | Supporting responsible forestry FSC® C013916

I read a story tonight. It ended unhappily. I was wretched until I had invented a happy ending for it. I shall always end my stories happily. I don't care whether it's "true to life" or not. It's true to life as it should be and that's a better truth than the other.

—L. M. Montgomery in *Emily Climbs*, chapter 16

TABLE OF CONTENTS

INTRODUCTION

In the early 1970s, a dedicated L. M. Montgomery reader and independent scholar, Rea Wilmshurst, made a trip to Prince Edward Island. One of the places she visited was Montgomery's birthplace in New London. There she found, piled in a corner, a stack of twelve scrapbooks. Intrigued, she opened them and discovered they contained clippings of hundreds of Montgomery's stories and poems that had been published in newspapers and magazines from 1890 until the mid-1900s. Montgomery herself had pasted them into the scrapbooks. Rea's curiosity was piqued—she had not known that Montgomery had written so many stories and poems in addition to the twenty novels she had published, starting with *Anne of Green Gables* in 1908.

Although Montgomery had added some of the titles of the periodicals in which the stories and poems appeared, most of the clippings in the scrapbooks had no information on the periodicals and did not include the dates they were published. Rea wondered where and when the stories and poems had appeared.

Rea soon discovered that Montgomery also kept a record of the stories and poems in a ledger, writing down the titles and how much she had been paid for each. However, she did not identify the publications themselves or the dates of publication in this ledger. Rea's detective work began. She travelled to many libraries and spent many days and hours in the collections of by then vintage periodicals. After a few years, she had identified publication information for most of the stories and poems in the scrapbooks; in the process, she also found stories and poems that were not in the scrapbooks. In 1986, her work was published as part of *Lucy Maud Montgomery: A Preliminary Bibliography*, issued by Waterloo University. In that bibliography, Rea also listed titles of works mentioned in the ledger but that she had not been able to find; in addition, she included titles that she had found in her search that were not in Montgomery's scrapbooks or ledger.

In 2016, *An Annotated Bibliography of L. M. Montgomery's Stories and Poems* (updating Rea Wilmshurst's original chronological bibliography from 1986) was published by the L. M. Montgomery Institute at the University of Prince Edward Island. A team of independent scholars in Canada, Great Britain, and the United States had identified even more sources of Montgomery's publications, including information on stories and poems that Rea had been unable to find. More sources are still being discovered from time to time. We learned that Montgomery's stories and poems were published in hundreds of periodicals, mostly in the United States and Canada; some were published simultaneously in different publications (*Forward* and *Wellspring*, for instance, and *American Agriculturist* and *New England Homestead*); others were picked up after their original publications and republished. The publications ranged from newspapers or magazines for boys, girls, and young adults to religious and general interest newspapers, women's magazines, and national, regional, and local periodicals.

About three hundred of Montgomery's five hundred stories were published before *Anne of Green Gables* made its appearance in June 1908. Her first published story, "A Baking of Gingersnaps," was published in 1895 in *Ladies' Journal*. Montgomery was paid $3. The average payment for each of her stories in the first few years was about $10; by June 1908, the average was about $34. In the last ten years of her story publishing (1926–1936), she earned an average of about $104 per story.

Nearly three hundred of Montgomery's stories have been republished, twenty-seven in Montgomery's lifetime. Since her death, 258 stories have appeared in published collections, including this one. Some of her stories were adapted for her novels, including *Anne of Green Gables*, *Anne of Windy Poplars*, *Emily of New Moon*, *The Story Girl*, and *Magic for Marigold*.

Many of Montgomery's stories and poems can be viewed in their original form in the Ryrie-Campbell Collection at the University of Prince Edward Island, online as KindredSpaces (kindredspaces.ca).

L. M. Montgomery's twelve scrapbooks are kept in the Confederation Centre archival collection in Charlottetown, Prince Edward Island. Some of the scrapbooks are displayed at the L. M. Montgomery Birthplace in New London, Prince Edward Island, when it is open during the tourist season. Her ledger is in the L. M. Montgomery Collection at the University of Guelph in Ontario.

ABOUT THE STORIES IN THIS COLLECTION

Rea Wilmshurst photocopied the stories as she found them in their original publications and included them in her files, now housed at the L. M. Montgomery Institute at the University of Prince Edward Island. When I discovered Rea's files, I wanted to share the stories she had found over the years, as well as some stories from Montgomery's scrapbooks that had not been republished since their original appearances. Those stories make up this collection, the seventeenth volume of Montgomery's stories to have been republished. (See Appendix II for a list of the books of stories.)

The twenty-seven stories in this collection were published in twenty-two periodicals from 1901 to 1932. Most were written before *Anne of Green Gables* was published in 1908; five were written within the next two years, and one was written in 1932. Nineteen of the periodicals were based in the United States, three in Canada (*East and West*, *Family Herald*, and *The Chatelaine*, precursor to today's *Chatelaine*). Some stories were published in more than one periodical. Some of the periodicals (including *The Advance*, *The Churchman*, *Boys' World*, *Children's Visitor*, and

Zion's Herald) Montgomery referred to as "Sunday school" papers and were published with a young audience in mind. Of the stories she composed for them, she wrote in her journal on August 23, 1901, that "I would like it better if I didn't have to lug a moral into most of them…like a spoonful of jam." Other periodicals (including *American Boy*, *Boys and Girls*, *The Chatelaine*, *Springfield Republican*, and *Waverly*) were independent, and Montgomery could send them her "fun for fun's sake" stories. (See Appendix I for more information on the periodicals in which the stories from this collection appeared.)

Readers may notice that in "Aunt Susanna's Thanksgiving Dinner," the feast seems to fall on a mild day, probably in October or early November, while in "Our Thanksgiving Day," there is a blizzard to contend with, likely in late November. Canadian Thanksgivings were celebrated at different times until 1957 when the second Monday in October was made the official day to celebrate. Since both of these stories were first published in American publications in November, it is likely that Montgomery tailored them to fit with their traditional Thanksgiving Day, the fourth Thursday of that month.

Most of the stories are set in Prince Edward Island, where Montgomery lived the first half of her life. One story, "A Friendship Won," is set in Western Canada. Montgomery spent a year (August 1890 to August 1891) with her father and his family in Prince Albert, Saskatchewan, and set this and a few other stories in that part of the country.

The characters in seven of these stories are young children, but the rest are a little older, from early teens to young adults in college to mature adults, and show Montgomery's ability to appeal to a variety of ages. Writing for the younger children, she used themes they could relate to, such as learning how to use their time more wisely (as in "Bessie's Dream"), resisting being envious of others (as in "Discontented Dorothy"), giving to others less fortunate (as in "In Place of Queen Mab" and "The Schoolma'am's

Donation Party"), and spreading cheer (as in "Why People Liked Amy" and "Dot's World"). The older characters in the stories deal with student rivalries (as in "Frank's Revenge" and "Ted Williams, Sneak"), which may remind readers of Anne and Gilbert's rivalry for top honours in school and college; cheating or robbery (as in "A Case of Mistaken Identity"); finding long-lost treasures (as in "The Pot of Gold at Rainbow's End" and "Our Thanksgiving Day"); keeping one's word (as in "The Word of a Kennedy"); friendships and romance (as in "A Thorny Rose" and "A Platonic Experiment"); adventure (as in "A Narrow Escape"); or overcoming challenges (as in "A Friendship Won" and "The Winning of Frances").

Quite a few of the stories highlight teachers and teaching, and many address the need to raise enough money to attend college. On the latter subject, in her story "Our Thanksgiving Day," Montgomery writes, "One of these problems was that old and exceedingly trite one, which is always figuring in stories just as it does in real life—how to get to college." Montgomery herself taught school for a few years after completing her teacher's training at Prince of Wales College in Charlottetown, PEI, and took one year of classes at Dalhousie University in Halifax, Nova Scotia, in 1895–96. Montgomery had saved a good portion of her teaching income to use for her expenses; she also received some financial help from her Grandmother Macneill. Still, she could afford only one year of college. Many college students had to struggle to find the necessary funds for tuition and room and board. Brothers Lee and Frank Taylor mull over how to pay for college in "Our Thanksgiving Day," as does Irving Kennedy in "The Word of a Kennedy," Miss Clayton in "Evangeline's Father," and Frances Porter in "The Winning of Frances." Indeed, the need for extra money figures in many of the stories collected here. Hazel Bruce in "The Chiffon Dress" has to find a job to pay for the dress she ruined. Meanwhile, Sophy Holmes is facing mounting debts and an uncertain future in "The Schoolma'am's

Donation Party," and Aunt Kitty Peterson is afraid of ending up in the poorhouse in "The Pot of Gold at Rainbow's End."

In addition to these various themes, there is also a good sprinkling of Montgomery's signature wit throughout most of the stories, notably in "A Chapter of Accidents," "Discontented Dorothy," "Aunt Susanna's Thanksgiving Dinner," and "The Letter Patricia Wrote."

Readers may notice similarities in some stories to scenes in Montgomery's novels. For instance, Montgomery entitles a chapter in *Anne of Avonlea* "A Chapter of Accidents," in which, just as in the story with the same title, several kinds of little accidents happen when company is visiting. Saving a child with a bad case of croup in "A Friendship Won" evokes chapter 18 of *Anne of Green Gables* when Anne helps treat Diana's little sister, Minnie May. Little Louise's anticipation of having "splendid times" with the new little girl next door in "In Place of Queen Mab" will surely remind readers of Anne's excitement in learning that a girl her age lives next door to Green Gables. Another nod to Anne is in "Evangeline's Father"—both Anne and Evangeline win the Avery scholarship and attend Redmond College. The physical description of Rosamond in "A Thorny Rose" is similar to the description of Kilmeny in *Kilmeny of the Orchard*. Both Rosamond and Frances (in "The Winning of Frances") have difficult personalities and must be won over, a similar situation between Anne and Katherine Brooke in *Anne of Windy Poplars*.

Montgomery read widely, and a few stories may remind readers of scenes from other authors' works. For instance, both "The Chiffon Dress" and "How Nan Went to the Party" may recall Jo March's having to wear a dress with the scorched mark of an iron to a party in chapter 3 of Louisa May Alcott's *Little Women* (1868); "Bessie's Dream" and "Discontented Dorothy" involve dreams of fairies and odd characters that are reminiscent of Lewis Carroll's *Alice's Adventures in Wonderland* (1865) and *Through the Looking-Glass, and What Alice Found There* (1871).

Whether one is a casual reader or a Montgomery scholar, reading the pieces chronologically, as presented in this volume, provides deeper insight into Montgomery's development as an author. And exploring more of her short fiction not only offers another chance to enjoy her rich array of characters and situations, but also provides further insights into this author's impressive body of work.

A NOTE ON LANGUAGE

The story "What Teddy and Gordon Saw in the Lane" includes the use of the term "Indian" to reference a game the boys are playing. This term is widely considered incorrect and offensive today. In order to preserve the text as it was originally published, I have not censored this word.

A CHAPTER OF ACCIDENTS
(1901)

It was Saturday afternoon, and I was washing up the dinner dishes in the kitchen. It was rather a late hour for washing dinner dishes, being about three o'clock; but I had been busy getting Mother ready for a shopping expedition to town and the dishes went unwashed until she got away.

Frank, my brother, who was home from college on his vacation, took her, and when I had seen them drive down the lane, I was left in sole charge. Father was cutting hay on the other farm, and our hired girl's mother had taken sick the day before, which necessitated Amanda Jane's going home to nurse her, as became a dutiful daughter. This left me with all the Saturday afternoon work to do, and as it was a very warm day, I economized heat by mixing up and baking a cake before the dinner fire went out. This, with other things, kept me busy, so that, as I have said, it was nearly three o'clock before I attacked that huge pile of greasy dishes.

It wasn't good management, I suppose—I know Aunt Marian would say so. She is one of those born managers who contrive to make everyone else feel uncomfortable in contrast with their own perfection in housekeeping matters. I shall never make a manager, I'm certain. Mother is the most patient mortal alive, and even she gave me up long ago. I can wade around and get work done in some fashion, but I never can do it systematically, and I always get myself into the most dreadful mess imaginable while I am at it. Aunt Marian, who could wash dishes and skim milk in her very best black silk without so much as flecking it, I verily believe, regards this as a striking evidence of total depravity on my part. Even Mother laments over it and says gently, "My dear, don't you think if you were more careful—"

Then she stops and sighs, as if she realizes the hopelessness of my case.

I caught a glimpse of myself in the hall mirror as I flew to and out of the dining room with the dishes, and I really had to laugh at the appearance I presented. My dark print dress was all daubed over with flour, my unruly curls were powdered with it, and there was a big blotch of stove blacking on my nose. Besides, I had contrived to tear a long rent in my apron, and had splashed my skirt carrying in a bucket of water.

"I hope nobody will come while I am in this state," I said as I dashed at the kettle. "If they do they'll likely get a shock. It's a mercy people hereabouts don't visit on Saturday afternoons. What would Aunt Marian say if she could walk in and see me now? I just think I can see her expression."

I saw it so plainly that I began to laugh while I was carrying a dipper of water, with the result that I spilled a third of it over my boots, and by the time I was through dishwashing, I had splashed myself and soaked my apron thoroughly. I was more forlorn looking than ever, and was beginning to feel dreadfully tired and impatient as well, so that when I had finished with those detestable dishes I did something that Mother is always lecturing me about, and which is really a very reprehensible practice, I admit.

I think I am cured of it now—I don't think I shall ever do such a thing again. We have two doors in our kitchen, one opens on the back veranda and the other on a little plot of green behind the house. We generally carry dishwater carefully over this, and empty it into the pig's barrel.

But, alas! I was in a tremendous hurry, so I snatched up the dishpan, flew across the kitchen, switched open the door, and threw the water out without so much as even looking, giving it an energetic swirl to send it well over the grass.

Then I saw what I had done! I wonder the awful sight didn't paralyze me. On the step before me stood a young man, who had just sprung upon it as I let the water go. He was dressed in what, two minutes before, had been an immaculate summer suit, with a natty straw hat on his head and a fawn overcoat on his arm. And the other arm had been literally drenched with dishwater.

I have no doubt that if, by any known or unknown possibility, Aunt Marian could ever be caught in such a predicament, she would carry off the situation so gracefully that it would appear that she was conferring a favour rather than not in showering a man with the contents of her dishpan.

But I shall never be worthy to untie Aunt Marian's shoe-strings, and all I could do was to drop the dishpan and stare at my unhappy victim for a few dreadful seconds; then I burst into undignified tears, and sat forlornly down on a stool by the door.

"Oh, don't!" said the stranger, in a pleasant, musical voice in which there was certainly an undertone of amusement. "Don't distress yourself. It is of no—well—I—however, it can't be helped."

"Oh, do forgive me." I sobbed hysterically. "I didn't mean to—indeed, I didn't."

This time he laughed outright.

"I am sure you didn't. It is only an accident—rather an unfortunate one, I admit. I suppose I deserve it for coming to this door. But I knocked for some time at the front door and got no answer, so I thought I would come around here, as I knew that was sometimes permissible in the country."

I wiped away my tears and stood up. I was feeling quite desperate; I didn't know what to say or do—and all the time he was standing there as calmly and composedly as if it were the most natural and agreeable thing in the world to be met with a deluge of dishwater at the threshold of a strange house.

"Oh, come in!" I said wildly. "I'm dreadfully sorry. Can I do anything? Perhaps my brother's coat would fit you—there is a suit upstairs."

"Your brother? Are you Frank's sister?"

I was sure there was a glimmer of laughter in his eyes. I remembered the splotch on my nose, my rumpled hair, and my generally disreputable appearance, and answered dolefully, as some repentant school girl might,

"Yes, sir."

"Oh, then, perhaps we are not altogether unknown to each other. Have you ever heard your brother speak of Sydney Prentice?"

If anything had been wanting to complete my humiliation, it had come now. Ever since Frank came home from college he had been singing the praises of that wonderful chum of his until I was devoured with curiosity concerning him. And now! Well, fate is a diabolical old witch!

"Oh, yes. I've heard Frank speak of you," I answered lamely. "I'm glad to see you—I mean—Frank is away, and Mother—but they will be home soon. Will you come in?"

He came in accordingly. He was undeniably handsome—tall and straight, with a crop of dark curls and merry, friendly brown eyes.

"I suppose I had better change my coat until mine is dry, if it is possible," he said ruefully. "You spoke, I think, of a suit of your brother's—"

I whisked him silently through the untidy kitchen and hall and sent him to Frank's room.

"You'll find Frank's blue suit in the closet," I said, and when he had disappeared I fled to my own room and looked at myself in the mirror. Such a sight as I must have presented to the critical eyes of the fastidious Sydney Prentice!

I tore off my disgraceful dress, washed my flushed, floury face, and combed my hair. Then I put on my prettiest muslin and went down with many inward tremors and quakings.

Mr. Prentice was down before me, and waiting in the hall. He and Frank were a good deal alike in figure and height, so that the blue coat didn't fit badly. He turned with a smile.

"I suppose I must account for my unceremonious appearance," he said gaily. "I happened to be visiting some friends at Grafton, and as I knew Frank's home was not far away, I thought I'd run over and spend Sunday with him. I walked over from the station, and having, as I have said, vainly tried the front door, I went around to the side one—"

"To be met by a deluge of dishwater," I interjected.

"Was it dishwater? I thought it seemed rather greasy. Well, what are you going to do with me?"

"Keep you until Frank and Mother come home and then flee to the uttermost parts of the earth to hide myself. I am always doing something dreadful, but this surpasses all my previous exploits. Frank will scold me terribly. I don't know how to apologize."

He laughed.

"If anybody ought to apologize, it is myself. Don't give the matter another thought, Miss Breynton, I beg you. I'll spike Frank's guns. No great harm has been done, after all; it might have been much worse."

"I don't see how it could be any worse," I said dismally.

"Why, Frank might not have had a spare coat lying around—or it might not have fitted me. Don't you admit that would have been worse?"

"Oh, I suppose so—but I think it is quite bad enough. Mother will say it is just what she expected of me. I am awfully careless, and I never seem to profit by my mistakes."

"Well, think no more about it. I'm not so badly off. Frank won't object to lending me his coat for awhile, I am sure. When do you expect him back?"

"About five o'clock."

"Well, don't let me keep you from your work. I am sure you are busy." He looked perfectly innocent, but I believed he was thinking of the disgraceful state of that kitchen, and I blushed to the eyes.

"Not very," I cried hastily. "I was only getting the Saturday baking done, and I am almost through. I hope you will amuse yourself any way you like until Frank comes to your rescue."

"Or Frank's sister. Don't desert me altogether, even if I have proved such a disturbing element to your peace of mind. I really feel as if I knew you very well. Frank used to talk about his little sister last winter in a manner calculated to make a sisterless man tear his hair for envy. Don't look upon me as a stranger. At college they call Frank and me 'the twins,' so please regard me as a sort of honorary member of the family."

His eyes twinkled as he spoke, and I blushed again. Why? I don't know. Fortunately, he turned to the shelves of my bookcase just then, and somehow we glided into a delightful conversation about our favourite authors. I had almost forgotten about the mishap, and was feeling positively animated and happy, when the sound of wheels recalled me to a sense of the stern realities of life. I excused myself and rushed to the backyard.

"Why, Mab, how blooming you look! Why all this thusness?" remarked my brother.

"Oh, Frank," I cried nervously. "Mr. Prentice is here. He came—"

I got no further, for Frank had flung the reins over the pony's back and dashed into the house.

"Oh, Mother," I said wretchedly, "I don't know what you'll say when you hear what I've done. It's dreadful, and I'm as sorry as can be, if that would mend matters. And oh, Mother! Can grease stains be taken out of a light summer coat? Can they?"

"What is the child talking about?" demanded Mother in a mystified tone. "And what is it you've done? Burnt up all the cake, I suppose."

"If it were only that! It's ten times worse."

And I confessed all. I expected a severe scolding; but I suppose I looked woebegone, and that, or something else, softened Mother's heart. She only laughed and said,

"Well, you've done it now, Mable. I do hope this will be a lesson to you. You know how often I've spoken to you about that very thing, so I don't pity you a great deal. What must Mr. Prentice think of you?"

"I don't dare to speculate. And oh! I was in such a mess myself! I looked five times worse than Amanda Jane ever did. He must have taken me for a very aggravated specimen of kitchen girl. He looked so surprised when I told him I was Frank's sister."

As we went in we heard shouts of laughter echoing through the hall, and I knew that Frank had heard the whole story. My face crimsoned with mortification, and even Mother looked as if she pitied me. But Frank and Mr. Prentice had both composed their faces by the time we got in, and not another reference was made to my misadventure that evening. I was surprised at Frank's unusual forbearance, but I guessed that his friend had something to do with it.

Mr. Prentice stayed over Sunday, and I must admit we all enjoyed his visit. When he went away on Monday morning, Mother invited him to come back again and spend a week or two with us, when his visit in Grafton was ended.

"Do come, old fellow," said Frank. "Mab won't drench you with dishwater again, I hope. She doesn't do things like that out of malice aforethought, you know. It's only her incurable carelessness. And the rest of us will try to make up for her shortcomings."

It was rather mean of Frank; but I had dreaded something worse and was thankful to be let off so easily. Mr. Prentice promised to come back. He wore his own light coat, which Mother had manipulated until it looked tolerably respectable once more, but Frank's after-remarks about the feelings of the fastidious Sydney Prentice at having to wear a coat like that made me writhe.

"One thing's plainer than a pikestaff," said my irrepressible brother, "Syd is dead gone on you. Any one could see it with half an eye. How did you do the trick? Is there any particular virtue in the application of dishwater?"

The first week passed away smoothly, and all seemed to enjoy themselves. Mr. Prentice never made any reference to his ducking, but I could not hope he had forgotten it, and every now and then I had a spasm of discomfort at the recollection.

One afternoon, Frank and Mr. Prentice drove over to call at Lilac Villa. The Vaughans lived at Lilac Villa, and Frank was badly smitten with Fanny Vaughan that summer.

Mr. Prentice did not seem particularly anxious to go, and put forth several excuses, but Frank overruled them and dragged him off.

When they had gone Mother said,

"This is a good chance, Mab, for you to wash the storeroom windows. I was looking at them this morning. The flies have specked them disgracefully. Take this bucket of warm water, and don't make a mess on the floor."

I was tired and warm, and didn't like washing windows; but there was no way out of it, so I took the pail and went up the back stairs to the storeroom.

This was a big room over the kitchen, with five large windows; it was no easy task to wash them all and leave them as spotless and shining as Mother would demand. I did them painstakingly, and when I got through I was as tired and cross as any one could be.

"I'm not going to carry this rinsing water down those narrow stairs again," I said, viciously, as I wiped up some dribbles that in spite of my pains had got on the floor. "I shall just open the end window and fling it out. I don't care if Mother does see me."

I did take the precaution, though, to poke my tumbled head out first and make sure that no one was within drenching distance. Then I marched across the storeroom, grasped my pail, returned, and tilted it over the sill, sending a cataract of warm fluid downwards. I heard a smothered exclamation below, and a shout in Frank's tones, and, popping my head out, I saw a harrowing sight.

Right below the window stood Sydney Prentice, dripping with water. Frank was a little way behind him, doubled up with laughter. They had come around the corner while I was crossing the room, and of course Sydney Prentice must be there at the precise moment I emptied that water out, when I supposed him safely at Lilac Villa, three miles away.

I saw it all in a dash, for I didn't stay there looking. I sprang back, slammed down the window, and began to cry.

I heard them come laughing into the kitchen below, and presently Frank came rushing up the stairs. But I wasn't ready to face him, so I plunged down behind some bags of feathers in a remote corner, and lay there while he hunted for me.

When he had gone down again concluding I had made good my escape, I crawled out, my hair and dress white with down, and sat huddled up on a chair, sobbing until Mother came up about half an hour afterward.

She was wonderfully kind and didn't scold me. I suppose hers was the patience born of despair.

"Why don't you come down, Mable; Mr. Prentice is asking for you."

"Do you suppose I can ever face him again?" I cried. "No, not for worlds! What must he think of me?"

Mother laughed.

"He seems to regard it as a huge joke—very good of him, too, I think. Child, why will you be so careless?"

"I tried to be careful," I protested, "and what business had he to be prowling about when everyone thought he was at Lilac Villa!"

"The girls were not at home, so the boys did not stay. What a little goose you are to sit crying here! Mr. Prentice knows it was an accident. Go and wash your face and comb your hair and come down."

"I can't, Mother," I declared positively. "I don't care whether he thinks it is a joke or not. I don't. You needn't say anything, for wild horses wouldn't drag me into his presence again."

"You ridiculous child! What sense is there in taking it so to heart? And how are you going to keep out of his way a whole week?"

"I'll not be here," I said, firmly. "I shall go right off tomorrow morning on the early train, before anyone is up. Aunt Ruth has been coaxing for me all summer, so I'll go now. You have Amanda Jane, and the haying is over, so you can do without me."

"Now, Mabel," said Mother severely. "I am surprised at this. This is nonsense. What will Mr. Prentice think if you run away like that?"

"It doesn't matter what he thinks—he won't think anything at all except that there will be no danger of his being ducked a third time. I shan't be running away from him; he's visiting Frank, not me."

Mother smiled peculiarly. That ruffled me still more.

"A nice goose I've made of myself. Yes, I'm going right off. I shall stay here until he and Frank are out of the way, and then I shall go and pack up."

"Well, you can do as you like, Mabel. I think you are behaving very rudely and very foolishly as well, and you will be sorry for it. Since you will go, go. I daresay Mr. Prentice will console himself at Lilac Villa."

I made no answer; but Mother's parting shot disturbed me not a little, although it did not shake my determination. Lou Vaughan was a perfectly correct young lady, who would never be guilty of my shortcomings; and she was very handsome, too.

Early next morning, before Frank or Mr. Prentice were up, I drove to the station and boarded the morning train. It was only twenty miles to Bridgeport, where Aunt Ruth lived, so I walked in upon them before their breakfast dishes were fairly out of the way.

The girls welcomed me jubilantly, and I unpacked and settled down for my visit with a sigh, partly of relief and partly of something else.

That evening, when I was sitting at the parlour window in the dusk, a bicycle wheeled up to the front gate; the rider dismounted therefrom and swung the gate open with a triumphant click of the latch. It was Sydney Prentice.

I sprang up with a wild impulse to run; but it was too late for that. He had already passed up between the geranium beds and was at the front door. My cousin answered the bell and ushered him into the parlour. Dot discreetly vanished and I was left to meet the situation.

"Mr. Prentice!" I said, helplessly.

"At your service," he answered cheerfully. "Do you know what I've come for, Mab?"

"To give me your opinion of girls who seem to make a hobby of drenching unfortunate men," I responded, with a weak attempt at hilarity.

"Not at all. I merely rode over this trifle of twenty miles on the worst bicycle road in the world to ask what you meant by running away from White Maple Farm in this unceremonious fashion, and leaving me to Frank's tender mercies. What did you think I would do with myself while he was away at Lilac Villa? Why, it was adding insult to injury. Wasn't it bad enough to duck a fellow when he wasn't dreaming of it without decamping afterwards and never even waiting to see if he caught his death of cold from the shower bath?"

"It was warm," I said, feebly; and then my little pretense of composure quite failed me, and I slipped humbly down in the corner of the sofa. "Oh, I felt so mortified I couldn't bear to face you after it, Mr. Prentice," I murmured, and in spite of my efforts there would come a quiver in my voice. "I was so careless. I don't know what you must think of me."

"Shall I tell you what I think of you?" he asked in a low tone.

I scented danger and straightened up hastily.

"No, never mind. It must be something very uncomplimentary, I know. What did Frank say?"

"Never mind what Frank said. I'm the injured party and I want satisfaction. I think, if it is my opinion you are anxious about, that you are the dearest little girl in the world, and I know, without any thinking about it, that I love you dearly, and will be the happiest man alive if you'll marry me. Will you, dear?"

He was on the sofa beside me by this time, and somehow my hands were held in his. And all I could say, with something between a laugh and a sob, was—

"Aren't you afraid I'll drown you sometime?"

"I'll risk it," he declared.

And I took his word for it.

A CASE OF MISTAKEN IDENTITY
(1902)

Burnham and I had arranged to watch in the barn for oat stealers that night. In common with many other Danford farmers, we had suffered all winter from sundry raids on our oat bins.

We strongly suspected the Lackeys of being thieves. Luke Lackey's brood of lazy, hulking boys was the plague of the village. But we had no proof of their guilt, so we hoped to catch them red-handed.

It was in early March. That day, a raw, northeast wind was blowing up over the ice, with the threat of a snowstorm in its breath. In the afternoon, Father started for Selkirk, ten miles distant, with a load of pork for market. As the road was in very bad condition, owing to several recent thaws, he decided to go by the ice, although it was rumoured to be getting very unsafe.

During the day, the wind came around to the northwest and the indications of a storm passed away, but the night was very dark. We expected Father back by nine, but at half-past nine, when Burn and I went out to the barn, he had not come. We did not feel anxious, however; very likely, we thought, as it had cleared up, Father would come by the road and in that case, would be about two hours late.

The barn was quite a long distance from the house. We decided to crawl into the dark corner between the wheat bin and the wall, close to the oat room door. Then, if an oat stealer came, we would let him go into the oat room, and while he was scooping up the oats we could slip from our hiding place, shut the door, and shoot the bar into place. Our thief would then be snugly caged, for the only window in the oat room was a small round one high up near the ceiling.

We arranged the bar in readiness, put out our lantern, and crept in behind the wheat bin.

The time passed slowly. The night was cold and we grew chill and cramped. At about twelve, as we thought—later we discovered it was only eleven—we decided nobody was coming after oats that night.

"Let us go in," I said, shivering. Then I started. "What's that?"

A door had opened and shut gently. Then we heard footsteps crossing the floor. Directly across from our lair was the window in front of the barn. As the form of the midnight intruder paused at the oat room door, it stood out dimly at the faint square of light—the figure of a tall, muffled-up man. Luke Lackey himself!

The next minute he had passed through the door and closed it behind him. This was better luck than we had hoped for. We rose softly and without the least noise shot the strong wooden bar into place.

Burn gave a soundless chuckle.

"Not a squeak, Milt," he whispered, "just let him find out for himself how snugly he is caged."

We tiptoed away, slipped out the side door, and ran down to the house. As we went in, the clock struck eleven.

Mother was watching at the window, looking out on the bay. She turned at our entrance and said in a troubled voice:

"Boys, your father has not got back yet. What could be the matter?"

Burn and I grew sober instantly. Eleven o'clock and Father not back! All remembrance of Luke Lackey went out of our heads like a flash.

"You stay with Mother, Milt," said Burn. "I'll run over to Uncle Sam's. Father may have called there on his way home."

When Burn came back with Uncle Sam, the latter looked very much alarmed.

"What's this, Mary? Robert not home yet! That's strange. But he may have come around by the road."

"Even so he would have had time to be home before this," answered Mother. "No, Samuel. I'm convinced Robert has got in the ice."

"Not a bit of it," returned Samuel with assumed confidence. "Robert's too old a hand on the ice to get trapped. Still, we'll start off and see if we can find him. I've got my mare and cutter right here—just got home from the Corners when Burnham came in. Burn, you'd better stay with your mother, and Milton will come with me. We'll meet your father or pull him out of a spring hole if he has got into one."

In a short time uncle and I were on the ice.

"Keep a sharp lookout on your side, Milton," said uncle. "Halloo every few minutes. I don't like the look of things, I must say. Robert was foolish to go by the ice. I told him so when he left. We'll have to look out we don't get in ourselves. Lucky the moon's just up. Hall-o-o-o!"

The tones of uncle's powerful voice rang far out over the glimmering whiteness of the bay and echoed back to us, in mocking elf-like intonations from the distant islets. But no answering human voice responded.

We kept a sharp watch and shouted every few minutes. Once the mare put her foot through a bit of rotten ice, but uncle pulled her up quickly and we got over it in safety. It was about six miles across, and we took an hour to make it. On the farther side we roused up the inhabitants of a little shanty to inquire but could learn nothing. Three miles up the road we got our first trace of Father.

"Robert Stearns?" said the gaunt farmer whom we had roused from his hard-earned slumbers. "Yes, he passed here about eight o'clock, or maybe half-past. Said he intended crossing from Glover's Point. I told him 'twasn't safe. There's a dozen oyster beds near that route. Sure's you live, he's got in."

It looked like it indeed.

"We must go back home," said Uncle Sam slowly. "He may have gone around by the road after all and be home this very minute. If not, we'll rouse the neighbours and search for him. Cheer up, Milt."

It was all very well for Uncle Sam to say "cheer up," but I could not do it. A horrible dread was upon me as we drove back over the silent, pitiless expanse of ice. Through the darkness I seemed to see a vision of my father struggling in the black, icy waters that were closing over his head.

When we reached home, Mother and Burn rushed wildly out, and we knew Father was not there. I groaned aloud.

"None of that, Milton," said uncle sternly. "This is no time to give up. No, Mary, we saw nothing of him—but Saul Peterby at the Seven Mile farm said he intended to cross from Glover's Point. We can't do anything until daylight. Burnham and I will go over to the Corners and get Si Warren. He knows the exact whereabouts of every oyster bed in the bay. Warm yourself well, Milton. You are chilled through."

In half an hour Uncle Sam and Burn were back with Si Warren, a weather-beaten old oysterman, with a face as brown and wrinkled as an old walnut shell. Aunt Meg had also come over to keep Mother company. We hung about restlessly, waiting for the dawn, while old Si told numberless anecdotes about hairbreadth escapes on the ice, none of which tended to cheer us much.

At last the first faint ashen white of morning was whitening over the dim world.

"Now, Milton," said Uncle Sam as he gulped down the steaming hot cup of tea Aunt Meg handed him, "Si and Burn and I will go this time. We'll not come back without news one way or the other. There is not much doubt that your father has got into the ice, but it's just as likely he's got out again. Men get into the ice every week of the winter. We'll probably find him getting dried at some house along the shore. You stay here and look after your mother and take care of the stock when it gets clear daylight."

I suppose it was uncle's mention of the stock that reminded me of the unfortunate oat stealer shut up in the barn all that cold winter night.

I had forgotten Luke Lackey completely. It seemed a lifetime since Burn and I had imprisoned him. My start of recollection seemed to touch the same spring in Burn's memory.

"I declare, Milt, what about Luke Lackey? I'd clean forgotten him. He'll be half frozen."

"Luke Lackey? What's this?" cried Uncle Sam impatiently.

In as few words as possible we told our story.

"The man will be half-dead with cold," said uncle. "I should think he has been punished enough. We must go and let him out, of course. A few minutes more or less now can't make any difference."

We all hastened to the barn. The great building was silent and still. We hurried to the oat room door, slipped back the bar, and opened it.

A figure, sitting on an inverted half-bushel measure, rose stiffly up. Burn held the lantern aloft and the light fell over the prisoner.

It was—Father!

Burn dropped the lantern promptly and it went out, leaving us in gloom. Si Warren said, "Well, I'm blessed," with tremendous emphasis, and Uncle Sam muttered something that sounded like "Thank the Lord."

The next thing I remember clearly is that we were all outside in the white light, with Father in the centre of the group, all talking and explaining at once, while Mother and Aunt Meg came running up the yard.

Afterwards, while father was thawing himself out at the fire, the rest of us stopped talking and gave him a chance to say something.

He had been detained at Selkirk longer than he expected, so that it was dark when he reached the ice. He had intended to cross from Glover's Point but at the last moment changed his mind and came around by the road.

This kept him so late that it was nearly eleven when he reached home. He had no bells and had come across the fields by a road that passed neither the house nor the barn, which accounted for our not having heard him. He had driven directly to the carriage house, about halfway between, left the sleigh there, and then stabled the horse. Finally he went to the barn for some oats. He had forgotten all about oat stealers and our self-appointed police duty but remembered both when he found himself securely imprisoned. He shouted himself hoarse for a while, but Burn and I were both out of hearing—for, as I have said, the barn was a long distance from the house, and nobody had gone near the farm the whole night.

"At last I resigned myself to spending the night in jail," said Father. "I thought I might escape freezing and supposed I would be found sometime."

"We took you for Luke Lackey," said Burn, "and then we got such a fright that it went clean out of our heads."

"And here we've been driving over the ice like mad half the night," said Uncle Sam, "thinking you were at the bottom of the bay—and you locked up in the barn for stealing your own oats."

"Well, there's not much harm done, I hope, beyond the loss of our night's sleep," said Father cheerfully. "Only next time, be sure of your thief, boys. You haven't caught him yet."

And we never did. But no more of our oats disappeared, for the story got out and the guilty persons took warning thereby. Burn and I haven't heard the last of it this day, and every time old Si Warren sees us, he asks us if we've been stalking oat stealers since.

WHEN HEARTS ARE TRUMPS
(1902)

Dave Morris had just returned from the mill, whither he had gone with wheat in the morning. It was late in the afternoon, and he was doing the chores and attending to the farm stock in the listless, mechanical way of one who does not care what he does. Dave certainly took little interest just then in anything apart from his own trouble. He went to and fro, through barn and yard, with slow step and sullen face. The little black mare missed her usual petting; his dog slunk away from the unwonted surliness of his tone.

He was a tall, good-looking young fellow, with a certain manliness of bearing; his eyes, though darkened just then by some suppressed feeling, were frank blue ones, and his hair curled thickly over his tanned forehead.

The sun was beginning to hang low when he finished his work, but instead of going into the house he went dejectedly and sat down on the woodpile. The sun was hidden behind the spruces at his back, but the sky above the treetops was a lovely creamy gold; the long stretches of snowy fields glowed pink in the light. Far down, at the end of the slope, he saw the sea, deeply azure between the floating masses of white ice. Far out, the sky, paling to a ghostly blue, met the white floe. But Dave had no eyes for all these things. He sat with his chin in his hands and stared moodily out over the cold Atlantic.

His father was looking at him from the kitchen window. He was a handsome, ruddy old man, with a magnificent white beard and keen, unyielding eyes. He peered out from the frosted pane with an amused, sarcastic smile.

"Dave thinks he's pretty badly used, doesn't he now?" he said aloud. "Well, I s'pose it is rather hard on him. But there has to be some end to this way of living. I've said so and I'll stick to it. Dave will find I meant every word of it. I wonder what went wrong between him and Lois? They're both pretty high-spirited—wouldn't care much what they said when they got stirred up. If Dave has any sense, this will drive him to go and make up with her. Anyhow, I wish he'd give up his sulking and come in and get tea."

Dave still sat on the woodpile. Only once had he lifted his eyes from the sea to the long stretches of gently swelling hills. Then he frowned and looked back to the ice floe as if even that were pleasanter to his eyes. Far over on the farthest hill, peeping out from a grove of birches whose white stems gleamed in the rosy light, was a handsome farmhouse whose windows, reflecting the sunset, were all ablaze. Perhaps they dazzled Dave's eyes that he turned them away so quickly. There may have been another reason; it was Lois Harding's home, and once there had been no more welcome visitor there than himself—he who was now forbidden to cross its threshold.

How well he knew that long lane of birch trees! Many a night had "Lottie" been stabled in that big barn while her master sat in the "front room" and talked to Lois about "socials" and parties and other village happenings.

Dave was reviewing his past life with more intent and earnest scrutiny than he had ever bestowed on it before. He saw himself first as a curly-headed schoolboy; he remembered the old schoolhouse where he and Beecher McQuarrie had always sat behind Rene Moore and Lois Harding—Rene, a pale, reserved little girl who never got into scrapes, and Lois, with her head of fair, tumbled curls, mischievous eyes, and teasing tongue, who was on the floor for misconduct half the time.

He had liked Rene best then, and used to carry her books and sharpen her pencils. And when he got to be eighteen, and thought himself grown up, he went home with her from singing school and took her sleigh-driving on moonlit nights. Lois had left Hope Bay then to attend school in a distant city. They had almost forgotten her in three years, so that her homecoming the previous winter had made quite a sensation in Hope Bay.

Dave had first met her at a little party. He had never been "much of a fellow with girls," as his companions said, but he had outgrown his shyness with them; therefore, he could not understand why he was so hopelessly confused when Lois came to speak to him. When it was over, and she had turned to greet Beecher McQuarrie, Dave, red-faced and nervous, retreated to a corner, where he looked her over in amazement.

How she had changed! She had grown slim and tall; her fair hair had darkened to a glistening brown and was drawn up in a strange, pretty knot on her head; her silver-grey gown, with its touch of crimson, had something about it foreign to Hope Bay dressmakers. But still the laughing blue eyes, the little ringlets curling above her arched eyebrows, and the quick, dimpled smiles were the same.

Dave felt annoyed to see how constantly Beecher stuck to her side. He himself did not venture to approach her during the whole evening, but when the party broke up and the guests went laughing out into the frosty moonshine, he reached Lois first and they walked home together across the white fields. That was in March, and from then on through the summer, Dave was as her shadow. The neighbours had ceased to gossip about them, regarding their marriage as a settled affair.

But it was very far from being so. Lois was always charming and friendly but very noncommittal, and Dave, straightforward as he was, could not venture to put his fate to the test.

And then came their foolish, bitter quarrel—a quarrel that began in so little and ended in so much. Both lost temper beyond finding, and when Lois, with anger-darkened eyes and cheeks aflame, pointed to the door and said, "Go!," Dave had not waited for a second bidding. That was in October; it was March now, and since then he had never crossed the threshold of the Harding homestead.

After their first anger had cooled, Lois and Dave were outwardly friendly; in their occasional meetings they were icily polite. But the old comradeship was gone completely, and Dave realized it.

He concluded his musings with a long sigh just as he became conscious of a figure coming toward him from the lane. The newcomer had a freckled, good-natured face and smiling light eyes. His trig, navy-blue reefer coat and long black overalls drawn up to his thighs gave him a boyish appearance. He carried two or three straws in his hands and was chewing on another. Dave smiled. When was Beecher McQuarrie not chewing straws! He hardly knew whether he was glad to see him just then or not. Beecher was not promising material for a confidant, and Dave wanted one.

The two had been chums from boyhood, and it was always a sort of standing wonder in Hope Bay that it should be so—they were so totally unlike in every respect. Beecher was such a "trot-around" fellow, with a stock of thin, funny sayings; besides, he was an inveterate gossip.

But the McQuarrie and the Morris farms joined, running side by side from the woods at the back down to the blue shore of the gulf, and so Dave and Beecher had grown up together. They had coasted in winter on "the hilly Morris field" and skated on "McQuarrie's swamp"; they had "trouted" up the brooks and gone together to school. When they grew up they went driving in partnership to concerts and socials; and when they were ploughing in adjoining fields, it was pleasant and convenient to rest their horses frequently at the line fence while they chatted over it.

Beecher came over and sat down beside Dave on the log.

"Hullo!" he said. "Thought you'd a been over this afternoon. What you been doing?"

"Was to the mill," said Dave, dully. "I felt kind of tired when I got back. Got any news, Beech?"

"Naw, not much. Hope Bay is getting to be a regular dry old place now."

"M'm," assented Dave, indifferently.

Beecher went on chewing straws and detailing small bits of gossip. Dave said "M'm" and "Yes?" at regular intervals, but at last Beecher awoke to the fact that he was doing all the talking.

"Say, Dave, what's wrong with you tonight?"

"I dunno," said Dave, stupidly. "Nothing that I know of. Why?"

"Well, one can't get a word out of you. All you do is grunt. What is the matter?"

This was Dave's opportunity. He was aching to unburden himself and get advice, so he plunged in desperately.

"Well, everything seems to be going wrong just now, and has been ever since Kate got married. You see, when she wanted to marry Allan, Father hadn't any objection to him, but he didn't see how we could get on without a housekeeper, so he just asked me plump and plain if I was expecting to get married, 'cause, you see, I was—thought—it looked—" Dave broke through helplessly, then gathered his wits together and went on recklessly, "Well, it doesn't matter. I was fool enough to say I was, and then he said Kate could please herself. Kate waited till Christmas and then got married. And you may believe I hadn't much thought of marrying then, because—well, because I hadn't. Anyhow, Father didn't say anything, just a hint or two, and we worried along last month some way or another—pretty queer housekeeping, I guess," with a grim smile, "but I did my best. I didn't like it any better than Father did; but you know what he is—must have everything as neat as wax and his meals just so. I tell you, Beecher, things got pretty well mixed up, and last night Father and I had a regular row. He ended up by saying that he wasn't going to stand this way of living any longer, and that if I wouldn't get married, he would. He said Ellen Ramsay would take him tomorrow. That's no news; everyone knows she would; but I might as well pick up and go if that old tartar comes here. And Father means it, too. If I go against him, he'll never forgive me. But I'm not going to give in. It's a pretty hard position for a fellow to be in when he's done his best and can't help the way things turn out."

Beecher had listened with such intentness that he quite forgot his straw. When Dave concluded he drew a long breath.

"Well, by George! What notion on airth has struck the old chap! Is he loony or what!"

Dave winced slightly. Angry as he was with his father, he did not like to have others abuse him. And there was something absurd in hearing the dignified old man alluded to as "the old chap." It jarred on him.

"You can't blame him," he said resentfully. "'Tisn't very nice for a man like him to be living as we are now."

"Oh, of course," assented Beecher, "I ain't blaming him; but it's kinder sudden for you, Dave. What'll you do?"

"Dunno."

"Does he want you to take anyone in particular?"

Dave had left that part out. He filled it in shamefacedly.

"Well, not exactly—but he hinted at Rene Moore; and I s'pose she is about the only one round here to mention."

Beecher whistled.

"Whew! Rene? Well, Rene's a nice girl." Dave wriggled uneasily. "But I know a nicer. What's the matter with Lois Harding, now?"

Beecher leered at Dave with a look of great slyness.

"Shut up!" said the latter with a sudden anger. "You know Lois wouldn't look at me."

"Well, don't eat me, Dave! How was I to know? You and Lois used to be chummy enough. Did you quarrel?"

"Yes."

"How'd it happen?"

Dave hesitated a moment and then went on.

"Oh, I dunno hardly how it started. I guess Lois wanted to pick a row. You know that concert over at Hillsboro last October? I'd been so used to taking Lois everywhere that I didn't think it was necessary to ask her in so many words to go. But when I drove up for her, she was gone with that young doctor over at Lilyvale. I tell you, I was pretty mad. But I didn't say nothing, and next night I went up to see Lois as usual. I wasn't intending to say a word about it, but she spoke of the concert and said it was good; then, quite sassy, 'Particular as I had such a pleasant companion,' says she. I got on my dignity a bit, for all I thought she was only teasing me, and said it was a pity she didn't have him all the time since he was so captivating. And Lois says, 'I was just thinking so myself.' And 'pon my word, Beech, for my life, I can't tell how it was, but we both kept on saying things and getting spicier and spicier, and finally it ended up in her just telling me to go. There, that's the whole story."

"Those girls beat all!" said Beecher, sagely. "You can never tell what they'd be at. But see here, Dave! Can't you make it up with Lois?"

"Yes, mebbe," said Dave, scornfully. "Did anyone ever hear of Lois making up when once she got real mad?"

"Naw," admitted Beecher, "but that's no reason why you shouldn't be the first. There always has to be a beginning to everything."

Dave shook his head and kicked a chip. Then he said,

"Now, Beech, what would you do in my place?"

"Oh, if it comes to what I'd do, why, I'd just take Rene mighty quick and be thankful. We all know Rene wouldn't object to you. A nice, smart, good-looking girl—and old Moore has money, too! What more would any reasonable fellow want?"

"But I don't care two chips for Rene," protested Dave.

"You like her, don't you?"

"Yes, of course; but—"

"Well, I'm sure that's all that's necessary."

Dave felt it useless to argue the point with one of Beecher's mould. He did not answer. Beecher got up and began to pick the scraps of straw from his blue reefer. Dave also got up.

"Going?" he said.

"Yes, guess I must. Come over when you make up your mind and let me know. I advise you to go in for Rene. Well, so long!"

He started off across the fields. Dave went with him as far as the line fence and watched him out of sight behind the trees. He leaned there till the sun went down and the snow seemed of a chill bluish tinge. Then he went in and got tea. After tea he went upstairs and dressed himself in his best. When he went out into the bright moonlight, his father watched him from the window until he saw that his son had taken the road to Silas Moore's. Then he went back to his pipe and his newspaper.

That was Tuesday night; on Wednesday Dave went to see Rene again, and on Thursday night he drove her home from prayer meeting. Friday he took her to a lecture at Lilyvale.

Saturday was still clear and frosty. Dave finished up his chores just before sundown, and, not knowing exactly what to do with himself, decided to walk down the road as far as the blacksmith's forge. The road had been drifted full of banks in a storm the preceding week, and though the track had been broken, the walking was still very bad. Dave stalked unconcernedly through the holes and pitches until he suddenly became aware that a girl was coming swiftly down a lane a few feet further on.

It was Lois Harding. The whistle died on Dave's lips, and a deeper colour leaped into his frost-reddened cheek. For a second he halted, and his vague impulse was to turn and go back. Then he called himself a fool and resolved to walk deliberately on. He did not wish to meet Lois just then, of all times, but he would not let her know that. So he went steadily ahead and reached the end of the lane just as Lois came out of it on the road.

"Good evening," said Dave, stiffly.

He was thinking how pretty she looked. She had a pink "fascinator" wound around her head; her curly hair clustered about it, and her eyes were shining like twin stars. The cold, and perhaps something else, had deepened the pink in her round cheeks to crimson.

"Good evening," she said easily.

Her manner was less formal than his. They found themselves walking down the road together.

"The walking's awful down here," said Dave, looking ahead at the long line of jogged banks and the track, full of holes. "It isn't fit for you to be on this road."

"It is bad," admitted Lois, "but the north and south road is good. It is only this piece as far as the turn that is bad. I was just up seeing Aunt Emma's folks."

Dave could not think of anything else to say. He wondered if Beecher or anyone else had told Lois anything. He felt very uncomfortable. A long silence ensued as they stumbled on. Presently Lois said suddenly,

"Dave, I hear you're going to be married."

Dave was taken by surprise; he started and turned very red, but he managed to say constrainedly, with a feeble attempt at carelessness,

"You don't say! That's a dreadful report to be spreading on a fellow."

"Yes," said Lois, airily. "I suppose it is true, then?"

Dave gave a stiff little laugh.

"Now do you really think a sober-going fellow like me would do such a wild thing?"

"Would you call getting married a wild thing?" asked Lois, innocently.

"Well, would you?"

"Oh, well, I suppose it would depend on circumstances." She gave him a teasing look. "In your case, now, I'd say it was the most sensible thing you could do."

Dave crimsoned still deeper. So she knew all about it! Well, he might have expected it.

"Who told you?" he said angrily. "But there's no need to ask. Of course it was that blatter-tongue up there," with a jerk of his hand toward the McQuarrie homestead.

Lois nodded.

"Yes. Beecher was at our house last night and told your tale of woe. Poor Dave!"

He winced at her mocking tone.

"I suppose," he said sarcastically, "he didn't leave anything for me to tell. Guess he informed you who the bride was and the day of the wedding and all!"

Lois nodded.

"Oh, yes. Trust Beecher for that. He always tells all he knows and a little more."

There was only one field's length now between them and the corner where the road turned at right angles. Dave scrutinized both; the field was not drifted, and the snow was not deep.

"Suppose we cut across," he suggested. "It's better walking."

They went through a gap into the field. Lois picked up the thread of the conversation again.

"I hope you'll ask me to the wedding, Dave—that is, get Rene to ask me. She would like to have me there, I think."

She looked wickedly at him as she pronounced the name. He would not notice it. He looked stolidly before him.

"If you'd wanted to, Lois, you might have been at my wedding before now and not as a guest, either," he said bluntly. His patience was getting frayed.

"Oh, indeed!" said Lois, trying to be unconcerned. "This is the first I've heard of it."

"Would it have made any difference if you had heard it before?" demanded Dave, bitterly, not as if he expected an answer, but merely as an indirect reproach.

"Perhaps it might have," faltered the girl with the downcast eyes.

They had reached the fence. Before them, on the other side, ran the smooth level road with the runner tracks stretching far into the distance like glistening satin ribbons. But neither made any motion to climb the fence. At Lois's words, Dave had stopped and put one hand firmly on her shoulder. A sleigh came by just then, and its occupants, two roguish-eyed boys, looked curiously at the pair. One clicked his tongue suggestively against his teeth. Lois crimsoned and tried to move toward the fence, but Dave held her back.

"Lois, did you mean that?" he questioned soberly.

"Yes—I—I—guess so," she said hesitatingly.

Her face was turned from him, but something in her voice encouraged Dave. He became eager and confused, and could not for his life find words.

"Oh, Lois, will you—will you?" he said with eloquent breathlessness.

Lois looked at him now with laughing eyes. Since he had fairly got to the point, it would have delighted her to tease him for a while. But a silver tinkle of bells up the road betokened the approach of another sleigh, and she was bound to get over that fence before it passed. She put her foot on the lowest log.

"Lois!" said Dave, imploringly.

She looked over her shoulder at him.

"Seeing you're in such a fix, Dave," she said. "I guess—yes, I will! There!"

She was over the fence like a bird, and at the edge of the track before he could follow her. He scrambled over and got to her side just as the sleigh passed. The occupant was Beecher McQuarrie. He had been down to the forge and was now going over to Lilyvale to see his girl. His sleigh was full of fur robes, and his sleek bay horse had rosettes of ribbon behind his ears. Beecher nodded at the pair with a quizzical look and a "Fine evening."

Neither had composure enough to answer. After he had passed, Beecher deliberately turned his head around and watched them. Thus surveyed, Dave could only be strictly businesslike.

"Lois, you don't know how happy you've made me! I've been awful miserable every way. I suppose that scamp there told you all about how I'm situated just now, so you'll understand how it is if I ask you to marry me soon."

Lois nodded.

"So I'm to be at your wedding after all, Dave. I didn't expect it half an hour ago. Would you have believed that the world could change so in half an hour! But I know pretty well how matters are with you, and so—well, if you can wait a month longer, I must have that much time."

But Dave was looking at Beecher. The latter had at last reached the turn of the road, and, however unwilling he might be to lose sight of the interesting pair, he was obliged to turn down and disappear behind a grove of spruce. Then Dave took Lois in his arms and kissed her.

"Oh, Lois dear," he whispered, "I love you so! Tell me, don't you care a little bit for me?"

Lois turned her face to him, and the happy light in her blue eyes was his answer. And they went together down the shining silver road, while the setting sun cast cold rose lights across the fields, and now and then came to their ears, with sweet, far-off distinctness, the tinkle of sleigh bells among the snowy hills.

THE SCHOOLMA'AM'S DONATION PARTY

(1903)

Miss Holmes fluttered along the one street of Middle Millerton that straggled over two hills and a bridge. A gusty wind was whirling the crinkled maple leaves around her, and in her brown dress and fluttering cape, she looked as much like a scurrying leaf on a large scale as anything you can imagine.

Just across the river, two girls were talking together at the gate of Dr. Putnam's house. Jess Putnam and Alberta Reid were inseparable chums. Their clear laughter echoed down the hill and struck on Miss Holmes's ears as she crossed the bridge. She shivered as if something hurt her, and her lips trembled.

As she passed the girls they both called out a good-evening. They had been her pupils for ten years in the little yellow schoolhouse beyond the second hill, and though they had left school two years ago, they loved Miss Holmes still, as all her scholars did.

Miss Holmes only nodded and passed on. Other evenings she would have lingered for a chat, but now she went straight along, under the bare maples, past the two rival Middle Millerton stores and the Methodist church, with its graveyard around it, until she came to a little yellow house, set back from around the corner of a maple grove.

On the flat doorstone an old, glossy-brown dog was sitting patiently. He thumped his tail with joy when Miss Holmes came around the maples. She always had a pat and a good word for him to warm up the cockles of his faithful, doggish heart. Tonight she did not even see him, although she half stumbled over him. She opened the door and went in, shutting him out in spite of his imploring whine. Boxer could not understand it at all. He felt heartbroken and there was dejection in every kink and curve of his body as he lay patiently down on the cold doorstone again. If the next-door cat, whom Boxer hated with all his power, had appeared just then she might have sharpened her claws upon his very back without let or hindrance. Boxer was too crushed to care how impertinent she might be.

The little kitchen into which Miss Holmes stepped was unlighted, save by a fire that was sputtering and crackling in a companionable way: Aunt Gina was sitting before it, with her hands folded, humming a hymn tune to herself. "Sophy, child, is it you? I didn't expect you home so soon. Didn't you go up to see Mrs. Allen?"

Aunt Gina always called Miss Holmes "child," although the latter was forty.

"No, I didn't," said Miss Holmes weakly. "I called at the post office and I couldn't go any further. Oh, Aunt Gina!"

The long-repressed tears came at last and trickled through Sophy's fingers as she buried her face in her thin hands. Aunt Gina was frightened. Something terrible must have happened when plucky little Sophy cried. In all her life Aunt Gina remembered seeing Sophy cry on only three occasions. One was when her mother died; the second was when Charlie went out West; and the third when Boxer got his leg broke and everybody said he would have to be shot. But Boxer had not been shot and his leg was set, and since then Sophy had never cried—before Aunt Gina at any rate.

"Sophy, dear heart, what is the matter? Is it—did that horrid, red-headed Fraser boy raise a rumpus in school again today? 'Tisn't worth crying over if he did. Them Frasers were always the pig-headedest, impudentest lot that ever was born. That old father of his was the only man I ever hated."

In spite of her tears Sophy had to smile over the idea of Aunt Gina hating anybody.

"No, it isn't Dan Fraser this time. It's only—I got a letter from Charlie at the post office."

"What has Charlie been doing this time?" asked Aunt Gina.

At any other time Sophy might have resented somewhat the inference in Aunt Gina's question, but now she only said sadly:

"He has been in the hospital for six weeks with typhoid fever. He is getting around now, but he lost his place, of course, and has got behind and—and—"

"And he wants you to send him some money, I s'pose?" said Aunt Gina rather crisply. Aunt Gina, with all her sweetness, could be crisp at times.

"Yes—just a little to keep him going until he gets another place. He'll pay it back when he does."

"How much does he want?"

"Well, he says he thinks he could get along with forty-five dollars, and—"

"A whole quarter's salary?"

"Yes, and I'm so worried. I feel as if I must send it to him, but I don't know where I am to get it. I can't draw my salary until the last of December and this is only November. I have thirty dollars to be sure—but I don't see how I can spare it. The house rent will be due next week, and there's all the coal to get and everything we need for the winter. I haven't got our supply of potatoes and flour yet."

"And there's the doctor's bill, too," said Aunt Gina with a sigh.

Sophy had not mentioned that for fear of hurting Aunt Gina's feelings. Aunt Gina had had a bad spell of rheumatic fever the preceding spring. It had crippled her sadly and the doctor's bill had been hanging over Sophy's head ever since. It was one of her greatest worries, but she would not have Aunt Gina suspect this, so she hurriedly passed the subject by.

"Oh, Doctor Putnam won't press us. And as for the rest, I suppose I can get things on credit until next quarter. And Mr. Greer won't press for the rent either. If only I were sure—I may as well tell you it all, Aunt Gina. I heard Caddie Fraser talking to Emmeline Wadmar in the school porch today. Perhaps she meant me to hear. She said her father and lots of people were saying that it was time they had a new teacher here—one that could keep up with the procession—and that I ought to resign."

"I wouldn't believe a word a Fraser said," said Aunt Gina with sympathetic indignation.

"Oh, I don't know. I'm afraid it is true. Maybe I have got old-fashioned and rusty. But I have tried hard to keep up with the times and the new methods. Anyway, what Caddie said just cut me to the heart. I haven't any course left. I never felt so before. And now there's Charlie."

"You are just tired out, dearie. Go to bed and have a good sleep. You'll feel all right in the morning. You know we've had hard times before—lots of them. But we've always come through all right, and so we will this time."

"Well, I'll try to believe it, Aunt Gina," said Sophy, endeavouring to speak cheerfully. She lit the lamp, poked up the fire, and got tea, chatting away meanwhile about the village news to Aunt Gina. But she carried a heavy heart to bed with her that night and lay awake for a long time, listening to the weird scraping of the bare maple boughs against the roof outside. For the first time in her life the plucky little woman felt utter discouragement.

"There doesn't seem any way out," she sobbed wearily.

Life had always been a hard struggle for Sophy Holmes. She could not remember the time when she had been free from care. When she was only fifteen she had got her certificate from the Academy at Sussex and had gone to teach over in the South Millerton school, coming home to Middle Millerton every Friday night and walking back on Monday morning in all weathers and over all roads. Her mother had been alive then, and Aunt Gina had lived with them. And Charlie, too—dear, chubby little Charlie, with his winsome blue eyes and tangled yellow curls.

Charlie was Sophy's nephew. When his mother, her older sister, died she gave Charlie into Sophy's care on her deathbed and implored her to be good to him always. Sophy had promised and she had kept her promise. Charlie was all in all to her.

After Sophy had taught five years in South Millerton she was offered the home school at Middle Millerton. That was twenty years ago, and she had been there ever since. Everybody under thirty in Middle Millerton had been a pupil of hers at one time or another. Other schools in adjoining districts changed teachers every year or so. Middle Millerton's record was considered phenomenal.

Mrs. Holmes died and Charlie grew up—a wild young rascal whose winning manners long blinded people to his faults of laziness and trickery. Sophy idolized the lad—spoiled him, the Millertonians said. But I think her love and trust were all that held him back from utter lawlessness. She never lost faith in him; she was heartbroken when he went out West and other people said "Good riddance."

Charlie had not made his fortune speedily. More than once Sophy had sent him money "to help him along," pinching and economizing in a dozen petty ways to do it and loyally silent about it, although Aunt Gina suspected it and the gossipy postmistress told far and wide that Sophy Holmes was always sending registered letters to that good-for-nothing nephew of hers who didn't know what the meaning of shame was or he'd never dream of taking it.

Miss Holmes looked back over all her hard past and then forward to the future. But there was no future. She seemed to have come to the end of hope and courage all at once.

Before Miss Holmes had passed Dr. Putnam's gate that evening, Jess and Alberta had been bemoaning a grievance. This was nothing more or less than that there was to be no donation party at Middle Millerton parsonage that fall for the first time within their recollection. The new minister was unmarried and boarded at Deacon Martin's. So he did not need a donation party.

This annual donation party had always been looked upon as one of the most exciting social functions of Middle Millerton. It was not one of those donation parties which we read of in the funny papers when a horde of inconsiderates are supposed to pounce down on the unfortunate clergyman, wreck his furniture and temper, eat him out of house and home, and leave behind them a collection of misfits and uneatables.

The ministers of Middle Millerton always enjoyed both the party and its aftermath. It was usually gotten up by the young people, the older folks contenting themselves with sending their donations. The guests took their lunch baskets with them, spent a pleasant evening, and set the minister's family up in apples and cranberries, pumpkins, potatoes and preserves, geese and turkeys, jams and jellies, and almost everything else you could think of necessary to supply their table for winter.

But there was no minister's family this year.

"It is too bad," grumbled Jess. "The donation party was about all the fun we had to look forward to in the fall. I do think the conference might have sent us a married man."

"Middle Millerton is the dullest old place on earth," said Alberta in a tone of deep conviction.

When Miss Holmes had gone past Jess said:

"Doesn't Miss Holmes look awfully miserable this fall, Bert?"

Alberta nodded.

"Yes—everybody is noticing it. She doesn't seem a bit like herself. Father says he believes she is just killing herself trying to make both ends meet."

"Why, she gets a fair salary, and there's only herself and Aunt Gina."

"Yes; but you know how sick Aunt Gina was last winter, and it must have cost Miss Holmes an awful lot. And folks do say that she just about keeps that scapegrace of a Charlie out West yet. Father says he wishes he could help her, but he doesn't see how. She wouldn't accept anything that seemed like charity, you know."

Then Jess had an inspiration.

"Bert," she exclaimed, "let us have a donation party for Miss Holmes!"

"The very thing!" cried Alberta. "Why didn't we think of it before?"

"Listen," said Jess excitedly. "It has all come to me in a flash what to do. There are dozens of Miss Holmes's old pupils around here. Let's get them all to join in—they'll be glad to. We can have a lovely time ourselves and set Miss Holmes up in provisions for the winter just as we used to do for the ministers. She can't look upon it as charity then, and it isn't either. She gives us her house for an evening's fun, and that is a fair exchange."

The girls hung over the gate and made plans until Jess's mother came to the gate and called her in. For the next two or three days, while poor Miss Holmes was going about like a person in a bad dream, there was plotting and planning galore in Middle Millerton. Alberta and Jess found that their idea met with favour. Middle Millertonians wondered why they hadn't thought of it before, and all bestirred themselves to make "the schoolma'am's donation party" a success. The rate-payers put their heads together and said it was time some public recognition was made of Miss Holmes's long and faithful service. It was decided that abstract Millertonian gratitude should take the concrete form of a purse.

Somebody discovered that Miss Holmes's birthday came the next week, and the donation party was set for that night. It was clear and crisp and beautiful. Miss Holmes, with red eyes, had just sealed up a letter to Charlie. Her thirty dollars were in it.

"Wasn't that a rap at the front door?" asked Aunt Gina.

Miss Holmes went out through the hall and opened it. She fairly blinked with astonishment. Jess Putnam and Alberta Reid stood together on the steps, each carrying a basket. Behind them the little yard was full of boys and girls and as many of the young married Millertonians as had not yet lost their taste for such dissipation.

"Miss Holmes, we've come to give you a surprise-birthday-donation party," cried Jess. "We haven't any minister's family, but we had to have a donation party so we decided to victimize you. Don't turn us out, please."

Donation parties in Middle Millerton had always been nice affairs, but everybody agreed that never before had they had such a splendid time as they had that night as Miss Holmes's. The little yellow house rang with laughter and jollity. And after supper somebody stripped Miss Holmes of her apron, which she had girded on to wash dishes, and marched her to the head of the parlour. Then the door opened and a solemn procession walked in. Miss Holmes recognized every member of the famous old "sixth class" of which she had been so proud two years before. There were fourteen in it, and it was acknowledged to be the smartest class that had ever graduated from the little yellow schoolhouse. Jess Putnam was at its head. She halted before Miss Holmes and began to read an address.

The young minister who was guilty of being a bachelor had written it for the occasion, and everybody who heard it thought that it was a literary masterpiece. The truth was that it was as flowery and conventional a composition as was ever written or read since the first presentation address on record, with not a spark of originality in it. It was full of "grateful pupils" and "long and faithful services" and "love" and "affection" and "appreciation," and so on. But Miss Holmes thought that there had never been such an address before, and every word in it was balm to her sore little heart.

When Jess finished she handed the paper to Miss Holmes and with it a purse of seventy dollars as a "small token of appreciation" from the rate-payers of Middle Millerton to the teacher who had been with them for twenty years and who, they hoped, would be with them for twenty more.

When Caleb Matthews, who was supposed to possess literary leaning, reported the donation party for the Sussex *Advocate* the next week, he said that Miss Holmes acknowledged the presentation in a "few appropriate and well-chosen" remarks. But that was a flight of imagination on Caleb' s part. What really happened was that Miss Holmes burst into happy tears and could only sob out a few disjointed words of thanks and pleasure. But they did just as well as the most flowery speech in the world, and everybody was satisfied.

"Goodness me, Sophy," whispered Aunt Gina when the last merry guest had gone in the autumn moonlight. "You ought to go out and look at the kitchen. There's enough stuff there to run a hotel—potatoes and apples and cranberries and a ham—and three geese—and Mr. Matthews's big gobbler that took the prize at the fair—and cabbages—and two jars of Mrs. Putnam's green gage preserves—and pumpkins—and a big fruit cake Mrs. Reid sent over—and a bag of sugar—and I don't know what there isn't. I haven't mentioned a quarter of the things."

But Miss Holmes, with flushed cheeks and shining eyes, was reading over that delicious complimentary address and did not hear a word of Aunt Gina's inventory.

A FRIENDSHIP WON
(1903)

"Is it our fault?" asked Grace Fielding.

"I don't see how it can be," answered Beatrice impatiently. "I'm sure we have shown ourselves as friendly as possible."

"Could our manner have seemed rather—well, patronizing?" speculated Grace.

Beatrice shook her smooth brown head in a manner quite positive. "I don't believe it could when we didn't feel a bit that way," she protested.

"Then it must be our clothes," said Grace.

But Beatrice would not listen to this either. "Our clothes are very plain and perfectly suited to our way of living here, Grace. Why, we've worn nothing but gingham shirtwaists and sailor hats since we came."

"I know. But then, they're different from what the Gordon girls wear."

"Well," said Beatrice emphatically, "if those girls won't be friends with us because our clothes are different from theirs, all I can say is that they are very silly, and I don't want their friendship."

Grace laughed. "That doesn't sound sincere, Bee. You know we do want their friendship very badly. They seem so nice and jolly between themselves, and it is lonely here by spells—you can't deny that. If we could only fraternize with the Gordon girls, we might have such good times."

"Well, we've done everything we could think of to win their friendship, and we've just got snubbed for our pains."

"Oh, I don't think they meant it that way," said Grace quickly.

"I think the truth is that they are very shy and somewhat in awe of us, and they try to hide it under an assumed brusqueness. We must seem rather foreign to them, you know, with our 'down East' manners and ways of thinking and talking. We haven't much in common yet and they feel it."

"You'd find excuses for anybody, Grace."

"Oh, I'm not trying to find excuses—only reasons. And I am not going to give up trying to make friends with the Gordon girls yet, either. They are the only neighbours we have, and we must in any case be neighbourly."

But after another fortnight, even Grace despaired. There seemed to be no way of overcoming the reserve of the Gordon girls.

Grace and Beatrice Fielding had always lived "down East." In the preceding spring, Mr. Fielding's health had failed. The doctor had recommended change of climate and occupation for a while.

Europe was talked of at first. Then came a letter from Mr. Fielding's brother out West in which he stated his perplexity over a certain prairie farm he owned. It had been rented by a farmer who had recently died. It was hard to get a trustworthy tenant in his place. Did Mr. Fielding know of any man down East who wanted to rent a good prairie farm on easy terms?

Mr. Fielding replied by renting the farm himself for the summer, and he and his family arrived there in June.

Grace and Beatrice liked Red Deer Valley. Farm life on the prairies was to them a distinct novelty, and they enjoyed its freedom and freshness. The prairies were so beautiful too, with their blue, gem-like lakes, their groves of white-stemmed poplars, their sheets of golden sunflowers, and their long, winding trails fringed with nodding bluebells and wild roses. The girls, who had always had a vague idea that prairies were all alike—flat, monotonous treeless plains—were surprised and delighted with Red Deer Valley.

But after the first few weeks, they found it rather lonely. Red Deer was fifteen miles from town. Their only near neighbours were the Gordons, who lived in a little white log-house about half a mile away. Anna and Ida Gordon were about the age of the Fielding girls. They were pretty and merry-looking girls, and at first Grace and Beatrice had hoped that they might be friends, but the Gordon girls proved quite unapproachable. Nothing Grace or Beatrice could do served to break the ice between them. And at last even Grace owned herself defeated.

"I shall leave them alone after this," she said.

"They're horrid," declared Beatrice emphatically.

"Oh, no, they're not," Grace responded seriously. "Don't let your disappointment make you unjust, Bee. If they were horrid we wouldn't want to be chums. They're very nice, and they could be splendid company, but they distrust us. They're not used to other girls, and they can't come out of their lifelong shells. I understand how it is, and I hardly blame them, but I'm very sorry."

Thenceforward the Fielding girls amused themselves as best they could alone. They spun along the dusty trails in natty bicycle suits, they cantered in picturesque riding habits over the green prairie slopes, and tramped on botanizing expeditions among the parks of poplar. In the long, purple prairie twilights, they sat on the little veranda and played on their violins and mandolins. The music drifted over the valley to the Gordon homestead, and the Gordon girls heard it.

"They have everything, and we can't have even an organ," said Anna resentfully.

"I wish we were smart and clever enough to be friends with them," sighed Ida.

"We are just as good as they are, even if we can't dress and talk like them," Anna flashed back. "I don't want to be patronized."

"I don't think they ever meant to patronize us, Nan. And they seem so jolly. I'm sure they must think us stiff and unfriendly."

"I don't care," said Anna quickly. "I didn't want to be friends with them. They made me feel rough and ignorant, but I dare say they didn't mean to do so. You know they are different from us, Ida. Why, their very voices sound different. They're only playing at farming—they're rich and well educated—and—and—we can't be the same as they are, and I won't try to be."

Ida said nothing more. She felt that there was a flaw somewhere in Anna's reasoning, but she seldom argued with her brusque, emphatic older sister.

"I wish Nan wasn't quite so independent," she thought. "I did like those girls even if they are different from us. But of course I couldn't be friends with them when Nan wouldn't. I didn't mind their being so much better educated and smarter than we are. And I don't believe they ever thought of it, either."

The summer was half over, and the prairie wheat fields were sheets of pale gold when a ripple of excitement reached Red Deer. A politician of note was to visit Raymond, the nearest town. Mr. and Mrs. Fielding went to Raymond to hear him speak. They intended to remain overnight, and as the two hired men were absent also, Grace and Beatrice were left in sole charge.

"I'm not a bit scared," said Beatrice stoutly, as they watched the buggy disappearing, "but it's going to be lonesome. If we could only have the Gordon girls over for company!"

"They're all alone, too," said Grace. "Mr. and Mrs. Gordon have gone to town, and the man is away at Loon Lake. There are just Anna and Ida and little Lottie at home. I believe there is going to be a thunderstorm before the night is over."

"Don't prophesy that," said Bee with a shiver. She hated thunderstorms.

They went to bed early, for Bee declared that everything was so deadly still it made her nervous. About midnight Grace awakened. The thunderstorm had come and outside the rain was pouring down. But Grace knew that it was not the noise of the storm that had awakened her. As she listened the sound came again. Someone was knocking at the kitchen door.

She quickly aroused Beatrice, and the two girls slipped on their wrappers and hurried downstairs. At the back door stood Anna Gordon, bareheaded and drenched, with white face and wild, frightened eyes.

"Oh," she cried hysterically, clutching at Grace's arm, "won't you come over? Lottie's got croup—she's dreadful bad—and we don't know what to do! There's nobody to go for the doctor, and our horses are all away—oh! oh!"

"We'll go at once," said Grace, "but I'm afraid neither of us knows much about illness."

"Grace," interrupted Beatrice, "you go over with Anna, and I will go to Loon Lake for Doctor Ames."

"Oh, Bee, you can't! Such a night, and you don't know the trail—"

"I'll take Red Roy. He's been down so often with Jack that I think he will know the road himself. There's nothing else to be done, Grace. Get me my habit as quickly as you can, and I'll go out and saddle Red Roy. Don't cry, Miss Gordon! I'll go as quickly as possible."

When Beatrice was fairly off she realized what she had undertaken. Loon Lake was five miles away. The trail was winding and crossed by many others. The night was densely dark save when it was illuminated by blinding flashes of lightning. The rain still fell heavily. Beatrice had a nervous dread of thunderstorms, but she shut her eyes and galloped on, realizing that she must trust wholly to Red Roy, for she could do nothing but keep her seat.

As long as she lived Beatrice never forgot that ride. The uncertainty was its worst horror. She could not even be sure that she was on the right trail. When at last the little trading station Loon Lake loomed up before her, she gave a sob of thankfulness.

Doctor Ames was awakened to find at his door a drenched and bedraggled young lady, holding her horse's bridle and gasping out her story. Ten minutes later the doctor was galloping back over the Red Deer trail, and Beatrice, almost exhausted, was in Mrs. Ames's charge.

She did not get home until the next evening when her father came for her in the buggy. When she reached the house, Anna Gordon met her at the door.

"O Miss Fielding, how can I ever thank you?" she exclaimed. "You saved Lottie's life. The doctor came just in time. I wish I could do something for you."

Tears came into Anna's eyes. Beatrice felt her own growing misty. She slipped her arm through Anna's and said:

"I didn't do more than anyone would have done. It is Red Roy you ought to thank. The splendid fellow went straight to the lake; I just stuck on. Come in and have tea with us. Grace and I so much want to be friends with you and Ida."

Anna flushed. "I'm sure you must have thought me dreadfully rude and queer, Miss Gordon. It was my fault. I—I think I was envious of you. And I felt awkward and stupid beside you, and imagined you thought me so too. I've been very foolish, but I do ask your pardon for it. I shall love you forever for saving Lottie."

"I'm sure we are going to be good chums all around," prophesied Beatrice jubilantly. And this was a prophecy that came true.

A PLATONIC EXPERIMENT
(1904)

"Between a man and a woman of anything like equal age and ordinary attractiveness, a platonic friendship is impossible, thanks to the laws of Nature."

Mr. Dallas, having made this statement, looked around the table with a tentative ruffling of his plumage, as if he challenged anyone to an argument on the subject.

The majority of the boarders did not notice his remark. They were all hungry and indifferent to Mr. Dallas's opinions. He was not popular among them, being a middle-aged man with a cynical turn and pessimistic views of life. Two faces, however, were turned protestingly toward him—Howard Elliott's, whose previous mention of platonic friendship had evoked Dallas's remark, and a girl's, who sat opposite Elliott and flashed a scornful look at Dallas out of her brilliant hazel eyes.

"You don't agree with me, Miss Chester," he remarked affably.

"No."

The monosyllable was defiant. Dallas laughed, provokingly, and shrugged shoulders.

"And you!" he asked, turning to Howard Elliott.

"I certainly disagree," returned the young man warmly. "I do believe in platonic friendship. Why should it not be possible? I am tired of this outworn idea that a perfect friendship, untinged by love, is impossible between a man and a woman. It is sheer nonsense."

"Have you ever proved it to be sheer nonsense?" asked Dallas imperturbably.

"I have. I have one woman friend at least for whom I have the most sincere and friendly affection. There is not a shadow of sentiment in our relations with each other. And I know many other instances."

"Is the lady in question young—and pretty?" questioned Dallas, prudently avoiding the vagueness of the "other instances."

Howard Elliott flushed impatiently.

"She is not very old," he answered hesitatingly, "and—I have never thought about her looks."

Dallas laughed aggravatingly.

"I thought as much. Don't look so savage, my young friend. By the time you have reached my age, you will have proved the truth of the trite proverb that things are not what they seem. I grant that under some circumstances, such as yours, a true and sincere friendship is possible between a man and a woman. Please remember the limitations of my first remark. I have been a participant in some of your so-called 'Platonics' in my day, too. They invariably led to something else. This is simply in the nature of things, and you couldn't change it if you tried. In most instances the culmination of a platonic friendship is marriage—or divorce. Miss Chester, there is a very decided tilt to that chin of yours that leads me to infer that my eloquence has not convinced you."

"It has not, indeed," said Madge Chester. "There is such a thing as platonic friendship that does not end in love."

"Have you ever proved it personally?'

"No-o. But I believe in it thoroughly."

"Illogical, very. I dare say you do believe in all that pretty nonsense; it is pretty. I believed in it once myself. But time will teach you better."

Madge Chester and Howard Elliott exchanged glances of baffled protest against his calmly assertive tone. The latter looked across the table at his vis-à-vis with new interest. He seldom felt interested in girls; he was too busy for that, he thought. He was a journalist by profession, and his belief in Platonics amounted to a fad. He had written a series of articles on the subject two years before that had attracted some attention and had thoroughly convinced himself, if no one else.

But he did feel a certain interest in Madge Chester, born, doubtless, of their mutual theory. After tea he followed her out to the garden and sat down by her under the maples.

"Do you like Mr. Dallas?" he asked.

"I detest him," answered Madge, calmly. "He seems to assume that he must be right about everything and everyone else in the wrong. And it is so impossible to argue with him; he puts you down some way and then looks around with that maddening smile of his, as much as to say, 'Has any other person anything to say on this subject before I close it? If so, let him speak now or forever after hold his peace.'"

Elliott smiled.

"There is a great deal of latent antagonism toward Mr. Dallas in me," he said. "I hope he has not converted you to his heretical doctrines."

"Regarding platonic friendship? No, indeed. I should dearly like to prove him in the wrong for once."

"Let us do it."

"How can we?"

"Let us be friends," said Elliott calmly. "Let us have the courage of our convictions and squelch Dallas effectually."

Madge Chester tapped her round chin reflectively with the tips of her slender fingers.

"It's not a bad idea—if it is practicable. But I'm not sure of its success."

"Don't you thoroughly believe in your own theories, then?"

"Oh, I didn't mean that," cried Madge, blushing scarlet. "What I meant was could we be real friends? We may not like each other well enough on closer acquaintance, and friendship wouldn't be possible if we didn't."

"No; but, I think we will. At least, there is no harm in trying. Will you?"

Madge Chester never took long to make up her mind.

"I will," she answered frankly, holding out her hand. They shook hands gravely.

"Thus is our compact signed and sealed," said Elliott. "We are to be firm friends without a shadow of sentiment or romantic nonsense about our friendship."

"For the noble motive of ultimately discomfiting Mr. Dallas."

"Well, we ought to find a pleasure in it, too. Of course, Dallas is a motive."

"It is delightful to think of putting him down for once," said Madge vindictively. "It will be a great satisfaction."

"What will be a great satisfaction?" questioned Dallas with lazy interest as he came around a clump of lilac bushes. He squared his back against a maple tree and looked at the two conspirators quizzically.

"I am neither a prophet nor the son of a prophet," he went on, "yet I think I can tell what you two have been planning out here. You came here, hotly indignant with my humble self for having trampled on your pet platonic corns. You have doubtless abused me freely in a well-bred way, and you have ended up with a formal compact to exploit your theories in your own intercourse and thereby completely crush me. Am I right?"

"I believe you have been eavesdropping," said Madge sharply.

"My dear young lady, I never eavesdrop. I am only mapping out your probable line of conduct from my general knowledge of human nature. I was right, it seems. Well, I give you both credit for sincerity—a rare virtue in this posing age. Your experiment is very interesting. Don't you want an umpire, though? Shall I act in that capacity? I promise to be strictly impartial. If, when you leave here, you can both say to me in all good faith, 'We have been close friends; we like each other; we enjoy each other's society; we are thoroughly congenial; but we are no more than friends and have no desire to be more'—if you can say this, I will haul down my flag and surrender unconditionally. If, on the contrary—"

"There will be no 'contrary,'" interrupted Miss Chester coolly.

"I am sure you believe so. But we must consider all possibilities. If you cannot say that to me, I will expect you to admit your defeat honestly. Is this to be our understanding?"

"Yes," said Elliott promptly. "You see matters from your own standpoint, of course, and are incapable of judging them from ours. Meanwhile, let us drop all reference to the subject."

[Extract Number One. From Howard Elliott's journal.]

It is a curious compact—I do not know how it will succeed. Dallas piqued us into it. Yet I think I rather like her. She is a college student and somewhat imbued with the "new" womanhood, I fancy. She is very pretty and seems like a jolly, good-hearted girl, clever enough to be entertaining and companionable but not too clever. There is no nonsense about her. Why should not this summer friendship of ours be a mutually pleasant and profitable one? I am getting to be rather much of a recluse. This girl will rouse me out of myself and bring me into closer touch with my fellow creatures.

She has remarkably fine eyes—I could not help noticing them this evening. In colour they are like the sunlit current of a woodland brook flashing over tawny pebbles, but their expression is quite indescribable. I don't think I ever noticed a woman's eyes before.

[Extract Number Two. From Madge Chester's letter to a college chum.]

You will say it is very absurd, of course, but you know me of old, also my "everlasting theories," as you are pleased to call them. Well, I am going to test them. I have no fear of the result. I like Mr. Elliott thoroughly. He is such a straightforward young fellow, and not a bit spoiled or conceited. There is a great deal of fun in him, too, though in general he is quiet and reserved. He is not all handsome but has such an interesting face and such brilliant, piercing steel-blue eyes. He is immensely clever and writes a great deal, I believe, or at least Mr. Dallas says so. We talk "shop" most of the time. I hold forth on college life and co-education, and he discourses on journalism. How you and the girls will laugh over this and say, "Isn't that like Madge!" But, indeed, my dear, there is a method in my madness. I want to establish my theories to my own satisfaction, as well as other people's. Besides, it is really nice to have a friend you can be chummy with without his thinking that you are throwing yourself at his head.

[Extract Number Three. From Howard Elliott's journal.]

Miss Chester and I are getting on famously. Our friendship is perfect. I never met a woman like her before; she is never the same twice, yet she is always charming. The spice of "infinite variety" is hers to the full. We walk and row and ride together. We discuss our work and our ambitions. She is very clear-sighted and sympathetic, a friend worth making and keeping. That freakish idea of mine has borne unexpectedly good fruit, as unaccountable impulses often do when followed out. Yet there is not a trace of nonsense about our friendship. It is absolutely sexless.

Her beauty is a fresh surprise to me every time I see her. She looked like a dream vision tonight. We are going for a tramp over the hills tomorrow.

[Extract Number Four. From Madge Chester's journal.]

I don't like Mr. Elliott as well as I thought I did. He behaved hatefully today. We all went for a row across the harbour, and coming home through the dyke meadows he walked the whole way with Emma Hawley, who is a regular flirt. She has been doing her best to attract him all along and is simply furious with me because she fancies I am her rival.

I don't want to monopolize him, of course, but he might have looked out now and then to see how I was enjoying myself. Of course, I don't care. It was not my suggestion that we should be comrades this summer, and he is entirely welcome to Miss Hawley's society if he prefers it. Perhaps he regrets that he did not choose her for a friend instead of me. I shall be very cool to him tomorrow. He need not think he is indispensable to my enjoyment. He gathered a bunch of poppies for her, too. After that, of course, I wasn't going to wear the bluebells he had given me before we went; I threw them away and replaced them by some field daisies Mr. Dallas gave me. I watched him after that—Mr. Elliott, I mean—to see if he noticed, but apparently he did not. I suppose he is getting tired of our friendship, and we were just beginning to have such nice times.

Mr. Dallas asked me if Mr. Elliott and I had quarrelled. That man does make me so cross.

[Extract Number Five. From Mr. Elliott's journal.]

I cannot imagine what I have done to offend Miss Chester. I certainly have offended her, for she has treated me very coolly since yesterday. She wore Dallas's flowers coming home from the shore—what business has he to give her flowers?—and threw mine away. Dallas hung around her all day, too.

She may be tired of our experiment. Yet I never thought her capricious. Perhaps Dallas has been saying something to her. I must find out. He shall not come between us if I can help it.

What pleasant, companionable days we have passed! My theory is perfectly correct—platonic friendship is possible. But why is she angry at me?

[Extract Number Six. From Madge Chester's letter to a college chum.]

The summer is passing so quickly. In another month, college will reopen. I have had a delightful time, thanks to Mr. Elliott. I knew you would tease me about him. Why can't you be sensible, Mary? I assure you we are nothing more than the best of friends.

We had a tiff last week. I felt annoyed because I felt sure he was trying to get up a flirtation with that odious Emma Hawley. But I suppose my imagination ran away with me. We are all right again now. I shall be very sorry when he goes. He has only another fortnight here. He is very clever and I am sure will succeed in life. I hope he will.

Mr. Dallas is as cynical as ever. I imagine he is a little piqued that Mr. Elliott and I have held our point so well.

[Extract Number Seven. From Mr. Dallas's notebook.]

I can generally see through a grindstone when there is a hole in it! But some people in this establishment cannot.

The little platonic comedy still goes on. Miss Chester is serenely confident that she has proved her point and is gloating over my anticipated downfall.

Yet one day, when her co-theorist walked home from the shore with Miss Hawley—blond, soft-eyed, brainless, different stamp from Miss Chester altogether—my lady grows very pale and dignified, adopts the "cool and severely classical" air, wears my daisies, and throws Elliott's bluebells spitefully into the brook. Purely platonic, of course! But I fancy Elliott had to work his way back into favour, and he fidgeted a good deal under the process. Yet he, too, is blind. "What fools these mortals be!"

[Extract Number Eight. From Madge Chester's journal.]

Mr. Elliott goes away next week and I shall miss him very much. We have had such a pleasant summer. He has seemed very quiet lately. I wonder if he will ask me to write to him. It will be lonely here when he goes, but I shall not be here much longer myself. I long now to get back to college and to my work.

I have a dreadful headache—I wonder what is the matter with me these days. I feel rather blue tonight. No sooner does one make a good, true friend whom one really values than one loses him again.

[Extract Number Nine. From Howard Elliott's journal.]

I go tomorrow. I cannot understand why I should feel so depressed about it.

I shall heartily regret to part with Miss Chester. Our friendship has been so pleasant. I shall ask her to correspond with me.

I do not want to drop out of her life altogether.

I had a letter from the editor of the Caterer *today. He wants me to write an article on platonic friendship for his magazine, but I don't think I will—I have lost active interest in the subject. Of course, I believe in it just as firmly as ever, but it is getting stale. Besides, nothing can be really proved. What is true for one person might not be for another.*

Madge Chester was standing under the maples at sunset, looking steadily and unseeingly at the masses of scarlet poppies before her. Howard Elliott came jauntily across the lawn and said with overdone carelessness,

"Shall we go for a walk in the dyke meadows, Miss Chester—our last one? A pleasant finale to a pleasant vacation. Afterwards we must interview Mr. Dallas. The hour of our triumph is approaching. It is a comfort to think he will have to own himself in the wrong, isn't it?"

He did not explain why comfort should be needed, nor did she ask. They walked silently across the lawn, between the ranks of flaunting poppies. Dallas, swinging in a hammock, watched them amusedly as they passed on to the dyke meadows, blossom-sown and sunset-lit. Neither spoke until they came to a low, straggling fence, half-buried in goldenrod and faint purple asters. In the cool air the dusk was struggling with early moonrise. Over the meadows, sweet and far away, came the refrain of a song sung by some gay boaters on the harbour.

Elliott laid his hand over the girl's as it rested white and small on a mossy rail.

"I suppose we shall not see each other again for some time," he said with studied composure. "I am sorry. This has been a—I have been—our experience has been a pleasant one. I think."

"Oh, yes," said Madge hurriedly. She turned away that he might not see the quiver of her lips.

"You must not forget me altogether, Madge," he went on nervously. "We will correspond, will we not? I shall want to hear how you are getting along at college, and I promise to write the most interesting letters about my work that I possibly can. Perhaps we will meet again next summer."

"It is not likely," answered Madge faintly. "I expect to travel abroad next summer."

There was another long silence. At last Madge turned with a little shiver.

"It is chilly here. I think I had better go in. You can tell Mr. Dallas yourself. I don't care about meeting him—my head aches."

Elliott held out his hand.

"Goodbye," he said.

"Goodbye," said the girl, with a little choke in her voice. Two irrepressible tears fell over her burning cheeks.

Elliott reached out wildly for her other hand.

"Oh, I will say it. I love you—I love you! I don't care what Dallas or anyone says—only what you say. Don't say that you can't care for me."

[Extract Tenth and last. From Mr. Dallas's notebook.]

The pretty little comedy has had its inevitable ending. The two platonic friends went off for a long stroll tonight, looking as if they were going to be hanged, and came back radiant and shamefaced. I let them down easy and spared them the necessity of owning up.

"Bless you, my children," I remarked, paternally.

Miss Chester pouted and looked pretty. She is an independent little puss, that, and could, I fancy, make it hot for Elliott if he ever tried Platonics with anybody else. I don't think he will, however. I imagine he is cured of that for good and all. Platonics, indeed! Stuff and nonsense!

THE CHIFFON DRESS
(1904)

Hazel Bruce walked slowly up the lane of the old Bruce homestead at Framely, swinging her hat in her hand. The lane was old and "homey" and beautiful, with a row of spruces, grey and gaunt below but green and plumy above, skirting it on each side of the lichen-grown fence. Early in spring, the first faintly sweet, white violets of the year were to be found there. Wild rosebushes lurked along it, blossom-pink in June. Late summer brought daisies and blue-eyed grass. Now, in early September, the corners were gay with clumps of goldenrod, and every twist of the fence was outlined with a scarf of smoke-blue asters.

When Hazel entered the kitchen she found Lois punching the big blue plums of the "Grandfather Bruce" tree with a long darning needle, preparatory to preserving them. She smiled brightly at Hazel over the frills of her pink cambric apron. Lois had a weakness for dainty aprons.

"Home again? Did you have a pleasant visit, dear?"

Hazel nodded as she perched herself on the table.

"Yes, a delightful one. Aunt Lesley and the girls did everything to make me enjoy myself. It has been a week of golden days. But I'm glad to be home again. Has anybody been here while I was away?"

"Yes—Ida. She came the day after you went and was here until yesterday. Then she went down to Branchtown to see Uncle Howard's folks."

"And I've missed her!" exclaimed Hazel, in a tone of vexation. Ida was her favourite cousin.

"O, she is coming back in a fortnight's time. She left her trunk and most of her things here. She is not looking well but is as dear and sweet as ever. I do think Ida is the loveliest girl I know."

"Did you hear Father saying anything about sending me to the business college at Kentville this winter?" asked Hazel after a moment's silence, giving utterance to the thought that had been uppermost in her mind all day.

Lois's smile faded out and left a wistful expression as she looked at her pretty young sister.

"No, dear. He is so sorry, but he says he cannot afford the expense of books and tuition this winter, even though Aunt Lesley has so kindly offered to board you free. We are all sorry, too; but you know it can't be helped. We have had such losses this summer and the crop is a failure—"

"O, I know," interrupted Hazel, impatiently. "It is always the same story. There," seeing Lois's pained look, "never mind my crossness, dear. I'm an ungrateful girl, I know. But I feel so discouraged. If there were only any way that I could earn the money myself. But there is no chance of that in Framely."

"Are you going to Felicia's party tonight?" asked Lois, by way of changing a sore subject.

"I don't know," said Hazel, discontentedly. "I haven't a dress fit to go in—you know that. My old muslin has been washed and darned and let down so often that I'm positively ashamed of it."

"I wouldn't mind that very much if I were you," said Lois, gently. "Felicia will feel very much hurt if you don't go."

"It's easy to say don't mind it," sighed Hazel. "But I *do* mind it, Lois. I can't help it, if it's ever so foolish and frivolous of me. All Felicia's city cousins will be there in pretty dresses. I will be the one shabby guest among them all. But I suppose I'll go. Alec and Phoebe March are going to call for me in the carryall. I saw them at the station."

"I pressed your muslin this afternoon," said Lois, brightly, "and made a fresh ribbon collar for it. You can have my new white sash and pearl pin and all the roses on my bush. They have burst royally into bloom since you went away."

Hazel leaned over and dropped a kiss into the biggest dimple in Lois's soft cheek.

"You are the dearest sister in the world, Lois. I'm ashamed of my grumbling and growling. Well, I think I'll go and brush myself up a bit before tea time."

When Hazel went to her little white room over the front porch she found traces of Ida everywhere. Ida's trunk was behind the door; Ida's hat was hanging on a chair-back; Ida's dresses filled one side of the wardrobe; and Ida's toilet knickknacks were scattered over the dressing table. Everything was very dainty. Ida was a rich man's daughter.

When Hazel pulled open her third bureau drawer she said "O!" It was full of dainty fluffiness. She lifted the fluffiness out and held it up with a little sigh of admiration.

It was a dress of pale pink chiffon over a slip of pink silk. It was the prettiest dress Hazel had ever seen in her life. She touched the frothlike frills and puffs and tucks, the dainty adornments of lace and ribbon, with careful fingers and little exclamations of pleasure.

"I'm going to try it on," she said at last. "Ida won't mind. She always lets me try on her things. Our figures are so much alike that it will be sure to fit me. I wonder how Ida came to bring it with her. She could not have expected to wear it here."

When Hazel looked at herself in the glass after putting on the pink dress she fairly blushed with delight. Pink was her colour. It suited her creamy skin, velvety brown eyes, and curling bronze hair to perfection.

"How becoming!" she said. "And a perfect fit! If I only had a dress like this to wear to Felicia's party tonight!"

Hazel stood very still for a few moments after this, facing a sudden thought that had come to her.

"O, I couldn't," she whispered. She hurriedly took off the chiffon dress and replaced it in the drawer. But the thought remained. When she went down to tea, it was still with her. When she went back to her room in the clear autumn dusk to dress for the party, it had taken full possession of her.

"I might wear that dress tonight. Nobody would ever know it wasn't my own. Lois is going to the station after tea. Of course, I'll tell Ida when she comes back. I know she wouldn't mind. She has often lent me her things. And I would be so careful and not spoil it in any way. It is a perfect evening, and I could pin the skirt up and wear Lois's long linen duster. And my old muslin is so shabby."

The old muslin was lying on the bed. Its darns seemed very prominent. Even Lois's new sash could not cover them. She opened the bureau drawer and looked again at the chiffon dress.

When the Marches called for Hazel she was waiting for them, shrouded from head to foot in Lois's duster. Her cheeks were flushed and her eyes were bright. She was very silent during their three miles' drive, responding absently to Phoebe March's lively chatter. She sat stiffly on the seat of the carryall, afraid to move lest she crumple her dress. Phoebe had no such care. She wore her old blue organdy and was light of heart.

When Hazel discarded her duster in Felicia's room, a chorus of surprise and admiration went up from the girls assembled.

"Hazel Bruce, what a perfectly lovely dress! Where did you get it?" demanded Felicia, who always asked questions before she thought.

Hazel flushed crimson, but she was spared the embarrassment of a reply by Phoebe.

"No wonder you sat all 'prunes and prisms' as we came," she laughed. "It is the sweetest dress I ever saw, and it becomes you so much, Hazel. You'll be the bright particular star of the evening."

All the other girls had something complimentary to say. Hazel longed to break away from them. She did not enjoy herself one minute the whole evening. She was afraid to move lest she should spoil the dress. Besides, it seemed to her that everybody must guess she had borrowed it without asking.

"I've done a mean, dishonorable thing," she kept restlessly thinking. "How grieved Lois would be if she knew! Why didn't I think of these things before I put it on?"

Long as the evening seemed, it came to an end at last. Hazel breathed a sigh of relief as she hurried to the dressing room.

"I've had a miserable time, and I've deserved it," she said to herself with a lump in her throat as she put on her duster, glad to shut the chiffon dress from her sight.

When she found herself on the road, she saw with a sinking heart that the night, so clear and fine in the early evening, was dark and cloudy. Before they were halfway home, big drops began to patter down, and soon a heavy rain was falling. In vain Hazel tried to protect her dress, aided by the good-natured Marches, who sympathized with her dismay. But in a very short time the linen duster and the rug of the carryall were soaked through, and Hazel knew that the chiffon dress was ruined.

When she got home she crept upstairs and looked at herself in the glass, with the limp, draggled frills clinging about her. Her face was white and her eyes burning and dry. Lois, who had come softly in in her dressing-gown to hear about the party, gave a little cry of dismay.

"O Lois!" said Hazel, breaking down. Then she sobbed out her confession.

Lois listened with a pained look in her frank blue eyes.

"O Hazel, do you mean to say that you took Ida's dress and wore it to the party without her knowledge?" she asked.

Hazel nodded. That look in Lois's eyes was her worst punishment.

"It was dreadful of me," she said, chokingly. "I realize it now; I didn't think of it before. That dress just seemed to infatuate me. O Lois, you can't be more ashamed of me than I am myself. But the dress is ruined. I must replace it, that's all. How much do you suppose it cost, Lois?"

"It is very like the cream one Ida had last summer, and you know that cost fifty dollars, Hazel. You can never get that much."

"Yes, I know a way I can earn it, Lois. I thought of it before when I wanted to earn money to go to the business college, but it seemed to me then that I couldn't do it, even for that.

Mrs. Carmody at the station hotel wants a cook. She will pay five dollars a week. I'm going to hire myself out to her. She is cranky and unreasonable and finds it hard to get or keep a cook. It will serve me rightly as a punishment, too. I'll confess to Father and Mother tomorrow, and get their consent."

Two days later Hazel was installed as cook at the station hotel. People wondered and gossiped over it greatly, but she accepted that as part of her deserved humiliation. She had to work very hard, and Mrs. Carmody was an exacting and fault-finding employer.

At the end of a week, news came that Ida was down with typhoid fever at Branchtown.

"The doctor says she is not dangerously ill," said Lois, who had walked over to the station to tell Hazel the news. "But it is likely to be a tedious case. I thought she was not looking well when she was at our place."

It was nine weeks before Ida was up again and well enough to come back to Framely. She arrived the very day that Hazel came home from the hotel. Hazel looked almost as thin and white as Ida did. She had had a hard ten weeks of it, but she had her fifty dollars, too, and she poured out the whole story to Ida before she took off her hat.

"Hazel Bruce!" exclaimed Ida. "Do you mean to say that you have been slaving at the station hotel all this time to earn money to replace that dress? Why, you poor, dear girl, that dress was your own! I brought it from home as a little present from Mother and me to you. And to think how you have worried yourself about it! You might have known I would never have brought such a dress here for just a short visit at this time of year."

"The principle remains the same," said Hazel, soberly. "I took it when I thought it was yours. That is what hurt Lois so much and myself, too, when I realized what I had done. But I have learned a lesson, and I don't think my vanity will ever lead me so far astray again. I'm not sorry I went to the hotel, either. I have enough money now to pay for books and tuition at the business college this winter. And I think I can get along without a party dress, Ida."

HOW NAN WENT TO THE PARTY
(1904)

Avis Murray opened and read her letter with a smile of pleasure. "From Grace Forrest," she said to her sister. "Listen, Madge:

"Dear Avis: My long-promised birthday party is to come off next Thursday evening. You know I could not have one last year because of Ella's illness; so I am determined to make up for it this time. I am bubbling over with plans. All the Westland young folks will be here, and the Palmer girls are coming up from Taunton, and a lot of my cousins from Stanley. Of course, you must come; so consider yourself invited herewith, and please bring with you any new ideas for entertainment you may have picked up lately.

"Lovingly yours,

"Grace Forrest."

"How delightful!" said Avis gayly. "Grace is such a lovely girl, and her home is an ideal place for a party! I know we shall have a delightful time. What dress had I better wear, Madge? Something crushable, for I'll have to carry it out in a bundle on my wheel. My yellow silk organdy is the thing. It will stand any amount of ill usage. Those lovely, pale-yellow roses of Aunt Mary's will go with it beautifully. And you'll lend me your feather fan, won't you, Madge, like the dear you are? I'll be as careful of it as if it were crusted with diamonds."

"O, you may have anything I possess," said Madge amiably.

"I'll wheel out to Aunt Mary's on Wednesday afternoon, carrying my war paint with me," went on Avis, as if everything was settled. "That will give me time to get nicely rested before the party. O, I wouldn't miss it for anything."

Avis carried out her programme, and on Wednesday afternoon a rather tired and very dusty girl alighted from her wheel at Aunt Mary's door. Westland was a pretty country village about ten miles from town, and Avis had spent her vacation there a year before, enjoying herself greatly and making hosts of friends among the Westland young people, all of whom liked the warm-hearted, sunshiny girl. Avis hugged Aunt Mary, kissed the baby, patted the cat, and shook hands with Miss Wright from across the street, who had run in to borrow a cup of sugar. "I'm glad to get here, for I'm tired out and fearfully hungry," she said. "I hope you've got something good for tea, aunty. How is Nan, Miss Wright?"

"Nan is well enough," returned Miss Wright rather grimly. Miss Wright had a habit of being grim. "She's gone party mad, like all the rest of the girls around here, and hasn't been able to think of anything else since Grace sent her the invitation. She wanted a new dress for it, but I put my foot squarely down on that nonsense. I wasn't going to allow her to cultivate a spirit of vanity and extravagance. I told her that her white muslin was plenty good, and she had to resign herself to that. She's been flying around all day, washing and starching and kerflummuxing it. I'm afraid Nan is going to be very frivolous." Miss Wright looked grimmer than ever.

Avis picked up the baby to hide her smile. "O, I don't think Nan is frivolous, Miss Wright," she said gently. "Of course she likes pretty things—we all do. You did yourself when you were a schoolgirl, didn't you?"

"Well, I suppose I did," conceded Miss Wright, thawing, as people were apt to do under the influence of Avis's sunny personality. "And of course I like to see Nan keep herself neat and tidy. She's a good girl the most of times, and I suppose a bit of nonsense now and then won't hurt her." With which modified statement Miss Wright took her cup of sugar and her departure.

At dusk next evening Avis was ready for the party, and she surveyed her dainty reflection in Aunt Mary's spare-room mirror with satisfaction. The yellow organdy, with its frothlike frills and laces, suited the slim, girlish figure to perfection, while the clusters of golden-hued roses from the garden and Madge's feather fan gave the crowning touches.

"Now," said Avis, "I'll run over for Nan."

Nan Lawrence was the orphan niece of Miss Wright. Avis had seen a good deal of her the preceding summer, and a close friendship had grown up between the two girls. Nan was always bright and pleasant, but sometimes Avis thought that she was not quite happy. Miss Wright really loved her niece, and was sincerely anxious to do her duty by her, but she was rather a grim guardian for a young girl like Nan, who, like most girls, was fond of fun and laughter and good times. Miss Wright thought that this betokened "frivolity" and did her best to repress it. As the Westland people expressed it, Nan was "kept down."

The little white house across the street was dark and silent when Avis reached it, but the hall door under the honeysuckles was open, and she ran in and upstairs to Nan's room. At the door she paused in bewilderment. By the dim light she saw Nan sitting at the open window with her head bowed on her arms and still wearing her everyday print dress.

"Nan Lawrence, why aren't you ready for the party?" demanded Avis.

Nan started and lifted her face. "I'm not going," she said in a choked voice.

"Not going? Why–e–e–e, Nan Lawrence! Why not?"

"I can't," said poor Nan. "I—I haven't any dress. Yesterday, you know, I washed and starched my white muslin, and this morning I ironed it and hung it before the kitchen fire. It looked real nice and crisp, and the darned spots didn't show much. Well, I went out then—and auntie was out, too—and I don't know how it happened, but I suppose a spark flew out on it. Anyway, it caught fire, and when I came back the skirt had great holes burned all over it. And so—I can't go."

"It is too bad," said Avis helplessly, sitting down on the bed.

"I suppose it is very foolish of me to care so much," said Nan in a quivering voice. "Aunt says it is—but I can't help it. I do care dreadfully. You don't know how much I've wanted to go to Grace's party, Avis. I've never been to a party in my whole life—not one."

Nan's curly head went down on her arms again. Avis sat very silent. She too wanted very much to go to Grace's party—so much so that she didn't see how she could give it up. Yet that was what the idea that had just come to her meant.

I have been to so many parties, she thought, *and Nan has never been to one.*

But Grace's party will be better than any of the others have been, protested Avis's other self, *and she wants you especially. Of course you must go. It isn't your fault that Nan cannot.*

Avis sat still for a few moments longer. Then she sprang from the bed with an emphatic "I'll do it!"

"Do what?" asked startled Nan.

"Nan, you are to go to the party," said Avis, speaking very rapidly. "You are going to put on my dress and go. No, don't say a word. Listen to me. I've been going to parties all my life. It is your turn now. It won't be a bit of use for you to refuse, for I won't go if you don't. We are both the same height and pretty much the same in figure, so I am sure my dress will fit you. You shall have my roses, and I'll do your hair. Nobody in Westland has ever seen this dress, so they won't know but that it is yours."

"But it isn't fair to you, Avis," protested Nan.

"Yes, it is. I want you to go. I'll write a note to Grace and explain how it is—you won't mind her knowing, will you? She will never tell."

Nan did not give in all at once, but Avis would take no denial, and at last Nan consented, with a sigh of mingled delight and regret.

It did not take long for her to get ready. In a very few minutes Avis had on Nan's print dress, while Nan blossomed out in the yellow organdy and roses. Avis helped her arrange her riotous brown curls and pulled out her frills and puffs.

"There! How sweet you look, Nan! Nobody would ever guess that dress wasn't made for you."

Nan did look very sweet and girlish and pretty. She put her arms about Avis lovingly.

"O, Avis, you're so good. I'll never be able to repay you, but I'll never forget this."

When Avis had seen her upon her way and had explained matters to Miss Wright, she went slowly back to Aunt Mary's.

"I'm glad I did it, and I hope Nan will have a time," she said softly to herself. But it cannot be denied that she felt a little bit lonesome. She had forgotten her lonesomeness, however, when Nan brought the yellow organdy home next morning.

"O, I had a lovely time," said Nan enthusiastically. "It was like fairyland. And Grace was so sorry you couldn't come, but she told me to tell you she thought it was lovely of you not to come, and I think so too."

"I'm so glad you enjoyed it," said Avis heartily. And there was no regret in her heart or her voice.

BESSIE'S DREAM
(1904)

Bessie Hill was a very forgetful little girl. Her intentions were good, and when she did do anything she did it carefully and painstakingly; but eight times out of ten she forgot all about it and it was not done at all, unless Mother or Aunty reminded her of it many times.

One warm Saturday morning, Bessie was swinging in the hammock under the big trees of the garden reading a very fascinating new storybook which her Uncle Red had given her on her birthday. Presently her mother came out and said:

"Bessie, I am going up to Aunt Ella's to spend the day. Now, my dear, don't forget to water your flowers and feed Dick and sew up that terrible rent in the sleeve of your muslin dress."

"All right, Mother," promised Bessie, and she meant it. She also remembered that she must rewrite her composition, which had to be handed in to the teacher early Monday morning. But she would just finish her chapter first; and that was the last Bessie thought about flowers or bird or dress or composition.

During the forenoon her dearest friend, Edna Longworth, dropped in, and Bessie coaxed her to stay to lunch and spend the afternoon with her. They went for a walk and they swung in the hammock and had a "good old talk." When Edna went home it was five o'clock and all Bessie's duties remained undone.

She watched Edna out of sight from the windows of her room, leaning her head on the sill. How dreadfully warm it was! Where had she left her book? She must go . . . and get it . . . and finish . . . her . . . st-o-ry . . .

Why, where was she? Surely this wasn't her room! She was in a big, gloomy apartment. Before her, at a desk, sat a grim-looking personage who was certainly a man and yet bore such an odd resemblance to the old grandfather's clock which stood on the stair landing at home that Bessie felt bewildered.

Behind him sat a row of people who grinned and winked at her and changed countenance with a rapidity that made her giddy, for now they all looked like the cups and saucers of Grandmother's china set and now like the series of watercolours in the hall at home and the next minute like a row of brooms, dustpans, and dusters.

At the right of the clock-like personage sat another who was busy writing and who looked just like a scribbling book. Presently this clerk arose, bowed to the judge and jury, and said:

"May it please your lordship and gentlemen of the jury to proceed to the hearing of this case. The prisoner is now before you, charged with serious crimes and misdemeanours. The first witness to be examined is Richard Dandy. Richard Dandy, step forward."

The next minute a fluffy yellow canary bird fluttered forward and perched on the edge of the witness box.

"Oh, Dicky!" cried Bessie, suddenly remembering that she had forgotten to feed him all day. Then she paused in sheer amazement, for Dick was talking in a faint, chirpy voice.

"I know the prisoner well. She is my mistress. She was told by her mother to be sure to feed me today, but she forgot, as she very often does. All this long, hot day I have been in my cage without one bit of food or one drop of drink. As you can see, my strength is almost gone and I can with difficulty speak. My mistress has been guilty of great cruelty, and if I had died of hunger my death would have been at her door."

"Oh, Dicky, I'm sorry," said Bessie with a little sob; but nobody paid any attention to her.

"You may step down, Richard Dandy. Call the next witness," said the judge, in a voice that was as much like the ticking of the clock as anything could be.

"Tiger Lily," called the clerk of the court, and a fierce-looking fellow strode forward with a gorgeous mantle of orange and crimson flung over his shoulders.

"Your lordship and gentlemen of the jury, I am here to witness on behalf of all my kindred and friends in Bessie Hill's garden. This morning she was told to water us, but she did not do so. All this hot day we have drooped and wilted in a burning sun while the earth baked about our feet. Many of my friends fainted, and some of them may be dead. We have all suffered terribly, and that cruel girl is the cause of it."

"Monday's Composition," called the clerk, and something walked into the witness box of so odd an appearance that Bessie would have laughed had not her terror prevented. It was tall and lank and white and all marked over with scratches and blots.

"Look at me," said a dolorous voice, "and see if my appearance does not call for compassion. I am Bessie Hill's composition and must be handed to her teacher on Monday morning. She ought to have rewritten me, but she has not done so, and I must go in this shocking state. Her teacher will write some biting criticism over me as if I did not already feel the disgrace of my position keenly enough. I will suffer for her fault. Gentlemen of the jury, I appeal to you for justice."

"Oh dear, oh dear, I never thought compositions could feel," wailed Bessie, but the composition, after one contemptuous glance in her direction, stalked out, and its place was at once filled by her muslin dress with the long rip from elbow to wrist in the sleeve.

"Bessie was told to sew this rent up," rustled the dress, "and she has not done so. Nobody knows what I have suffered in this mutilated condition. I have been like this for a whole week. Just think of my feelings. Justice, my lord and jury, justice."

"Oh, what are you going to do with me?" cried poor Bessie. "If you'd only give me another chance! I'll sew you up right now if you'll let me . . . indeed I will!"

"Silence in the court," ticked the judge threateningly.

Then the jury held a consultation. Presently the foreman arose and announced that they had come to a decision.

"Do you find the prisoner guilty or not guilty?" demanded the judge.

"Guilty," said the foreman solemnly. He looked very like a teapot that had been broken in the Hill household the previous week because Bessie had forgotten to put it in its proper place.

"Elizabeth Hill," said the judge gravely, "have you anything to say before sentence is passed on you?"

"Oh, I'm so sorry," sobbed Bessie. "If you'll only let me off this time, I'll never forget again . . . truly I never will. Please forgive me. I didn't know compositions and dresses and things felt that way."

"You knew that your canary bird had feelings, and yet you left him to starve," said the judge sternly. "This is your punishment. You shall be deprived of our food for a whole day as he was; you shall be left without water to drink for the same time as your flowers; you shall be mutilated like your composition; and finally you must wear that dress everywhere you go for the rest of the summer."

What a terrible punishment! Bessie felt helpless. On every side she saw only angry, unsympathetic faces. She gave a pitiful little shriek as she saw the clerk of the court advancing toward her, and the dingy room, stern faces, judge, and jury vanished, and there she was sitting by the window of her own room while the old clock was ticking majestically outside her door.

"Oh, it was only a dream," cried Bessie, with a gasp of relief. "But how dreadful it was."

She flew downstairs to the sitting room where poor Dicky was twittering feebly in his cage. In a few minutes he was rejoicing over a plentiful supply of food and drink. Then the drooping flowers in the garden were liberally watered. The torn sleeve was next attended to, and when Mrs. Hill came home Bessie was rewriting her composition.

When she had finished it she sat down by her mother's side and told her the story of her funny dream.

"But it didn't seem very funny to me at the time," she concluded. "I never was so frightened in my life. How glad I was when I wakened up. Of course, I know that dresses and compositions can't really feel, but poor Dicky can and perhaps the flowers, too, and I was a very cruel girl. Dear me, I can see that horrid old judge's face yet. When you find me forgetting anything again, Mother, just say 'dream' and that will be enough."

WHAT TEDDY AND GORDON SAW IN THE LANE

(1904)

"I really don't know which you would better take," said Papa Porter. "They are both bright little chaps—but I think Gordon is the brighter. His teacher says so."

"They are both good-tempered little fellows and have been taught to look after themselves," said Mama Porter. "But," she said with a sigh, "Gordon never will wash behind his ears if you don't watch him."

"I can take only one," said Uncle Ralph, "and I want that one to be the boy who has the sharpest powers of observation, because he will be the one who gets most good out of the trip."

"I'm sure I don't know which you'd better take," said Mama Porter doubtfully. She was a good housekeeper and a better mother, but she was very far from sure that she knew just what Uncle Ralph meant by his "powers of observation."

Uncle Ralph's eyes twinkled.

"I'll soon find out," he said. "Call the boys in. I have a test to put to them."

Teddy and Gordon, ages eleven and twelve, respectively, were thereupon summoned from the carriage-house loft, where they were having a glorious game of Indian ambush. Uncle Ralph looked at them approvingly. They were really very nice little chaps to have for nephews.

"I wonder," he said, "which pair of eyes are the sharper—your blue ones, Gordon, or your grey ones, Teddy?"

Ted and Gordon maintained a prudent silence. That was always the best way with Uncle Ralph, unless you knew exactly what he was driving at.

"In order to find out," went on Uncle Ralph, "I am going to take both of you through the lane behind the barn. You will walk through it and not say one word. Then you will each write me a composition describing what you saw in the lane. And to the boy who writes the composition which pleases me most I shall award a prize."

Teddy and Gordon instantly grew excited. Only, Teddy did not feel very hopeful—teacher always said that Gordon's compositions were so much better than his. But he resolved to try his very best.

They had their walk through the lane, and then the boys were dispatched to separate rooms to write their compositions. After tea they brought them to Uncle Ralph. Papa and Mama Porter were likewise on hand to hear them read.

"Mine is short," said Gordon, looking with some surprise at the sheet of foolscap that Teddy handed in. "It was pretty hard to write much about the lane. I didn't see hardly anything to write about."

Uncle Ralph put on his specs and read Gordon's first.

"There is a very beautiful lane behind our barn," Gordon had written. "It is all arched over with trees, and I love to walk there, because it is always shady and cool and pleasant. Teddy and I go through it every night and morning when we take the cows to pasture and bring them home. I think I like the morning walk best, but the evening is very pleasant, too. Uncle Ralph and Ted and I walked through it today, but there was not much to see, only trees and ferns and flowers. The wild roses are in blossom at one end. I love wild roses. And we saw a rabbit; it ran across the road right before us. This is all I saw in the lane. But I enjoyed my walk through it very much."

"Humph!" said Uncle Ralph. Then he took up Ted's. Ted was feeling blue. He knew that his composition, although longer, was not so well-written and expressed as Gordon's, and teacher had always assured him that quality was so much more important than quantity. He never could begin or end gracefully, and his sentences were short and "wouldn't hang together somehow," as he complained.

"There are fourteen wild cherry trees in the lane," Ted's composition began, abruptly. "There are three birches, eight maples, two willows, one beech, and one mountain ash. There are no cherries this year. The frost killed them in June. There are no beechnuts, either. There is a robin's nest in the beech tree. There are six kinds of ferns in the lane. The curly kind smell nice. They fade quick, though, and the stiff green ones don't. They have seeds on the under side of their leaves. There is a lot of rice lilies growing in the grass at the far end. We call them rice lilies, but teacher says they are wild orkids. They are cream colour. They smell awful sweet. I saw three bluebirds. One was sitting on the fence. One was flying. One was hopping on the ground. He had a worm in his mouth. One of the birch trees has a strip of bark torn off it all round. The inside is an awful pretty golden brown colour and shiny. There is a yellow-hammer's nest in the gatepost. There are three eggs in it. There is a dead bough on one of the birches. It has turned yellow. I saw a rabbit. He came out of Abner Keech's spruce woods and went over into our clover field. He hopped. He was all grey, and about as big as a cat. I saw two squirrels on the beech, and a ground squirrel on the fence. He was grey with brown stripes. The other squirrels were red. I saw a lot of feathers on the ground. I guess a hawk had killed a bird. I saw a broken robin's egg. I guess a crow had taken it. There is a bush at one end with fourteen roses on it. This is all I saw in the lane."

"From a literary standpoint," said Uncle Ralph, folding up Ted's composition, "there is no doubt that you have yet much to learn in the gentle art of expression, Theodore. Considered as a composition, Gordon's is much better written, and 'orchids' is not spelt with a 'k,' Theodore. But you will remember that I did not say the best composition, but the composition that pleased me most. Ted's pleases me most because it shows that he can use his eyes to more purpose than you can, Gordon. You saw almost nothing in the lane. Ted saw a great deal. Hence, Ted goes with me to Montreal next week. He will there have a chance to see a good many things."

Ted drew a long breath. He looked a little doubtfully at Gordon. But Gordon was not a bit jealous or sulky. He would dearly have loved to go to Montreal, but since he couldn't, the next best thing was to have Ted go.

"But I'm going to learn to use my eyes, too," he told Ted, when they talked it over in the carriage-house loft. "I never thought about it before. It's s'prising how much you can see when you look."

FRANK'S REVENGE
(1905)

It was noon recess at Appledale School, and in one corner of the building was an excited group, of which Lisle Andrews and Frank Merwin were the central figures.

Lisle and Frank had had a brush that morning over a problem in the geometry class; and later on, when Mr. Sanderson had given back the history examination papers, Lisle was four marks ahead of Frank and had displayed some ill-timed triumph.

Frank was feeling very sore over his double humiliation, and Rose Chalmers put the last touch to it by taunting him with his defeat before the class at recess. Frank crimsoned hotly. "Well, I don't cheat at examinations, anyhow," he exclaimed impetuously "If I did, perhaps I would always come out first, too. But that isn't *my* way."

Lisle Andrews's grey eyes flashed ominously. "Do you mean to insinuate that I cheated, Frank Merwin?"

"I know you did," retorted Frank. "I saw you peeping into your history twice when Mr. Sanderson wasn't looking."

"You never saw anything of the kind," cried Lisle, losing her temper completely. "It *wasn't* my history. It was the dictionary. I wanted to see how a word was spelled."

"That's a likely story. I guess there's not many will believe that, Miss Andrews."

"O, go on—call me a storyteller, too, as well as a cheat," cried Lisle, bursting into tears of anger. "Just wait until Mr. Sanderson comes, though, and see if I don't tell him."

"You're welcome to," retorted Frank as he flung himself out of the school; but he felt rather uncomfortable, nevertheless. It was one of Lisle's unpopular characteristics that she was too much disposed to be a telltale, and Frank did not relish the idea of having his foolish and unguarded accusation brought up before Mr. Sanderson.

Frank and Lisle both belonged to the seventh grade in the Appledale School and were considered the cleverest two in it. The rivalry between them was rather sharp. Frank was a general favourite in the school, while Lisle was disliked. She was considered to be sulky-tempered and vain, and some called her spiteful and envious. Nevertheless, like everyone else, Lisle had her good as well as her bad qualities and might have made friends in plenty had it not been for her pronounced tendency to crow over defeated rivals, a fault more fatal to popularity than almost any other.

Between Frank and Lisle, as I have said, a class enmity existed that wanted but little to become bitterly personal. That little was supplied by the outcome of that unlucky history examination and its consequent skirmish. Mr. Sanderson, coming in at noon, found Lisle at her desk with red eyes and an injured expression. Inquiry was followed by a resentful explanation of her wrongs and an investigation into them by the master, with whom Lisle was rather a favourite pupil. The result was that Frank got a severe rebuke. Moreover, Mr. Sanderson told him that, as he had insulted his classmate before the whole class, he must apologize to her before the class for such ungentlemanly behaviour.

Frank would have preferred almost any other punishment. Lisle's eyes sparkled with triumph, and she tossed her head expressively, regardless of the angry looks cast at her by Frank's partisans.

Mr. Sanderson turned to his desk and wrote out a brief and comprehensive form of apology. This he handed to Frank. "Now, sir," he said sternly, "sign your name to that, and then read it aloud."

Frank took the paper with a crimson face. Left to himself, he would probably soon have repented of his rude speeches to Lisle, but this public humiliation roused his boyish anger to white heat. He blamed Lisle for it all, and mentally added another to his list of grudges against her as he read the apology slowly, feeling as if every word would choke him.

"Now go to your seats," commanded Mr. Sanderson, "and don't let me hear any more of this squabbling among you." He dismissed the matter from his mind forthwith. But not so Frank. He vowed to himself that he would pay Lisle back sooner or later. Lisle herself felt uncomfortable and sorry but would not show it, and was sneered at by some as a "telltale" and let severely alone by others.

One Wednesday quite a sensation was caused by an announcement from Mr. Sanderson. It was to the effect that Mr. Keyworth, the Appledale minister, had offered a prize for the best essay of not more than a thousand words to be written by a member of the seventh grade. The subject of the essay was "Poetry," and the prize was to be several beautifully bound volumes of the standard poets. The competition was open to the whole grade, and the essays were to be handed in to Mr. Sanderson in a fortnight's time; a committee would decide on them, and at the semi-annual public examination of the school the following week, the prize was to be awarded and the prize essay read.

When school was dismissed, the excited Sevenths clustered on the playground in agitated swarms. Some nine or ten declared their intention of competing, although, as a sort of safeguard against probable mortification, each ended up by saying that the prize would be between Frank Merwin and Lisle Andrews.

A distinct excitement pervaded the seventh grade for the following two weeks. Most of the competitors discussed their essays freely, but Frank and Lisle were markedly reticent, from which fact the Sevenths concluded that this competition was to be a tug-of-war between them.

On the day upon which the essays were to be given to Mr. Sanderson, eleven students of Grade Seven handed in their rolls of manuscript. Lisle Andrews was not present, and curiosity was aroused. She did not come until recess, when she suddenly appeared on the playground with such a woebegone expression that even her bitterest enemies relented enough to crowd around and ask what was the matter.

"I've—I've lost my essay," said Lisle chokingly. "I put it in my basket this morning and came by the wood road. I suppose it slipped out. It was on top of my books. I missed it when I got to the hollow and went right back. I've been hunting ever since, but I couldn't find it. I suppose it has gone for good and so has my chance of the prize." Lisle's voice trembled into a sob, and she hastily walked into the schoolroom to hide her tears.

The Sevenths were disposed to be sympathetic, with the exception of Frank Merwin, who would have been more than human not to have experienced a little satisfaction. He went home to dinner by the wood road and paused on the bridge across the brook to peer for a moment into its dim, golden-brown depths. As he did so his eye fell on something white, caught in a crevice of the cross logs under the little rustic bridge. He stooped down and drew it out with a face suddenly flushed. It was Lisle Andrews's essay and must have fallen from her basket as she crossed the bridge. For an instant Frank hesitated. Then he stooped down and replaced the essay between the logs. "I don't care," he muttered as he hurried up the road. "I said I'd pay her back, and I will. She'd serve me the same way quick enough. I wasn't looking for her essay. I just happened to see it, and it is there exactly as I found it. I didn't hide it. Someone else is quite likely to find it. If so, all right."

Mr. Sanderson's patience was sorely tried in the senior geometry class that afternoon. The wits of his two star students seemed to be wool-gathering. Lisle Andrews was brooding gloomily over her loss, and Frank Merwin made mistakes that would have disgraced a fifth-grade boy. When the class was dismissed, he asked permission to go out; and when the scholars swarmed out for recess ten minutes later, it was to see Frank Merwin spring over the wood fence, breathless with haste and with a roll of manuscript in his hand. Straight to the moody Lisle Andrews he went. "Lisle, here is your essay. I found it under the bridge at dinnertime, and at first I thought I'd leave it there to pay you out. It was mean of me, and I felt mean, so I went and got it." It cost Frank a good deal to say this to Lisle, but he brought it out manfully. Lisle turned very red and took her essay in a silence that seemed to Frank both sulky and ungrateful, but he did not care for that. His conscience was clear once more, and he felt that he could look anyone squarely in the face.

The examination day came; the schoolroom was filled with visitors. All the exercises went off smoothly, but the real excitement came when Mr. Heyworth got up to announce the prizewinner and award the prize. His speech was brief. The essays, he said, were almost all good, and a credit to their writers, but there were two—here everybody looked at Frank and Lisle—which in style and vigour had been judged best. Over these the committee had hesitated for some time; but, as the essay marked "B" was a trifle exaggerated in style, they had finally decided to award the prize to essay "G," which was simple and more clearly written. He was pleased to announce Master Frank Merwin as the successful competitor. Miss Lisle Andrews was a close and excellent second.

The Seventh boys went wild and cheered vociferously. Those near Frank thumped him on the back until he was purple. In the general excitement, very few noticed Lisle at all, but she did not seem disappointed.

When all was over and the scholars were crowding about Frank on the playground, Lisle came calmly down the steps, through the group, and held out her hand. "I want to congratulate you, too, Frank—and thank you. I've behaved abominably to you, I know. Please forgive me, and—and—I'm glad you got the prize," she concluded lamely.

Frank shook her hand with impulsive heartiness. "It's all right, Lisle. I was just as much to blame, and more. I ought not to have said what I did about the history examination. Can't we be friends after this?"

The others had fallen back out of hearing. Lisle flushed gratefully. "I'd like to. I know the others don't like me, but after this I mean to try to be nicer and not so cranky. I've often felt ashamed of myself; but I was too stubborn to give in, and one thing led to another some way."

"Let's just rub out the slate and begin over again," said Frank.

"Agreed," responded Lisle.

Hence it was that the Sevenths were surprised beyond measure at the sight of Frank Merwin and Lisle Andrews walking amicably down the street together.

WHY PEOPLE LIKED AMY
(1905)

"I wonder why Amy hasn't been over this week," said Aunt Min to Grandma, as they went around the hollyhock curve. "It seems such a long time since we saw the dear child."

"It's five days," said Grandma, promptly. "Five days without Amy is too bad. I must scold her for it when she comes."

"As if anyone could ever scold Amy!" laughed Aunt Min, as they passed out of earshot.

Flo and Jennie, sewing at the window over the honeysuckle porch, heard this little dialogue. They had come to spend the summer with Grandma, and they had been long enough in Riverdale to become pretty well acquainted with the younger set.

"I wonder why everyone likes Amy so much," said Flo, thoughtfully. "She is the most popular girl in Riverdale, but I'm sure I can't tell why."

"She isn't pretty or witty, but she is certainly the one loved best," said Jennie. "Let us try to find out the secret of her popularity the next time she comes over."

Amy came that afternoon. She was short and plump, with bright brown eyes that were always shining and rosy cheeks that were always dimpling. She was not a bit pretty herself, but her smile was so bewitching that you never got past it to the consideration of her face.

She had brought a big bunch of old-fashioned, pink English roses for Grandma.

"I just remembered as I came through our yard that you liked our old roses so much, so I picked all the very nicest ones for you," she said.

There was a magazine for Aunt Min.

"Aunt Laura sent it out from town, and the minute I saw that article on lace-making, I thought you would like to see it, Aunt Min. O Flo, I've just wanted to see you, ever since you wore your new pink organdy, to tell you it was sweet. It is the prettiest dress in Riverdale. Jennie, everybody says you outdid yourself in the anthem last Sunday night. Professor Dawson admires your voice immensely. Well, I must toddle up and see Aunt Marcia. I've brought her some heliotrope."

Aunt Marcia was a shut-in, who spent her days on a sofa in the southeast sitting room. Amy kissed her with the heartiness of one who kisses from choice, put the heliotrope in Aunt Marcia's blue vase, and then sat down and chattered for a bright half-hour, telling Aunt Marcia all the Riverdale doings and sayings, describing all the merrymakings and all the girls' new dresses, forgetting none of all the little things Aunt Marcia liked to hear about, even if she were an invalid.

"Come again soon, dearie," she said, lovingly, when Amy went away.

On the stairs Amy met Tom, who insisted on carrying her off to his workshop to show her some new contrivance of his. Tom was always inventing things. Amy listened and questioned and gave Tom all the chances he wanted to display his darling bit of work and explain it fully to so interested a listener.

"It's a pleasure to show one's work to a girl who understands it," said Tom, patronizingly. Whereas the truth was that Amy hardly knew the difference between a rivet and a screw.

Then there were the twins, Davy and Jill, who had kittens and puppies in the barn to show her and who were prouder than peacocks when Amy pronounced the kittens half Maltese and thought the puppies very intelligent for their age. She helped name them all, discussing the appropriateness of various names as gravely and earnestly as the twins themselves. Davy and Jill thought Amy a very sensible girl; she clearly understood that it made a great deal of difference whether the grey kitten with tan points was called Daffy or Rusty.

Coming back through the kitchen, Amy hunted Hannah Jane out of the pantry to tell her that her jumbles had been pronounced the most delicious things contributed to the Flower Band social the week before and that her mother wanted the recipe. Hannah Jane beamed all over her broad red face and set to work to write it out at once with her floury hands.

Then old Mrs. Lane came with her basket, and when it was well-filled with leftovers by kindly Aunt Min, Amy said brightly:

"I think we're both going the same way, Aunt Jessie"—Mrs. Lane, who wasn't anybody's aunt, loved to be called so—"so just let me carry your basket for you as far as I go. I'm glad of company on the way home."

So away went Amy, as pleasant and agreeable to a bent, crooked, not over tidy old woman as if her "company" had been one of her bright young girl friends.

Flo and Jennie looked at each other.

"Well?" said Flo, questioningly.

"Thoughtfulness," said Jen.

"And unselfishness," said Flo.

"And a power of interesting herself in what interests other people—not just pretending to do so, but really doing it," said Jen.

"She makes you feel glad and cheerful just because she is so," said Flo.

"And she likes to tell people nice things she's heard about them. There isn't a particle of envy about her," said Jen.

"In short, she really loves her neighbour as well as herself, no matter whether the neighbour is an invalid, or a twin, or a servant, or old Mrs. Lane," concluded Flo. "I think that is why people like Amy."

DISCONTENTED DOROTHY
(1905)

Dorothy was a very discontented little girl indeed. She was much given to grumbling and was apt to say a great many times a day that it would be *ever* so much nicer if she could be like Kitty Glover or have a hat like Minna Sherwood or go out, riding in a pony carriage whenever she pleased like Hazel Lawrence. At times Dorothy really thought that she was more to be pitied than any other little girl in the world. O, she was quite sure she was.

One warm, drowsy summer day she was surer than ever. Everything was poky and horrid and hateful. "I'm just sick and tired of being Dorothy Kirke!" said Dorothy decidedly. She had gone out into the garden to say it and was sitting on the grass under the big silver maple, her head resting against its trunk, with a rosebush all pinked over with roses before her and a big clump of splendid, fierce tiger lilies, all very gorgeously bedecked with orange and crimson, behind her.

Now perhaps you don't know any more than Dorothy knew that it's a very dangerous thing to grumble near tiger lilies.

"Why are you sick and tired of being Dorothy Kirke?" said a voice behind Dorothy—such a tiny, piping voice that if you hadn't been very close, you might have thought that it was just the wind whistling through the trumpets of the tiger lilies.

Dorothy jumped up and wheeled around. There, sitting right on the middle of the biggest, most splendid tiger lily of all, was a fairy, with his arms folded across his breast and his feet hanging over the edge of a red-freckled petal.

Dorothy knew at once that it was a fairy, although she had never seen one before. There could be no mistaking it. He wasn't quite three inches tall, and two lovely, gauzy wings sprouted from his shoulders. He wore a funny little peaked yellow cap, a doublet of crimson silk, and long hose of pale green. His feet were shod with funny yellow shoes with twisted points at the toes.

"Who are you?" cried Dorothy in amazement.

"O, I'm the prince of the tiger lily fairies," he said carelessly, "but it doesn't matter about me. You are the one concerned. You've been grumbling around the lilies today and yesterday and the day before, and so I've been obliged to come and see what the trouble is. I can't be worried like this all summer. It's really getting on my nerves. Now why are you tired of being yourself?"

Dorothy thought the fairy looked cross and impatient, so she hastened to answer: "O, because I never have any good times, like—like the other girls. I haven't a pony like Hazel Lawrence, and my new hat isn't half as pretty as Minna Sherwood's, and I have to mind the baby when I want to play, and I have to learn long, horrid lessons and new patchwork and wash dishes, and O, I'm just tired of it!"

"Well, you are in a pretty predicament, I must say," said the fairy reflectively. "But I'll soon remedy that. I'll change you into any other little girl you'd like to be in a jiffy."

"O, how perfectly splendid!" cried Dorothy in delight.

"Well, well, tell me who you want to be," said the fairy crossly. He really didn't seem to be a very good-tempered fairy, but that is the way with the tiger lily folk. You can never depend on them. "I haven't time to stay here all day. They are waiting for me at court this very minute. If you hadn't vexed the tiger lilies so, I wouldn't have come at all. But I had to attend to their complaints. Now who will you be?"

"O, I think I'll be Hazel Lawrence," cried Dorothy, all in a flutter. "But no, no! How could I have forgotten? She hasn't any mother, and I wouldn't be without a mother for any amount of pony carriages. Kitty Glover—but Kitty Glover has red hair, and I think that would be dreadful. Minna Sherwood—but O dear, Minna is so stupid in school! The teacher is always scolding her. Then there's Alice Gray. She lives in a lovely big house; but then she hasn't any brothers or sisters to play with, and she must be dreadfully lonesome. Jennie Larkins hasn't to learn lessons or sew; but her parents are very poor, and Jennie has to go barefooted. Milly Martin has a pug nose, and Bertha Clark's big brother is horrid to her, and—and—and, O dear fairy, I can't think of any little girl I'd really like to be, after all."

"Then what were you grumbling for?" asked the fairy severely. "I have a good notion to change you into one of those girls anyway, just to punish you."

"O, don't do that!" entreated Dorothy in sudden terror. "O please, dear, good, kind fairy, don't do that! I really don't want to be changed. And I'll never, never grumble any more. Indeed I won't."

"Will you promise me solemnly that you will not?" demanded the fairy.

"Yes, indeed; cross my heart," answered Dorothy eagerly.

"Very well, then. Mind you don't," said the fairy just as a sudden gust of wind came along and mixed the tiger lilies all up together. When the wind passed and the lilies stopped nodding, the fairy was gone and Dorothy was sitting down on the grass with her head against the maple, although she was quite sure she had been standing up while she was talking to the fairy.

Dorothy told her mama all about it, and her mama laughed and said that she had dreamed it. But Dorothy has been very careful not to grumble or give way to discontent since that day; for she thinks that *perhaps* it wasn't a dream and the fairy *might* hear her, and it's better to be on the safe side.

DOT'S WORLD
(1906)

"Oh, dear me!" said Dot, crossly, "this is a horrid old world. It's the very worst world ever was!"

Aunt Meg smiled.

"I've been thinking it was a real nice world. What is the matter with it?"

"It rained all morning," said Dot, "and I couldn't go down to play with Sallie, and I've nuffin to do, and I'm tired of all my books and games. Nobody pays any 'tention to me, and it's a horrid old world."

Aunt Meg laid down her work and looked seriously at seven-year-old Dot. Dot liked to have people look seriously at her. It made her feel so nice and grown up.

"I don't really think it is a horrid world, Dot," she said. "It is just the kind of world we make it. Would you like a recipe for making it a nice world?"

"'Course I would," said Dot, promptly.

"Then," said Aunt Meg, decidedly, "you must go and do things for other people."

"What things?" asked Dot, opening her eyes.

"Oh, I can't tell you that. You must find out what things for yourself."

"Are you in earnest?" demanded Dot.

"Indeed I am. Just try my recipe. You'll see that it will change your opinion about the world."

Privately Dot didn't believe it would. She wasn't at all sure she knew just what Aunt Meg meant, but she thought it over very carefully as she went downstairs.

In the sitting room she saw Grandma getting ready to wind a skein of yarn over two chairs. Dot knew it made Grandma's arms and rheumatic fingers ache to wind yarn, but Dot didn't like it, either, and she was just slipping out when she thought of what Aunt Meg had said. Was this what she meant?

"Grandma, I'll wind your yarn for you," she said.

And wind it she did. When it was done, Grandma gave her a kiss and a pineapple drop.

"I'm ever so much obliged to you, dearie. You're a thoughtful little girl."

Dot slipped out to the kitchen, and there was Nora getting ready to bake a cake.

"Can't I seed those raisins for you, Nora?" she said.

"Shure, and it's meself that'll be obliged to yez if you will," said Nora, heartily. "I've got forty other things to do this blessed afternoon. If ye'll seed the raisins for me, I'll bake yez two little pattypans out of the cake for your doll house."

"Where is Ethel?" said Mama, coming into the kitchen when the raisins were done. "I want her to amuse Bobby while I stitch up her shirtwaist."

"Ethel is busy doing her arithmetic for Monday," said Dot. "I'll play with Bobby, Mama."

So for an hour Dot played woolly bear and building house with two-year-old Bobby.

"That's my little woman," said Mama.

When Bobby fell asleep, six-year-old Teddy strayed in with tears on his face.

"I tan't learn my letters," he sobbed.

"Oh, yes, you can," said Dot, brightly. "I'll help you. Come along, we'll go up to the hall window seat and find out all about them."

In half an hour's time Teddy had got his alphabet so well straightened out that he knew every letter in it. Then Dot ran down to the Corners and did an errand for Ethel, for the rain had stopped and the sun was shining gloriously. The flowers in Dot's garden plot were all wide open and fresh when she came back.

“I b’lieve I’ll pick a bunch and take them down to old Mrs. Brown,” said Dot to herself. “I know she likes flowers, and she hasn’t any.”

“Bless your kind little heart, dearie!” said Mrs. Brown, as she took the big sweet bouquet of blossoms. “It’s a sweet thing of you to think of bringing me such lovely flowers. I’ve been wishing for some all day. And you’re like a flower yourself, pet.”

That evening Aunt Meg came into the little white bedroom where Dot had just gone to bed.

“Well, Dot, what do you think of the world now?” she asked, merrily.

“It’s a nice, splendid world,” said Dot. “I’m ever so much obliged to you for your recipe, Aunt Meg, and I’m going to use it every day.”

THE POT OF GOLD AT RAINBOW'S END
(1906)

In the spring of '86, Father sold his farm at Edgehill and moved to one over Rainbow's End, fifty miles away. I was a boy of twelve at the time, and my principal memories of our moving are connected with the jokes indulged in by our neighbours, who kept asking us if we were going to Rainbow's End in hopes of finding a pot of gold. I had often wondered, when I heard the settlement of Rainbow's End mentioned, how, why, and when it had acquired such a curious name, and as soon as we were settled there, I proceeded to find out.

Our right-hand neighbour was William Temple, and to him I propounded the question:

"Why is Rainbow's End called Rainbow's End?"

"Because there's a pot of gold buried here, of course," said Mr. Temple, with a twinkle in his eye. I was sick of hearing about that pot of gold. I felt indignant, for I thought Mr. Temple was making fun of me.

"Why don't you dig it up, then?" I asked, with twelve-year-old pertness. "A pot of gold isn't much use if it's buried."

Mr. Temple laughed.

"We'd dig it up mighty quick, if we knew where it was, sonny. Old Aunt Kitty'd be glad to find it. It'd belong to her. 'Twas her brother buried it, so they say. You can spend your spare time projecting for it—it's the favourite amusement of our Rainbow's End gilded youth."

"Is there really a pot of gold?" I asked, curiosity getting the better of my fear of a trap.

"Certain," said Mr. Temple. "Never heard the story? Well,

you know old Aunt Kitty next door to you over there? James Peterson was her brother, and a queer old miser and hermit he was. He lived alone in that house Aunt Kitty lives in now, and he was supposed to have a pile hid somewhere round, all in gold, for notes he'd never keep. If he had to take one in payment for anything, straight to the bank he'd go and get gold for it. He was always called 'Old James Peterson,' because he was so queer and close, but he wasn't really old—not mor'n forty. And when the war broke out he enlisted, to the astonishment of everybody. In a year's time he died of fever. Two of his mates, Sam Gorrall and Percy Whitman, were with him when he died, and he told them he had put all his money in a stoneware crock and hid it safely before he left home, and that it was all for his sister, Mrs. Abner Moore. He didn't tell them where he'd hid it, but he wrote his sister a letter and told her where she'd find the money, and he gave the letter to Sam Gorrall to take to her. Sam promised he would, but the next day he was taken prisoner in a skirmish and died down south in a prison, and that letter was never seen or heard tell of again. Percy Whitman came home and told what he knew of the story. Mrs. Moore was James Peterson's only living relative, so his house was hers, and she came and lived in it, her husband being dead. Everything was done to find that pot of gold, and the home was ransacked a dozen times, and every inch of ground near it has been dug up, but 'twasn't ever discovered and never will be, I reckon. Folks laugh at the story, and say there never was a pot of gold buried, and that Perce Whitman either made the yarn up—Perce was fond of yarning, it can't be denied—or, that James Peterson was raving. But it's certain not a cent of his money was ever found, and he must have had a little, at least. This settlement was always called Milligan's Road until about six years ago, when folks began to think it wasn't high-sounding enough, and they had a meeting in the schoolhouse to select a new name. There were two factions, and they couldn't agree on a name and came near fighting about it. Then the schoolmaster suggested

Rainbow's End, and they decided to call it that rather than give in to the other side."

I was not a little excited over Mr. Temple's story, but later I found that the pot of gold was looked upon as a myth by most of the Rainbow's End people, who said that James Peterson was a poor man who had made no more than a bare living by lobster fishing in summer and job work in winter.

"Old Aunt Kitty," as she was called, was our left-hand neighbour, a tiny, bent old woman of seventy, yet as smart and active on her feet as a girl. She lived in a little house in the hollow below our farm, with big birch trees growing about it and a fertile garden of gooseberry bushes behind it. As a rule, Aunt Kitty was not fond of boys; she had been much pestered by adventurous youths who wanted to poke and pry and dig about for the pot of gold. But she seemed to like me and always made me welcome when I went over to see her.

Aunt Kitty was in mortal dread of the poorhouse. Her husband had left her poorly off, and what little money she had was almost gone.

"I'm too old to work," she said to me one day, when she had been telling me all her troubles, "and I don't see anything for me but the poorhouse. Oh, it's dreadful to think of! I know they're going to send me there this fall. It'll break my heart. The thought of it just haunts me night and day. It's such an awful disgrace. If I could only find my pot of gold!"

Old Aunt Kitty firmly believed in the pot of gold and bitterly resented any doubt cast upon its existence. She was somewhat childish on the subject and spent much of her time poking about with the hoe and spade looking for it. She believed that it was concealed somewhere in the cellar, probably because she often dreamed of finding it there.

I had my spell of prospecting for it, too, like every other boy who had been born in or immigrated to Rainbow's End. After a time, however, my enthusiasm waxed cold, and I took to hunting ferns instead of gold, having got the notion of making a collection of ferns from a boy's magazine I took. Rainbow's End woods abounded in ferns, and by September I had a fairly good assortment.

That summer is yet remembered in Rainbow's End as the dry summer. The drought was phenomenal. From the first of June until the third week in September there was only one rainy day. The crops failed; everything was parched up; the brooks and springs ran low and in most cases dried up altogether. Among Aunt Kitty's many troubles was the fear that her well was going dry. It was lower than it had ever been at any time in her recollection, except the summer her brother had enlisted. It was a large, open well, with stone walls out of whose crevices long ferns grew abundantly. It was surmounted by a kind of hood of mossy, crumbling boards, and the water, which was exceedingly cold and sweet, was drawn up by means of windlass and rope.

One day in early September it struck me that a certain fern I wanted to complete my collection might possibly be found in Aunt Kitty's well. I went over to her house and, finding it deserted, betook myself to the well. I could not reach the ferns with my hands, but I knelt down in front of the well and leaned far over the curb, peering downward into the cool gloom to scrutinize the ferns. Suddenly, the rotten board against which I was too heavily pressing gave way, and I pitched headforemost into Aunt Kitty's well.

If I had fallen unhindered to the bottom, I would certainly have been killed. But by great good fortune I struck on the bucket, which was swinging loosely about a third of the distance down. I blindly and half involuntarily grasped at it, the windlass whirled wildly around, and bucket and boy sped down to the bottom together. There was enough water in the well to break my fall, and I was not at all injured except for some bruises, but for a few moments I was blind and dazed, not understanding what had happened to me. I soon came to myself, however, and found that I was doubled up at the bottom of Aunt Kitty's well in ice-cold water to my neck. I managed to get on my feet, and then the water reached to my waist. When my dizzy head grew better, I had some thought of trying to climb out of the well by means of the rope and the rough stones in the sides. But I soon abandoned the idea.

The rope was none too strong, and the stones were mossy and slippery. I was in no danger, and although the situation was an uncomfortable one, I decided I would better remain where I was until Aunt Kitty returned home and I could send her to summon assistance.

When my eyes got accustomed to the gloom, I began to examine my surroundings—cabined, cribbed, confined they were, indeed! The last few feet of the well had been drilled through solid rock, from which gushed the ice-cold spring. Above this rock basin, which was generally covered with water, were the roughly stoned walls of the well, but just at my elbow was a space between the rock and the masonry about half a foot high, looking like a deep, dark shelf. I poked my hand in to explore it out of simple curiosity. My fingers came into contact with something round and hard. I clutched it and drew out—an old crock of brown stoneware!

For a moment I stared at it incredulously, disbelieving the evidence of my eyes. Then I lifted the round cover; inside were James Peterson's gold pieces, unharmed by their long seclusion, as potent for good or evil as they had ever been. I had found the long-lost treasure.

I forgot my bruises and aching head and almost freezing feet, and gave vent to my feelings in a whoop of delight that sounded unearthly in that narrow tunnel. Oh, why didn't somebody come?—not so much to get me out of the well as to hear my great news! I was bursting with it.

It was all of an hour later when Aunt Kitty returned home from a neighbourly call and came to the well for a bucket of water. As she peered over the curb of the well, grumbling at finding the front board broken and the bucket down the well, I called out heedlessly:

"Oh, Aunt Kitty, I'm down the well! Please get—"

I got no further, for, with a shriek of terror, Aunt Kitty disappeared. I had frightened the poor old soul nearly to death by my thoughtless shout.

As I learned later, Aunt Kitty fled over to our place at once with her tale of woe, but at the time I did not know what had become of her, and I feared she had fainted. Besides, I was getting very anxious to be rescued from my uncomfortable position. After what seemed to me a long time but which was really only about a quarter of an hour, I heard voices, and presently Father was peering down the well.

"Father, won't you please get me out of this?" I exclaimed.

"It's Tom!" said Father. "How did you get down there? Are you hurt?"

"I fell in," I answered, with chattering teeth. "I'm not much hurt, except that I'm black and blue with bruises, but I'll catch my death of cold if you don't get me out of this mighty quick."

"Can you climb a ladder, if we put one down?" said Father.

I said that I could, and, after a little more delay, two ladders were secured, lashed together, and cautiously lowered down. I took the pot under my arm and stiffly scrambled up the swaying rungs. As I stepped out on good solid ground once more, Father, and my brother Ted, and Mr. Temple, and Mother, and Aunt Kitty, who were all standing around, gave a simultaneous cry of surprise—not over my dripping and battered appearance, but over what I carried.

"What have you got there?" demanded Father.

It was the proudest moment of my life. I bowed to Aunt Kitty and extended my treasure trove.

"Here is your pot of gold, Aunt Kitty," I said. "I found it on the rock shelf at the bottom of your well."

I was the hero of Rainbow's End for weeks and had to tell and retell the story until I was sick of the very sound of it. The affair made quite a sensation in our quiet community. Reporters came out from town to write it up, and photographs of Aunt Kitty, myself, the house and well, and the famous old pot itself adorned the columns of all the city papers.

As for Aunt Kitty, she was perfectly happy. The old pot contained between two and three thousand dollars—a sum sufficient to maintain her in comfort for the rest of her life. She insisted on my taking twenty of the gold pieces and would have made me take more if I had not flatly refused. Father did not wish me to take any, but when he saw how hurt Aunt Kitty was over his decree, he relented and allowed me to accept the two hundred dollars she was determined I should have. It paid my expenses at the Roxdeane High School the next year, something we could not otherwise have afforded for several years, if at all. So I owe my start in life to Aunt Kitty's kindness and my lucky tumble down her well in the dry summer. As the punning news editor of the *Morning Gazette* put it, "All is well that ends well."

EVANGELINE'S FATHER
(1906)

There was a tap at the door of Evangeline's room, and Miss Clayton popped in, a trim, glistening little figure in her dark raincoat and tam, looking as if wind and weather had no manner of influence on her engagements.

"The maid said I was to come right up. Don't touch me," she said as Evangeline sprang to meet her, "I'm as wet as a duck—wait till I get my things off. Do you suppose they turned me out of my boarding house, because I'm wandering the streets in such a downpour? Not a bit of it! I merely got lonesome, desperately lonesome, and a wee bit blue; so I came to see you to get cheered up."

Miss Clayton dropped into Evangeline's cushiony rocker, with a sigh of comfort. She was small, and slight, and dark, and much older than the other girls in her class. She had a thin, eager, wistful little face with some lines on it indicative of many things suffered and many difficulties overcome; but she was so bright and jolly that all the other girls liked her and went to her with their perplexities and problems.

"I don't know whether you've come to the right place for that," said Evangeline, with a rueful smile, as she snuggled down into her cozy corner. "I'm blue myself—blue as the famous Alsatian mountains—and I want cheering up, rather than to cheer."

"You blue, Eva! My dear girl, it must be simply indigestion in your case," laughed Miss Clayton. "You have nothing to give you the genuine blues, you fortunate mortal. Let me recount your blessings to you, if you've forgotten them. You are to be graduated tomorrow with honours after a brilliant arts course at Redmond College, during which you have had a splendid time socially, made hosts of friends, and incidentally picked up almost everything in the way of scholarships going, including the notable Avery prize, which no girl ever has captured before! Hence every co-ed looks upon you as a credit to your sex in general and to Redmond co-eds in particular. You have a lovely home and a father to be proud of you. You are leaving college to step into the social position that is yours by right of birth, and fitness, and which you will adorn to perfection, seeing that nature has gifted you with beauty, brains, and charm. Oh, you enviable Evangeline! How dare you talk of being blue! Suppose you were in my place, a poverty-stricken little old maid, without a relative in the world, who has taught 'deestrick schools' all of her life—it really seems as if I had been teaching all my life, I began so young—to save money to put herself through college. Suppose you'd spent your four arts years in a grubby little boarding house and mended the stockings of luckier girls to help yourself along. Suppose you weren't very brainy and had to grind every spare moment to pull through examinations at all. Suppose you were short, and meagre, and pale, and possessed of a carefully concealed but certainly consistent grey hair or two, instead of being tall and pink and sweet nineteen. Suppose all these things, and add thereto the fact that, lacking a brilliant record of prizes and honors, your BA would only suffice to get you an underpaid position in a high school in a faraway little town you never saw in your life and where you don't know a single person. Suppose all these things, my dear, and then give yourself over to the dismals."

Evangeline laughed a little uncertainly.

"I suppose it does sound ungrateful in me to talk of being blue," she admitted, "but 'the heart knoweth its own bitterness,' Miss Clayton. Besides, I am going to teach—I have taken the position of English teacher in the Bonner Seminary."

"Evangeline Foster! You!" protested Miss Clayton in amazement. "Why, I never thought you wanted to teach!"

"I'm not sure that I do want to. I don't know if I shall like teaching. But I must have some purpose in life—do something. I would not be satisfied to give myself over to society and live the aimless, butterfly life of so many girls of my set. It wouldn't content me—I'd die of inanition. So I'm going to Bonner."

"But your father?" said Miss Clayton wonderingly. "Does he want you to go away? Won't he be dreadfully lonely? Wouldn't it be—excuse me for speaking so plainly, but I simply must—wouldn't it be the best and most satisfying aim and purpose you could possibly find to live for your father, to make his home bright and happy, adorned with your education and your gifts? I'm sure that couldn't be an aimless, butterfly life. I only wish that I had a chance to live it! I've envied you the possession of a father, Evangeline. I've never envied you anything else—your beauty, or talents, or popularity—but I do envy you a father's love. If only I had a father to be proud of me and to work and live for—oh, I never would have blue spells then!"

Evangeline was silent so long, looking soberly out of the window where the rain was splashing through the elm boughs, that Miss Clayton was afraid she had vexed her.

"You're not displeased with me, are you?" she said anxiously. "Perhaps I shouldn't have spoken—it really isn't any of my business, I know—but I'm such a lonely, desolate mortal that I can't understand anyone not living up to their privileges of relationship."

"I'm not a bit displeased," said Evangeline slowly; "but I want to tell you something, Miss Clayton—if I can."

She slipped from her cozy corner to the rug at Miss Clayton's feet and laid her head in the other girl's lap.

"I've never told it to anyone else before—I couldn't. It hurt me too much to think about it, let alone speak of it. But I must tell you, because I don't want you to misunderstand me. Father doesn't care. He isn't particular whether I go or stay. He never has cared. He isn't proud of me, and he isn't at all interested in my work or attainments. If he realizes I am to be graduated tomorrow, it's about all. He has no more interest in the fact than if I were some other girl."

"Oh, dear. Are you very sure of this?" said Miss Clayton soberly.

"Yes, only too sure. It has hurt me cruelly all my life. Mother died when I was born. Sometimes I have thought that that turned my father against me. I never have felt that he loved me at all. He has given me everything I wanted, and let me do just as I liked, but he never has said an affectionate or encouraging word to me. He is a cold, reserved man—honestly. I don't even feel really acquainted with him. He never talks to me as other girls' fathers do, never asks me about my studies, or my pastimes. He seems completely wrapped up in his business, and nothing else on earth has any interest for him. When I told him I had won the Avery prize, he merely said, 'Very good,' and nothing more. I don't think he even knew what it signified. When I told him I thought of teaching, he said, 'Please yourself, Evangeline,' in an impersonal tone that seemed to set me thousands of miles away from him. Understand, Miss Clayton, he never has been unkind or severe—only indifferent. I mean nothing to him, either in affection or pride. He'll not miss me when I go. If he would—oh, I'd never go! I'd be only too glad to stay here, and make his home as happy as I possibly could, and live for him through my whole range of capacities. But he doesn't care. Oh, you don't know how bitterly I feel this! This why I was blue before you came."

Evangeline's voice choked and broke into a little sob. Miss Clayton patted the rich brown hair with careful fingers, wondering what she should say. She knew that it was no use to attempt to smooth over the matter with platitudes. She knew that the relation between parents and children is, in theory, the most beautiful thing in the world, and really is so in many cases. In many others it is far from being so, owing to faults on one side or the other.

"I'm so sorry! I know it must be very hard. But isn't it possible you may be mistaken after all, Eva? You admit your father is a very reserved man. Don't you think that he really loves you dearly, and is proud of you, although he may be one of those unfortunate mortals that can't show it? It is hard for impulsive, demonstrative people, such as you, to understand the other sort. And are you quite sure you have done everything on your side to win his confidence? You're such a sensitive little thing—perhaps you have been too easily rebuffed by his reserve."

Evangeline coloured.

"I don't think so. And if I thought Father really cared, Miss Clayton, I really wouldn't mind his not showing it. Please, let's not talk of it. I only told you so you would understand why I am going away to teach. I want to be useful to somebody. Let's make some fudge. In view of that severe bachelor's gown and mortarboard hanging up in my wardrobe there, I want to be as frivolous as possible."

Understanding that the subject was dismissed, Miss Clayton said no more, but she wondered sadly if Mr. Foster could really be as indifferent to this clever, charming daughter of his as the latter believed. And if he wasn't, what a pity it all was!

The Redmond convocation was held the next day, and Evangeline was the bright star of the co-eds. But there was a bitter little smile on her face as she noticed the other girls with their proud fathers and brothers around them. Her father was talking stiffly to the president of Redmond, and his dark, stern face expressed as little emotion as ever. When they met in the evening at dinner, he said nothing to her about the day's doings, and Evangeline cried herself to sleep that night.

After midnight, she awakened with a grumbling toothache; rising, she slipped on her dressing gown and went downstairs in search of toothache drops. To her surprise, there was a dim light in the library and the sound of somebody talking. From her position on the stairs, she could see her father through the open door, standing before her mother's picture, talking aloud to it. As the meaning of his words penetrated her mind, the girl caught her breath, and a flood of emotion swept over her whole being.

"Hasn't our little girl done splendidly, Mary?" he was saying with a tenderness in his voice that Evangeline never had heard before. "I wish you were here to be proud of her with me, Mary. But you are proud of her—somewhere else—and you know all about it. She graduated today with honours, and won the Avery prize—think of it, Mary, the Avery prize! And she's everything you would have liked your daughter to be, Mary—sweet, and beautiful, and good, as well as clever. I wish I could tell her how proud I am of her; but you know how hard it is for me to express my feelings, Mary. It was the same way with you when I had you here—I could never tell you how much I loved you, until it was too late. But I've tried to do my best for our daughter, Mary. I remembered what you said to me the night you died. I've fulfilled every wish of hers as far as it lay in my power. She wants to go away and teach now, Mary. When she told me so, my heart sank. I don't see how I'm going to live without her, or how I am going to bear this great, lonely, empty house, if she goes away and takes its life with her. But if she wants to go, I will not hinder or thwart her. It's dull for our girl here, Mary. I'm poor company for her. But I don't see how I'm going to live without her. Oh, Mary, if only you had lived! And now, Eva is going to leave me—my dear, bright, clever little girl."

He bowed his head on the table before his wife's picture, and Evangeline heard a sob. The girl's own eyes were full of tears, but they were tears of happiness. She never had been so happy in her life. Her first impulse was to rush down and into the library, to throw her arms about her father's neck and assure him that she would never leave him. But she felt that, with a man of his reserved temperament, shrinking almost morbidly from any outward display of emotion, this might not be the most tactful course. Instead, she quietly went back to her room, her toothache forgotten and her whole soul filled with delight and thankfulness.

"He does love me; he is proud of me," she murmured joyfully. "Oh, I've misunderstood him terribly. But I never will again; and I'm going to Bessie Clayton the very first thing in the morning to tell her I was mistaken and that there never was a mortal so glad and willing to admit her mistake."

The next day, as her father was leaving the breakfast room, Evangeline timidly laid her hand on his arm. "Father," she said gently, "I wanted to tell you, I've changed my mind about teaching at Bonner. I'm not going to teach there, or anywhere—I'd rather stay with you."

"Well, please yourself, Evangeline," Mr. Foster said again, with as much apparent indifference as ever. But Evangeline, grown suddenly clear-sighted and observant, had seen the swift flash of surprise and pleasure in his eyes; and after her long years of blindness, she understood.

THE WORD OF A KENNEDY
(1907)

Big nephew Irving towered above his grand-aunt Agatha. "So you are John's boy?" the little woman said, in a voice that, despite her eighty years, was strong and vibrant. It seemed to be the only strong thing about her; she was a wisp of a little white-haired lady, looking as if a breath of wind might blow her away, as she leaned on her cane under the elms of the Lansdowne church and glanced up at her tall grand-nephew with very bright black eyes.

"So you are John's boy," she repeated, holding out her tiny hand. "The last time I saw you, you were a baby in arms. I would have declared it was only yesterday, and here you have shot up overnight nearly as tall as your father. Are you going to stay long in Lansdowne?"

"Just a week," said Irving Kennedy, smiling. "I came up yesterday, and I'm going to stay here till next Saturday with Aunt Elizabeth."

"Well, you must come and see me then," said Aunt Agatha.

"Of course I will."

"I want you to come and spend a whole day with me," persisted the little old lady. "What day will suit you? I always like to know just when people are coming to see me. Suppose we say next Thursday?"

"All right. I'll come up in the morning, and we'll gossip the whole day," promised Irving, laughingly.

"Well, I'm fond of gossip," admitted Aunt Agatha, candidly, "but I want to hear you play more than gossip. They tell me you are a good musician and a genius on the organ. I am very fond of music, especially organ music, and I never hear it except in church. You will promise to come next Thursday then, and play for me? You won't disappoint me?"

"Indeed, no. And I'll be glad to play for you if you will like it; only don't expect too much. I'm not at all a genius."

"I shall look for you then on Thursday," said Aunt Agatha, nodding.

"You must be sure and go to see Aunt Agatha," said Aunt Elizabeth, as she and Irving walked home from the church. "She will be so pleased. She has a very lonely life and suffers a good deal, although her spirit is wonderful. She will be looking forward to Thursday all the week."

"I'll be glad to go," answered Irving. "I've heard Father talk so much about his Aunt Agatha and Maywood. He says Maywood is the quaintest, most charming old spot in the world."

"It is indeed, but it is not kept quite so nicely now as it used to be. Aunt Agatha has only a small annuity, you know. It is enough for her needs, and she is quite comfortable, but there is nothing over for any 'frills,' and the Maywood grounds have rather gone to seed. But they are quaint and pretty still."

"So is Aunt Agatha," said Irving, admiringly. "She looks as if she had just stepped out of an old miniature. I'm proud of her for a great-aunt."

"Be sure and tell her all about your college and your studies. By the way, do you think you'll manage to go back next year, Irving?"

"I don't know," said Irving, a shadow falling over his face. "Father can't send me, that is certain, and there are so few ways a fellow can earn money while going to college in a small town like Trenton, Aunt Els, even if he is willing to do anything. I am trying to get the position of organist in the Fourth Street Church, and, if I do, the salary will enable me to get through next year, with a few other things I can pick up. I've applied for it, but of course my chance is rather slim. If I can't go back this year, I'll teach, and earn enough that way to go back next. But a fellow hates to drop out of his class, Aunt Els."

Irving enjoyed himself in the days that followed. Lansdowne possessed young people galore, and there were picnics and drives and sails. The tall, bright-eyed young fellow was a general favourite, and as for Aunt Elizabeth, she petted and spoiled him shamefully, as he laughingly declared. "A Kennedy can't be spoiled," said Aunt Elizabeth.

"You are loyal to the Kennedys, aren't you, Aunt Els?" smiled Irving. "You think a Kennedy is about right, don't you?"

"Yes, I do," said Aunt Elizabeth, candidly. "Of course, we have our faults. But no Kennedy ever did a mean thing, or broke his word in large or little. That's the record you have to live up to, Irving."

"It pretty nearly covers the ground," answered Irving, thoughtfully. "Well, at least I don't think I've ever broken my word yet, and I shall try not to."

Wednesday evening Irving came home from the post office without his usual whistle. He gravely handed his aunt her mail and then went to his own room, where he sat down and reread his own letters with a very sober face. One was from his father, telling him he must come home on Friday instead of Saturday; the other was from his college chum, Mark Hazelwood, who lived in Carmody. It ran as follows:

"Dear Irv, I want you to come up to Carmody on Thursday, without fail. Professor Edgeley is here visiting the Martins. You know he is the head of the Trenton Conservatory, and he has been asked by the Fourth Street Church committee to keep his eyes open for a suitable organist for them. I've been talking to him about you, and he wants to hear you play. He's going away Thursday evening, so be sure you come that day. If he once hears you, you'll be sure to get the position, I know."

Irving laid down the letter and went to the window. He *must* go to Carmody, he thought. But what about his promise to Aunt Agatha? She would be expecting him and would be bitterly disappointed if he failed to come. To go to Carmody would take the whole day. "If I could only stay till Saturday it would be all right," he reflected, ruefully. "I could go over to Maywood tonight, tell Aunt Agatha all about it, and arrange to spend Friday with her in place of Thursday. But as it is, it is simply a choice between disappointing Aunt Agatha and practically losing my chance of getting that position."

Irving strode up and down the room a few times. Then he exclaimed, "No, there's more to it than that—it means breaking my word if I go to Carmody. And no Kennedy has ever done that—so Aunt Els says—'in large or little.' This is 'little,' I suppose, but the principle is the same. Am I going to keep my word or break it, that is the point. Well, I'm going to keep it, that's what, if it does cost me my chance of college next year."

Having made up his mind, Irving wasted no more time in vain regrets, and early the next morning he set out on his four-mile walk to Maywood. Arriving there, he found Aunt Agatha expecting him, and, in spite of his own disappointment, Irving felt heartily glad he had come, so pathetic was the little old lady's joy. She was as delighted as a child, and Irving soon found himself enjoying his visit. Maywood was, as his father had told him, a most quaint, delightful old place. Aunt Agatha took him all over it and told him the history of everything. Then he played for her in the dim, old-fashioned parlour, which was scented by rose leaves in a huge old Chinese jar. Aunt Agatha's organ was a bit squeaky and out of tune, but Irving coxed such music out of it as it had never given forth before. When he finished with the simple old-time hymns that Aunt Agatha loved, the little lady's black eyes were softened through a mist of tears.

"You've given me more pleasure than I can ever tell," she said, wistfully. "This day will give me pleasant memories for a long, long while to come. You are so like your father, Irving. He was just such a thoughtful, manly boy as you."

They had a long talk then, over many things, for Aunt Agatha had a genius for asking questions. She discovered that Irving did not expect to get back to college the next year, but she did not find out about Professor Edgeley and Mark's letter.

Irving would rather have liked to go home soon after tea, for he knew that a moonlight sail was being planned by some of his friends; but Aunt Agatha's heart was set on reading him a packet of old letters, written long ago by a clever brother of hers. Irving did not find them particularly interesting, but he did not wound Aunt Agatha's feelings by letting her see it, for she was evidently very proud of them. "Wasn't he a beautiful writer?" she said, when she had finished, holding an envelope across the table for him to see. "You don't see such writing nowadays. You young fellows do scrawl so dreadfully. Why, what is the matter?"

For Irving, with an exclamation of astonishment, had caught the envelope up and was examining the stamp in the corner. "Aunt Agatha," he exclaimed excitedly, "this is a red stamp of Canada—a very, very rare one. Do you know that it is worth about four hundred dollars?"

"Nonsense," said Aunt Agatha.

"Indeed it is. I know a good deal about stamps, Aunt Agatha. I have a friend who is a collector. I am sure that any dealer will give you that much, at least, for this stamp, for it is in splendid condition. I wonder if there are any more here like it."

"No, all the other letters were written from Europe," said Aunt Agatha. "It seems impossible to believe that that old stamp is really worth as much as that, but if it is I am very glad, because I shall give it to you, Irving."

"Oh, no, I couldn't think of taking it, Aunt Agatha," exclaimed Irving.

"You must. I've wanted to help you in some way—I've been wishing I could help you to go to college next year. You have discovered the stamp, and you have the best right to it. I don't need the money. I have everything I want, and nobody to come after me. You have to take it, Irving. If you won't, I'll just simply throw it in the fire."

Aunt Agatha was a very determined old lady, but Irving was also a very determined boy. They had quite a spirited argument, and finally Irving said, "Well, Aunt Agatha, since you insist, I'll tell you what I'll do. I'll accept half the value of the stamp. That will be plenty to put me through next year and enable me to graduate with my class. You must keep the other half yourself."

"Very well, since you are too stubborn to take it all," said Aunt Agatha reluctantly, "I daresay I can do some good with the money. I won't spend it on myself, that is certain."

"Thank you, Aunt Agatha," said Irving, with shining eyes. "I can't tell you what this means to me."

"Oh, I can imagine it," laughed Aunt Agatha. "I'm old outside, but you'd really be surprised if you knew how young I am inside. And it makes me younger than ever to know I can help you a little. Take the stamp and sell it for me, and when you come up to divide the booty, I shall make you play on the organ for me till your fingers ache. That's all the thanks I want."

THE AFFAIR OF THE SHY PROFESSOR
(1907)

"Bashful Bertie seems to be getting worse instead of better," said Sally Alexander. "I asked him after class today why the pluperfect was used in that fourteenth line, and he said, 'Yes, I—I think—that is the reason.' I went out then—I was sorry for him. Who can have been responsible for turning a man like that loose in a co-educational institution?"

We were talking about the new professor of classics. "We" were five Dalhousie seniors—to wit, Juliet Andrews, who went in for philosophy, Meg Dean, who was the class beauty, Gwen Smith and Sally Alexander, both of whom leaned to mathematics, and myself, Mary Tupper, commonly known as Poll and possessing no especial hobby. This story is not about us, however, so nothing need be said of us save that we were a jolly little crew and fitted into one another's angles admirably—which is something to be thankful for when five girls are sharing a flat for precious economy's sake.

The new professor's real name and title was Dr. Robert Sherwood, with enough capital letters after it to fit out the tail of a respectable comet. His shyness was already proverbial at Dalhousie. The boys nicknamed him "Bashful Bertie," after their affectionate fashion, and almost worshiped him. In fact, we all did, and would have gone through fire and water any day for our shy professor, but that did not prevent us from considering him in the light of a standing joke. Some story about him was always floating around among the "Dals," and when things got dull at a class party, they could always be enlivened up again by an allusion to Bashful Bertie.

He was very good-looking. In fact, in a college where most of the other professors were as ancient and weather-beaten as the everlasting hills, he might have been called handsome. He had fine, dark-grey eyes, when one got a chance to see them, and a clear olive complexion—when he wasn't blushing brick-red, as was usually the case when girls were around. He was tall and broad-shouldered, too, which made his shyness seem all the more ridiculous. He was reputed to be capable of thinking in Latin and dreaming in Greek, if he so elected, and was credited with having forgotten more about the dead languages than any of his predecessors had ever known. Apart from his ancient lore, he was very modern and went in for athletics and fraternities, heart and soul. All the boys, from the greenest freshie to the most blasé senior, declared that he was the finest fellow in the world when there were no girls to bother him.

In Paradise Lost—that is to say, in our study and den—it was our unanimous opinion that Prof. Sherwood would have gone to the electric chair as a cheerful alternative to asking a co-ed to translate in class. But he was so conscientious that he forced himself to do it, and his mode of proceeding was invariably the same. He would wrap his gown nervously about him, cast an anguished glance over the class, and stammer out, "Will Miss So-and-So be kind enough to construe the next passage?"

The girl referred to would make a wild guess at his meaning, more because he had looked in her direction than because she had made out what he said, and the ordeal would be over for that time.

Bashful Bertie was always late for class. This was because he would never leave the library as long as a co-ed was prowling about the halls. Now and then he would pop out his head and look around. If he saw the flutter of a feminine garment, back he went. But if the coast seemed clear, he would make a frantic dive along the hall and up the stairs, with his gown streaming out behind him. At first some of the co-eds, in order to tease him, would stand at the door of the dressing room and open it as he went by. But public opinion frowned this down, as taking an unfair advantage of a fellow creature in distress.

It was at our college receptions and class functions that the professor distinguished himself most brilliantly. He seemed to think that it was his duty to patronize them, and he attended religiously, wearing a faultless evening dress and an expression compared to which that of an early Christian martyr, assisting at a Neronian illumination, would have seemed gay and frivolous by contrast.

That poor professor! What agonies he must have endured at those affairs when designing students would take him up to a bevy of strange town girls and introduce him, while the rest of us stood afar off and looked on! We used to be very sorry for him, but we could never prevent the boys from doing it. They declared that it was too good fun to give up for a mere principle.

At first we thought that the professor's shyness would wear off after a time—that he would get acclimated, so to speak, and learn to regard his class as a mere sexless conglomerate of cultivatable grey matter. But he did not; he got worse, if that were possible, and we all pitied and loved him more than ever.

When the winter term opened after the Christmas holidays, Betty Howard came to college. She brought a letter of introduction from a friend of Juliet's, and as we had room for another girl, we admitted her straightway into the fraternity of Paradise Lost. Although Betty was a senior, she was a stranger to us. She had taken her sophomore and junior years before we came to Dalhousie and had been teaching ever since to earn enough money to come back and finish her course.

By the end of a week we all loved Betty devotedly. She was sweet. I am quite well aware that this adjective, through misuse and abuse, has become utterly threadbare; nevertheless, I am obliged to use it as the only one fully descriptive of Betty. She was sweet, and you knew it when you looked at her.

She was pretty, too, although her beauty was secondary to her sweetness. She had lovely, long-lashed brown eyes and a milky complexion all sprinkled over with tiny golden freckles, especially on her nose where they were so thick that the ground colour hardly showed at all. Betty used to worry about her freckles, but the rest of us thought them becoming. She had a crooked, clever little mouth and a habit of going about with her head drooping that, Gwen said, made her look like a violet bending its head in the woods. Gwen, between mathematical spurts, leaned to poetry, which accounted for this outbreak.

Betty had not been one of us long before we discovered that she was as hopelessly and miserably shy as the professor himself. Among girls she was jolly and off-handed, but if any men were about, she shrank into herself and became mutely wretched. We fairly had to drag her to our class functions, and when she got there, she crept away to the nearest dim corner and stayed there until it was time to go home.

Once or twice in class Prof. Sherwood asked her to translate; but he could not be said to be personally acquainted with her until the night of the senior co-ed's "At Home," when Bobby Douglas towed him up to Betty and introduced him.

Everybody knew that Bobby did it out of malice prepense, since theoretically at least, the professor was supposed to know all his students. A lot of juniors and seniors were grouped around to see the fun, but they were disappointed. The professor bowed and blushed as usual, and Betty turned a lovely peach colour, but neither of them spoke a word. Most girls on such occasions tried to put him at ease by random remarks about the weather or exams, and the fun came in with the professor's desperate attempts to follow up this small talk.

But Betty said nothing and did not even lift her eyes, so Bobby's mean joke fell as flat as it deserved to. There was a vacant chair beside Betty, and the professor, after standing foolishly before her for a full minute, sat down in it. They sat there the whole evening in silence. Nobody could get at the professor unless they climbed over Betty, and he was left unmolested.

When we broke up we saw him turn to Betty and stammer out something.

"I believe he is actually asking if he may walk home with her!" gasped Meg.

When the men were invited to the co-ed's affairs, they held it to be a sacred duty to see the girls safely home, and a man, if unpledged elsewhere, usually looked after the co-ed to whom he happened to be talking when the Mrs. Professor who was chaperone for the occasion gave the signal for departure.

The professor might have really wanted to see Betty home, but his inclination alone would never have bolstered him to the point of asking her. It was simply the idea of duty that steadied his nerves. If our dear shy professor thought that he ought to do a thing, why, he did it, and that was all there was to it.

Bobby Douglas and I walked home behind them. Betty crept along by the board fence of the rink grounds, as far as it went and then by the railings of the poorhouse. The professor walked so close to the edge of the sidewalk that it was a mystery he didn't fall off in the gutter.

When they got to No. 187—our number—they kept straight on. At first we supposed that they were going to the little restaurant at the corner for ice cream, but when they passed it also, Bobby insisted on tearing down the street after them and shouting at them to stop. Otherwise they might have gone on until they walked over the wharf at the end of the street. We wormed it out of Betty later on that neither she nor the professor had spoken a word since they had left the college. She admitted she knew they had passed our number, but she could not get up sufficient courage to tell him so.

I think the professor began liking Betty because she did not torment him with conversation, and she liked him for the same reason. At any rate, it soon became an established thing for him to see Betty home from various places. But we did not think it serious until he called on her one evening. Then we knew.

We saw plainly—the poor man couldn't hide it—that the professor was in love fathoms deep with our dear little freckled Betty. As for Betty, we didn't know but we guessed, and we all banded together in a solemn league and covenant to help the professor's wooing along in every lawful way. We knew the poor things needed all the help we could give them.

It was a curious courtship. The professor carried it on mainly by flowers. He sent Betty the most beautiful ones every day. The chair of classics at Dalhousie was well endowed, which was fortunate, for those flowers must have made a big hole in his income that winter. He was perfectly reckless with them, and, as Betty couldn't possibly use them all, she shared them lavishly with the rest of us.

We girls effaced ourselves religiously that winter. But even with all the assistance we could give them, the professor and Betty did not get on very fast. When the term drew to a close and every day brought a new crop of bristling examination rumours, they really did not seem to be much further ahead than at the beginning. We had done our best for the professor, but we couldn't propose for him. It was Juliet's opinion that he would never get up enough courage to speak.

"If it were any other girl than Betty," said Juliet sagely, "she might help the lame dog over the stile so neatly that he would never know it before it was done. But Betty can never do that. I feel almost in despair about those two. If the matter isn't settled before convocation, it never will be. Betty is going out West to teach, and they may never meet again."

"We must simply trust to Providence after this," said Gwen in a sort of "last forlorn hope" tone. "If the professor doesn't speak up, it isn't our fault. We've given him every chance."

When examinations came on we had no time to think of anybody but ourselves. After they were over, we employed the lull before convocation in making our bachelor gowns and worrying over Betty and her professor.

"How I'd love to shake him!" groaned Meg. "What business has any man to be so shy!"

Convocation was to be in the afternoon, and that evening we senior girls intended to give an At Home to some visiting alumnae. As it would be our last college function, we wished to make it as successful as possible, and we spent all the morning building sandwiches and decorating the Monro room, where all such affairs were held.

All our family friends had come up to see us graduate. Betty's only living relative was an aunt. None of us had ever seen so grim a person as Miss Jordan. We knew Betty was in mortal awe of her and never dreamed of disputing her commands.

Miss Jordan said she thought this Convocation Fuss—she spelled both words with a capital—was all nonsense, but since Elizabeth wished it, she had come up to see her graduate, and they would start for home on the early morning train. She thought Elizabeth looked thin and peaked and supposed she had been killing herself over her books. For her own part, she considered all this college business for women tomfoolery; but the girls of this generation seemed bitten with a craze for making a neck-and-neck race of it with the men. She hoped that now Elizabeth had got her education, she would settle quietly down and become a sensible young woman like her mother before her.

It was dreadful to hear our dear Betty called Elizabeth!

"The professor's last chance has vanished," moaned Meg. "That awful woman will never let Betty out of her sight, and she will whisk her off tomorrow morning. The professor won't even dare to ask Betty if he may take her home from the reception tonight."

Convocation was a brilliant success. Juliet took honours in philosophy, and the rest of us got along respectably. Betty looked like an angel in her gown and mortarboard. Then came our At Home. The Monro room was quite dazzling that night. Generally it was a long, ghostly apartment, hung with photographs of departed classes and defunct professors, with a lot of bare chairs and a piano by way of furniture. But we had decorated it lavishly with flowers and palms and flags, and our reception went off beautifully. We graduates wore our gowns and mortarboards over our evening dresses, and, having stowed our refreshments safely away in the Modern Language room, felt that we were free to enjoy ourselves.

Betty looked sweet and sad. Miss Jordan was grimmer than ever. The professor seemed so forlorn that even Sally lost patience with him.

"Why doesn't he do something, instead of moping in that corner?" she demanded fiercely.

"What can he do with that dragon mounting guard over Betty?" protested Gwen.

Betty grew paler and sadder as the evening wore away. Once she actually sent a timid, wistful little glance at the professor, but he was looking moodily down and did not see it.

"The idiot!" said Sally, who always got bitter when things did not go to suit her. "Oh, the unspeakable idiot! He doesn't know that she is going right away in the morning, or he might make an effort. I hope I shall never be mixed up in an affair of this kind again. It is too hard on the nerves."

Finally Miss Jordan told Betty that it was time to go home. Betty humbly prepared to obey. I felt that a crisis had come, and I made a frenzied dash across the room to the professor. Sally always declares that I caught him by the shoulder, but I have no recollection of doing that. But I know I spoke with tremendous earnestness.

"Professor Sherwood! Betty's aunt is taking her away! They leave on the early morning train. Do something!"

Of course, I only meant that he should go and ask permission to see her home as usual, and I thought he understood, for he stood up and threw back his head. I had never seen him look like that before.

He stalked across the room and touched Betty's arm. Betty paused. Miss Jordan went on, supposing that her niece was behind her. We Paradise Lost girls closed around them in a little circle, shutting them off from the rest of the guests, most of whom were crowded about a distinguished alumna at the upper end of the room.

The professor's lips were set and his eyes were blazing. He seemed utterly unconscious that he and Betty were not alone in the world, and I believe he thought they were. He looked her straight in the face and said, steadily and calmly,

"Miss Betty, will you marry me?"

Betty did not blush; she turned very pale. Just at that moment, Miss Jordan missed her and looked back.

"Elizabeth!" she called severely.

Betty looked at her professor.

"Yes," she said softly.

Prof. Sherwood bowed and drew her hand through his arm. They went down the room together, and the professor took an introduction to Miss Jordan without turning a hair. We watched them out of the room and through the hall beyond until they disappeared down the staircase. Juliet, as became a philosopher, was the first to recover herself.

"And that is your shy professor!" she said.

"I feel weak," said Sally feebly. "Let's go into the Modern Language room and have a sandwich."

AUNT SUSANNA'S THANKSGIVING DINNER
(1907)

"Here's Aunt Susanna, girls," said Laura, who was sitting by the north window—nothing but north light does for Laura, who is the artist of our talented family.

Each of us has a little pet new-fledged talent that we are faithfully cultivating in the hope that it will amount to something and soar highly some day. But it is difficult to cultivate four talents on our tiny income. If Laura wasn't such a good manager, we never could do it.

Laura's words were a signal for Kate to hang up her violin and for me to push my pen and portfolio out of sight. Laura had hidden her brushes and watercolours as she spoke. Only Margaret continued to bend serenely over her Latin grammar. Aunt Susanna frowns on musical and literary and artistic ambitions, but she accords a faint approval to Margaret's desire for an education. A college course, with a tangible diploma at the end and a sensible pedagogic aspiration, is something Aunt Susanna can understand when she tries hard. But she cannot understand messing with paints, fiddling, or scribbling, and she has only unmeasured contempt for messers, fiddlers, and scribblers. Time was when we had paid no attention to Aunt Susanna's views on these points; but ever since she had, on one incautious day when she was in high good humour, dropped a pale, anemic little hint that she might send Margaret to college if she were a good girl, we had been bending all our energies toward securing Aunt Susanna's approval. It was not enough that Aunt Susanna should approve of Margaret; she must approve of the whole four of us or she would not help Margaret. That is Aunt Susanna's way. Of late we had been growing a little discouraged. Aunt Susanna had recently read a magazine article that stated that the higher education of women was ruining our country and that a woman who was a BA couldn't, in the very nature of things, ever be a housewifely, cookly creature. Consequently, Margaret's chances looked a little foggy; but we hadn't quite given up hope. A very little thing might sway Aunt Susanna one way or the other, so that we walked very softly and tried to mingle serpents' wisdom and doves' harmlessness in practical proportions.

When Aunt Susanna came in, Laura was crocheting, Kate was sewing, and I was poring over a recipe book. That was not deception at all, since we did all these things frequently—much more frequently, in fact, than we painted or fiddled or wrote. But Aunt Susanna would never believe it. Nor did she believe it now.

She threw back her lovely new sealskin cape, looked around the sitting room, and then smiled—a truly Aunt Susannian smile.

"What a pity you forgot to wipe that smudge of paint off your nose, Laura," she said sarcastically. "You don't seem to get on very fast with your lace. How long is it since you began it? Over three months, isn't it?"

"This is the third piece of the same pattern I've done in three months, Aunt Susanna," said Laura presently. Laura is an old duck. She never gets cross and snaps back. I do; and it's so hard not to with Aunt Susanna sometimes. But I generally manage it, for I'd do anything for Margaret. Laura did not tell Aunt Susanna that she sold her lace at the Women's Exchange in town and made enough to buy her new hats. She makes enough out of her watercolours to dress herself.

Aunt Susanna took second breath and started in again.

"I notice your violin hasn't quite as much dust on it as the rest of the things in this room, Kate. It's a pity you stopped playing just because I came in. I don't enjoy fiddling much, but I'd prefer it to seeing anyone using a needle who isn't accustomed to it."

Kate is really a most dainty needlewoman and does all the fine sewing in our family. She coloured and said nothing, that being the highest pitch of virtue to which our Katie, like myself, can attain.

"And there's Margaret ruining her eyes over books," went on Aunt Susanna severely. "Will you kindly tell me, Margaret Thorne, what good you ever expect Latin to do you?"

"Well, you see, Aunt Susanna," said Margaret gently—Maggie and Laura are birds of a feather—"I want to be a teacher if I can manage to get through, and I shall need Latin for that."

All the girls except me had now got their accustomed rap, but I knew better than to hope I should escape.

"So you're reading a recipe book, Agnes? Well, that's better than poring over a novel. I'm afraid you haven't been at it very long though. People generally don't read recipes upside down—and besides, you didn't quite cover up your portfolio. I see a corner of it sticking out. Was genius burning before I came in? It's too bad if I quenched the flame."

"A cookery book isn't such a novelty to me as you seem to think, Aunt Susanna," I said, as meekly as it was possible for me. "Why, I'm a real good cook, 'if I do say it as hadn't orter.'"

I am, too.

"Well, I'm glad to hear it," said Aunt Susanna skeptically, "because that has to do with my errand here today. I'm in a peck of troubles. Firstly, Miranda Mary's mother has had to go and get sick, and Miranda Mary must go home to wait on her. Secondly, I've just had a telegram from my sister-in-law who has been ordered West for her health, and I'll have to leave on tonight's train to see her before she goes. I can't get back until the noon train Thursday, and that is Thanksgiving, and I've invited Mr. and Mrs. Gilbert to dinner that day. They'll come on the same train. I'm dreadfully worried. There doesn't seem to be anything I can do except get one of you girls to go up to the Pinery Thursday morning and cook the dinner for us. Do you think you can manage it?"

We all felt rather dismayed, and nobody volunteered with a rush. But as I had just boasted that I could cook, it was plainly my duty to step into the breach, and I did it with fear and trembling.

"I'll go, Aunt Susanna," I said.

"And I'll help you," said Kate.

"Well, I suppose I'll have to try you," said Aunt Susanna with the air of a woman determined to make the best of a bad business. "Here is the key of the kitchen door. You'll find everything in the pantry, turkey and all. The mince pies are already made, so you'll only have to warm them up. I want dinner sharp at twelve, for the train is due at 11:50. Mr. and Mrs. Gilbert are very particular, and I do hope you will have things right. Oh, if I could only be home myself! Why will people get sick at such inconvenient times?"

"Don't worry, Aunt Susanna," I said comfortingly. "Kate and I will have your Thanksgiving dinner ready for you in tiptop style."

"Well, I'm sure I hope so. Don't get to mooning over a story, Agnes. I'll lock the library up, and fortunately there are no fiddles at the Pinery. Above all, don't let any of the McGinnises in. They'll be sure to be prowling around when I'm not home. Don't give that dog of theirs any scraps either. That is Miranda Mary's one fault. She will feed that dog in spite of all I can do, and I can't walk out of my own back door without falling over him."

We promise to eschew the McGinnises and all their works, including the dog, and when Aunt Susanna had gone we looked at each other with mingled hope and fear.

"Girls, this is the chance of your lives," said Laura. "If you can only please Aunt Susanna with this dinner, it will convince her that you are good cooks in spite of your nefarious bent for music and literature. I consider the illness of Miranda Mary's mother a Providential interposition—that is, if she isn't too sick."

"It's all very well for you to be pleased, Laura," I said dolefully. "But I don't feel jubilant over the prospect at all. Something will probably go wrong. And then there's our own nice little

Thanksgiving celebration we've planned and pinched and economized for weeks to provide. That is half spoiled now."

"Oh, what is that compared to Margaret's chance of going to college?" exclaimed Kate. "Cheer up, Aggie. You know we can cook. I feel that it is now or never with Aunt Susanna."

I cheered up accordingly. We are not given to pessimism, which is fortunate. Ever since Father died four years ago, we have struggled on here, content to give up a good deal just to keep our home and be together. This little grey house—oh, how we do love it and its apple trees—is ours, and we have, as aforesaid, a tiny income and our ambitions; not very big ambitions but big enough to give rest to our lives and hope to the future. We've been very happy as a rule. Aunt Susanna has a big house and lots of money, but she isn't as happy as we are. She nags us a good deal—just as she used to nag Father—but we don't mind it very much after all. Indeed, I sometimes suspect that we'd really like Aunt Susanna tremendously, if she'd only leave us alone long enough to find it out.

Thursday morning was an ideal Thanksgiving morning—bright, crisp, and sparkling. There had been a white frost in the night, and the orchard and the white birch wood behind it looked like fairyland. We were all up early. None of us had slept well, and both Kate and I had had the most fearful dreams of spoiling Aunt Susanna's Thanksgiving dinner.

"Never mind. Dreams always go by contraries, you know," said Laura cheerfully. "You'd better go up to the Pinery early and get the fires on, for the house will be cold. Remember the McGinnises and the dog. Weigh the turkey so that you'll know exactly how long to cook it. Put the pies in the oven in time to get piping hot—lukewarm mince pies are an abomination. Be sure—"

"Laura, don't confuse us with any more cautions," I groaned, "or we shall get hopelessly fuddled. Come on, Kate, before she has time to."

It wasn't very far up to the Pinery—just ten minutes' walk, and such a delightful walk on that delightful morning. We went through the orchard and then through the white birch wood where the loveliness of the frosted boughs awed us. Beyond that there was a lane between ranks of young, balsamy, white-misted firs and then an open pasture field, sere and crispy. Just across it was the Pinery, a lovely old house with dormer windows in the roof, surrounded by pines that were dark and glorious against the silvery morning sky.

The McGinnis dog was sitting on the back-door steps when we arrived. He wagged his tail ingratiatingly, but we ruthlessly pushed him off, went in, and shut the door in his face. All the little McGinnises were sitting in a row on their fence, and they whooped derisively. The McGinnis manners are not those which appertain to the caste of Vere de Vere; but we rather like the urchins—there are eight of them—and we would probably have gone over to talk to them if we had not had the fear of Aunt Susanna before our eyes.

We kindled the fires, weighed the turkey, put it in the oven, and prepared the vegetables. Then we set the dining room table and decorated it with Aunt Susanna's potted ferns and dishes of lovely red apples. Everything went so smoothly that we soon forgot to be nervous. When the turkey was done, we took it out, set it on the back of the range to keep warm, and put the mince pies in. The potatoes, cabbage, and turnips were bubbling away cheerfully, and everything was going as merrily as a marriage bell. Then, all at once, things happened.

In an evil hour we went to the yard window and looked out. We saw a quiet scene. The McGinnis dog was still sitting on his haunches by the steps, just as he had been sitting all the morning. Down in the McGinnis yard everything wore an unusually peaceful aspect. Only one McGinnis was in sight—Tony, aged eight, who was perched up on the edge of the well box, swinging his legs and singing at the top of his melodious Irish voice. All at once, just as we were looking at him, Tony went over backward and apparently tumbled head foremost down his father's well.

Kate and I screamed simultaneously. We tore across the kitchen, flung open the door, plunged down over Aunt Susanna's yard, scrambled over the fence, and flew to the well. Just as we reached it, Tony's red head appeared as he climbed serenely out over the box. I don't know whether I felt more relieved or furious. He had merely fallen on the plank guard inside the box; and there are times when I am tempted to think he fell on purpose, because he saw Kate and me looking out at the window. At least he didn't seem at all frightened and grinned most impishly at us.

Kate and I turned on our heels and marched back in as dignified a manner as was possible under the circumstances. Halfway up Aunt Susanna's yard we forgot dignity and broke into a run. We had left the door open, and the McGinnis dog had disappeared.

Never shall I forget the sight we saw or the smell we smelled when we burst into that kitchen. There on the floor was the McGinnis dog and what was left of Aunt Susanna's Thanksgiving turkey. As for the smell, imagine a commingled odour of scorching turnips and burning mince pies, and you have it.

The dog fled out with a guilty yelp. I groaned and snatched the turnips off. Kate threw open the oven door and dragged out the pies. Pies and turnips were ruined as irretrievably as the turkey.

"Oh, what shall we do?" I cried miserably. I knew Margaret's chance of college was gone forever.

"Do!" Kate was superb. She didn't lose her wits for a second. "We'll go home and borrow the girls' dinner. Quick—there's just ten minutes before train time. Throw those pies and turnips into this basket, the turkey too—we'll carry them with us to hide them."

I might not be able to evolve an idea like that on the spur of the moment, but I can at least act up to it when it is presented. Without a moment's delay we shut the door and ran. As we went I saw the McGinnis dog licking his chops over in their yard. I have been ashamed ever since of my feelings toward that dog. They were murderous. Fortunately I had no time to indulge them.

It is ten minutes' walk from the Pinery to our house, but you can run it in five. Kate and I burst into the kitchen just as Laura and Margaret were sitting down to dinner. We had neither time nor breath for explanations. Without a word I grasped the turkey platter and the turnip tureen. Kate caught one hot mince pie from the oven and whisked a cold one out of the pantry.

"We've—got—to have—them," was all she said.

I've always said that Laura and Maggie would rise to any occasion. They saw us carry their Thanksgiving dinner off under their very eyes, and they never interfered by word or motion. They didn't even worry us with questions. They realized that something desperate had happened and that the emergency called for deeds, not words.

"Aggie," gasped Kate behind me as we tore through the birch wood, "the border—of these pies—is crimped—differently—from Aunt Susanna's."

"She—won't know—the difference," I panted. "Miranda—Mary—crimps them."

We got back to the Pinery just as the train whistle blew. We had ten minutes to transfer turkey and turnips to Aunt Susanna's dishes, hide our own, air the kitchen, and get back our breath. We accomplished it. When Aunt Susanna and her guests came, we were prepared for them: we were calm—outwardly—and the second mince pie was getting hot in the oven. It was ready by the time it was needed. Fortunately our turkey was the same size as Aunt Susanna's, and Laura had cooked a double supply of turnips, intending to warm them up the next day. Still, all things considered, Kate and I didn't enjoy that dinner much. We kept thinking of poor Laura and Maggie at home, dining off potatoes on Thanksgiving!

But at least Aunt Susanna was satisfied. When Kate and I were washing the dishes, she came out quite beamingly.

"Well, my dears, I must admit that you made a very good job of the dinner, indeed. The turkey was done to perfection. As for the mince pies—well, of course Miranda Mary made them, but she must have had extra good luck with them, for they were excellent and heated to just the right degree. You didn't give anything to the McGinnis dog, I hope?"

"No, we didn't *give* him anything," said Kate.

Aunt Susanna did not notice the emphasis.

When we had finished the dishes, we smuggled our platter and tureen out of the house and went home. Laura and Margaret were busy painting and studying and were just as sweet-tempered as if we hadn't robbed them of their dinner. But we had to tell them the whole story before we even took off our hats.

"There is a special Providence for children and idiots," said Laura, gently. We didn't ask her whether she meant us or Tony McGinnis or both. There are some things better left in obscurity. I'd have probably said something much sharper than that if anybody had made off with my Thanksgiving turkey so unceremoniously.

Aunt Susanna came down the next day and told Margaret that she would send her to college. Also she commissioned Laura to paint her a watercolour for her dining room and said she'd pay her five dollars for it.

Kate and I were rather left out in the cold in this distribution of favours, but when you come to reflect that Laura and Maggie had really cooked that dinner, it was only just.

Anyway, Aunt Susanna has never since insinuated that we can't cook, and that is as much as we deserve.

IN PLACE OF QUEEN MAB
(1907)

If a good fairy had suddenly appeared to Little Louise and granted her three wishes, Little Louise's first, last, and middle wish would have been for a sister. But the days of fairies seem to have gone by, and all even Santa Claus could do for Little Louise was to bring her the most beautiful dollie you ever saw—a doll almost as big as Little Louise herself (to be sure Little Louise was *very* little), with lovely long, golden hair, brown eyes that opened and shut, and a trunkful of beautiful frilly clothes.

Of course, nothing could really make up to Little Louise for not having a sister; but that wonderful dollie came very near it. Little Louise called her Queen Mab and loved her next best to Father and Mother and Auntie May, and Nora, the cook.

In the spring a new family moved in next door, and when somebody said there was a little girl in it, Little Louise's big round blue eyes almost popped out of her head. She couldn't sleep for ever so long that night for excitement, and when she did sleep she had the most exciting dreams about the little girl next door and the splendid times they were going to have together.

Bright and early the next morning, long before foolish grown-up people would think of making calls at all, Little Louise had crept through the gap in the spruce hedge into the next-door yard with a big bunch of sweet peas picked from her own garden plot to give the new little girl next door.

Now, would you believe it? There was the new little girl next door lying back in a wheelchair under the big apple tree; and when Little Louise got acquainted with her—when you are seven years old it never takes long to get acquainted—she found out that the new little girl's name was Amy Burns and that she couldn't walk a single step, or run and play, or do *anything* except be wheeled around in a chair or lie on a sofa. Little Louise gave Amy the flowers and kissed her and promised to go back soon, and then Little Louise went home and cried with disappointment for herself and pity for Amy.

The next time Little Louise went over to see Amy she took Queen Mab with her. Amy thought she had never seen anything so lovely as Queen Mab; she begged to be allowed to hold her for just a minute, and Little Louise let her hold her all the time she was there. After that she took Queen Mab over every day, and Amy loved the doll as much as Little Louise did, and they were all three very happy together. But there were some days when Little Louise was not allowed to see Amy, and Little Louise knew that on those days Amy had to stay in bed all day and suffered a great deal.

"If I only had a doll like Queen Mab with me, I wouldn't mind so much," Amy said one day, wistfully. She was very white, for she had had a bad day the day before.

"Why doesn't Santa Claus bring you a doll?" asked Little Louise.

"My Santa Claus is too poor," said Amy. "He is not rich like your Santa Claus, you know."

"Well, maybe he'll get richer by next Christmas and bring you a doll," said Little Louise, cheerfully.

But Amy had not much hope of that, and, besides, Christmas was so dreadfully far away.

As the hot weather came on, Amy got thinner and paler, and her "bad days" came oftener and oftener. Little Louise felt dreadfully about this, for she had learned to be very fond of Amy. She went over often and talked and sang and told fairy stories to Amy; but somehow Amy did not take much notice of anything except Queen Mab. She never lost her interest in Queen Mab.

One day when Little Louise went over, she found Amy quite bright and excited.

"O Louise, I have such splendid news! Look what Tommy Adams gave me! It's a wishbone; and Tommy says that, if I take it on my birthday and wish three times for whatever I want, I'll get it sure. Tommy says it can't fail. Wasn't it good of him to give it to me? And, O Louise, tomorrow is my birthday, and I'm going to wish for a doll exactly like Queen Mab!"

Little Louise was silent from very dismay. She hadn't a bit of faith in Tommy Adams, not she! She knew Tommy Adams had just been hoaxing Amy, and Amy would be so dreadfully disappointed. Little Louise felt quite sure that a disappointment would be a very bad thing for Amy just then.

"She'll cry herself sick when she doesn't get a doll," thought Little Louise, sorrowfully, as she went home through the gap in the spruce hedge. "And she'll have a lot of bad days one after another. Tommy Adams is a hateful, wicked boy, and just as mean as he can be."

Little Louise felt so worried that she couldn't bear to go to see Amy the next day for ever so long. At last she tiptoed to the hedge and peeped through. There was Amy in her chair under the big apple tree crying as if her heart would break, with the wishbone on her lap.

Little Louise sat down on the grass on her own side of the hedge and thought what a hard world it was. There was really nothing but trouble. Mama was sick upstairs and they wouldn't let her go up to see her; Auntie May was busy waiting on her; Papa was so worried about something he had hardly noticed Little Louise all day; Nora had neuralgia and nerves combined; and now, to crown all, here was Amy breaking her heart because the wishbone hadn't brought her a doll.

Little Louise got up with a long sigh. She went into the house and took Queen Mab and her trunkful of clothes. Then she marched over into the next-door yard.

"Amy, I've brought you Queen Mab," she said, resolutely. "I'm going to give her to you for your very own."

Amy stopped crying and looked at Little Louise in amazement.

"But—don't you want her yourself?" she gasped.

"I want you to have her more," said Little Louise. "You just take her and keep her. But, O Amy, do be good to her!"

"Oh, I will, indeed," promised Amy, all flushed and dimpled with delight, as she took Queen Mab in her arms. "O Little Louise, I just love you—you're so good. Oh, I'm just going to be so happy after this! I don't feel as if I'd have a bad day for ever so long; and when I do, I'll just have Queen Mab lying beside me all the time, and I won't mind it a bit."

Little Louise hurried away home because she wanted to get out of Amy's sight and have a good cry; but at the door she met Papa, and Papa was all smiles.

"Run up to Mama's room, Little Louise," he said, "but don't make any noise. There is something there you'll like."

Little Louise mounted the stairs without much enthusiasm. She didn't believe there was anything in the world she could like now that Queen Mab was gone.

Mama was lying on her bed, very pale and smiling; and Auntie May came forward, holding something all tiny and fat and dimpled.

"Here is your new sister, Little Louise," she said. "Isn't she sweet?"

Little Louise gave one enraptured glance. The whole world was simply made of rainbows then, and her happiness was too great for utterance.

"O Auntie May!" she gasped. "How long will it be before I can have her to hold?"

THE WINNING OF FRANCES
(1908)

Pauline Wilson came down Corridor Two and joined the group of girls chatting on the landing of the front staircase. Instantly arms were about her, and she was drawn into the centre of the group.

"Oh, but it's good to have you back again, Polly," said Cornelia White, with an affectionate squeeze. "We were so afraid you wouldn't be able to come. And Oakburn Hall without Polly Wilson is just cake with the flavouring left out."

A general laugh of assent greeted Cornelia's smile. Pauline had been the pet of Corridor Two the previous year, as well as the acknowledged leader, from a social point of view, of all the Oakburn Hall girls. She was rich and pretty and clever; and, more than all, she was lovable. Even the poor and plain girls, who were apt to hold aloof from the richer set, liked Pauline, and she had many friends among them. She had not been able to return to the Hall when the school opened in September, owing to her sister's illness; but now in mid-October she had come.

"I'm glad to be back," said Pauline, gaily. "It's good to see all you dear girls again. Mother thought I might as well wait until after the Christmas holidays, since it was so late in the term, but I said I must come right away. As it is, I feel half a stranger—there are so many new girls. What are they like? Are they nice?"

"Oh, *you* will discover that they are *all* nice before you've been here a week," laughed Emily Millar. "The rest of us now, not being gifted with your discernment, think some of them are nice, and some most decidedly not. And, speaking of that, here comes one"—Emily dropped her voice to a careful undertone—"whom we count among the 'nots.'"

Pauline looked around to see a girl coming down the corridor. She was very tall and plainly, one might almost say shabbily, dressed; she had a dark, intense face, and rather too firmly set lips, looking as if they never relaxed into girlish smiles. Her whole air and bearing bespoke a reserve bordering on positive ungraciousness. She passed the group of girls with a distant bow, although some of them smiled in a friendly fashion and said, "Good morning, Frances."

"That is Frances Porter," explained Cornelia, when Frances had passed out of earshot. "When I see her coming, and have time, I always put on my coat. She positively gives me a chill. You have a genius for winning friendship, Polly, as I've known ever since you thawed Josephine Campbell out, but I prophesy you'll never thaw Frances. She'll freeze you right up, as she has frozen all the rest of us. We *can't* make friends with her, that is all there is about it."

"Have you honestly tried?" asked Pauline.

"Yes, we have, honestly. We were just as nice to her when she came as we could be and asked her into everything. But she wouldn't come, not she. She seems to be a naturally reserved person; and then, of course, the way Kate White acted tended to prejudice her against us, though it isn't fair of her to dislike us all because Kate was mean. Miss Carson wanted Kate to take her as a roommate. But Kate—well, you know she's a snob anyway—wouldn't, because Frances was poor. Of course, she didn't give *that* reason to Miss Carson; but she showed plainly that she didn't want Frances, and Miss Carson didn't insist, because I suppose she thought Kate would make it terribly uncomfortable for a new girl if she did. Frances is rooming alone in the little corner room at the end of the corridor.

"The rest of us tried to make up for Kate's behaviour, but there, you can't melt an iceberg. Frances shuts the door of her soul slam-to in our faces, and I, for one, have given up trying to open it."

The other girls agreed with Cornelia, but Pauline shook her pretty golden head.

"Polly's going to have a try," laughed Betty Moreland.

"Yes, I am," admitted Pauline. "I wasn't here when Kate acted up, so she can't have that against me. I'm going to win Frances Porter's friendship."

"Well, I hope you'll succeed, I honestly do, but I don't believe you will," finished Cornelia, pessimistically. None of the others believed it either.

Frances Porter had gone down the stairs to her shorthand lesson, with more bitterness in her heart than ever. So Pauline Wilson had come—the wonderful Pauline Wilson, about whom those giddy Corridor Two girls were continually talking—and was being bowed down to and worshipped by her satellites.

"Just because she is rich and wears fine clothes," thought Frances, resentfully; and she hardened her heart against Pauline.

Frances Porter was poor—how poor none of the Oakburn Hall girls really knew, or, to do the most of them justice, would have cared a straw if they had known, although you could never have convinced Frances of it. Her home was on a little farm out at North Hill, and Frances, by dint of teaching the district school and pinching and economizing, had managed to save enough for a year at Oakburn Hall. She was naturally a reserved girl, and her proud spirit had been much galled by her poverty. The Oakburn Hall girls would have found it difficult to make friends with her, in any case, for Frances had a belief that the richer girls would look down on her for her poverty. Kate White's snobbishness intensified this belief, until it became positively morbid. It did not make any difference that Kate White was the most unpopular girl in the school. In Frances's eyes they were all birds of a feather. Frances, as Cornelia said, shut the door of her soul in their faces and never opened it for as much as a peep. The kindnesses they offered made no impression on her.

"They're just trying to be condescending and patronizing, because Miss Carson tells them they should be friendly with everybody," she told herself, stubbornly. "They look down on me just the same. Their kindness is all put on. There isn't one of them would really put herself out to do me a favour."

Frances did not ask herself why they should unless she showed herself worthy of it. Many of us, you know, look grimly on the world and then resent it because the world doesn't beam on us. Frances went on encouraging her foolish and uncomfortable bias against the girls and never for a moment doubted that she was quite right. Her ungracious reception of the girls' advances she counted proper independence—she would show them she wasn't going to be patronized!

Pauline Wilson made up her mind that she would win Frances Porter's friendship, and she opened her first battery that afternoon when she came up the stairs and found Frances looking out of the window on the first landing. Pauline stopped and held out her hand.

"Nobody has introduced us yet," she said, with the smile few people could resist, "so I think we must dispense with that formality. I'm Pauline Wilson, commonly known as Polly, and you are Frances Porter. I'm a little late getting back to school this term, so I'm in a hurry to be friends with all the new girls, by way of making up for lost time."

Frances surrendered her hand in a very unresponsive clasp. "Thank you," she answered coldly, "but I am so busy with my studies that I have no time to form friendships with strangers."

And Frances passed on down the stairs, leaving Pauline staring rather foolishly after her. "Have—I—been—snubbed?" said Pauline. "Yes, I have—the first time it ever happened to me. Well, every new experience is broadening. Cornelia White, what are you grinning at?" For Cornelia was hanging over the upper stair railing, with a broad smile on her face.

"At your blank expression, dearest Poll. Didn't I warn you? You'll believe your Cornelia next time."

"Never mind, I'm going to win that girl yet," vowed Pauline, determinedly. "It may take a long while, but I'll do it."

"I suppose even an iceberg would melt in time, if you kept hot blankets to it," returned Cornelia, airily. "But the question is, would it be worthwhile?"

"In Frances Porter's case, I think it would," answered Pauline, thoughtfully. "I like her face, in spite of its coldness. There's a lot in that girl—she'd be a jolly good comrade if she hadn't got so warped. I'm going to bring her back to her normal self, you'll see."

"Wish you luck," said the skeptical Cornelia.

That evening, Pauline, with a plate of ruddy apples in her hand, knocked at the door of the little corner room on Corridor Two. No cheerful "Come" responded. Instead, Frances opened the door and stood inhospitably, with no invitation to enter.

"I've brought you some of my apples," was Pauline's greeting. "I brought a big boxful with me from home, and I want all the girls to help me eat them up."

"Thank you, but I don't care for apples," said Frances icily, "and I am very busy just now. Good evening."

And the door was shut in Pauline's face, literally as well as figuratively. Pauline walked down the length of the corridor before she said a word. Then, being a girl with a sense of humour, she leaned against the wall and laughed softly.

"Snub number two—and such a snub! Well, I'm glad Cornelia wasn't by to laugh at me. Frances Porter, the day will come when you'll love me like a sister and welcome me to your room with open arms. But I foresee that day will be more distant than I at first supposed."

It was, indeed. As the weeks went by, there were times when Pauline herself despaired, although she would never admit it to the other girls, who watched the "experiment," as they called it, with amused interest. Pauline left no means untried to break down the barriers of Frances Porter's reserve, but she was tactful enough not to let the object be too evident. She asked Miss Carson's permission to sit beside Frances at the table, and she talked to her persistently, winning only cold monosyllables for her pains.

"There isn't a trickle from the iceberg yet, as far as I can see," remarked Cornelia.

"I don't know," mused Pauline, thoughtfully. "Today at lunch she actually asked me to pass her the crackers. She never volunteered a remark before. I consider that encouraging."

"She was probably hungrier than usual and couldn't get the crackers any other way," objected Cornelia. "Let's talk about something more cheerful. Betty Moreland's violin recital is coming off next week. Betty is in agonies of nervousness. But her recital will be the best of the year. Emily Millar is going to sing, and Miss Tait is going to play the piano. There's a galaxy of talent for you."

"And Cornelia White is going to recite," laughed Pauline. "Don't be too modest. Miss Crockett says you are the best elocution pupil she ever had."

"Nonsense," protested Cornelia, blushing and looking enormously pleased.

Betty Moreland's recital came off in due time, and was, as Cornelia predicted, the best of the year. Betty was an excellent violinist; Emily Millar a remarkably sweet singer; Miss Tait, one of the music teachers, a finished pianist; and Cornelia White, a capital reciter. Everyone enjoyed the programme.

Pauline Wilson, on her way back from the assembly room, found Frances Porter gazing out of the corridor window at a young moon shining between the elm boughs. For a moment Pauline was tempted to pass on in silence. She had grown almost discouraged and was about ready to give up. What was the use of trying to win over this cold, moody, unresponsive girl? Then she turned back from the staircase and went to the window. "How did you like the recital tonight, Frances?" she asked.

To her surprise, Frances spoke almost cordially. "It was splendid."

"Betty can make her violin speak," said Pauline, "and laugh and cry, for that matter."

"I was just wishing my sister Margaret could have heard her—her and Emily too," said Frances, slowly. "Margaret is so fond of music." Frances had never mentioned any of her family before.

"Can't she come in to the recitals?" suggested Pauline. "You know you can send tickets to anybody you like."

"No, she can't," answered Frances, brusquely. "She—she is a cripple with spinal trouble. She never leaves her couch."

"Oh, I am so sorry," sympathized Pauline, gently.

But Frances, as if already repenting her confidence, had wheeled about and started down the corridor, without another glance at Pauline. The latter, however, went to her room greatly encouraged. She really was making headway. Then, just as she opened her door, an idea came to her.

During the following week, it was evident that something was brewing among the Oakburn Hall girls. Even Frances Porter felt it and scornfully attributed it to some scheme for an unlawful midnight spread. Pauline Wilson seemed to be the centre whence radiated all the plotting. There were notes, and whispers, and conferences; an air of mystery pervaded the corridors; scraps of conversation might have been heard here and there.

"We must put on our very prettiest dresses," cried Betty Moreland.

"Miss Tait has consented to go as chaperone," announced Emily.

"Miss Carson says that, for once, we may buy all the things we want from the corner grocery, and take them out," added Pauline. She was so interested that she did not notice Frances going by, and Frances went downstairs with an odd feeling of disappointment in her heart. There was no doubt of it, Pauline Wilson had not seemed so friendly this past week; she was preoccupied and forgetful. Frances was illogical enough to feel hurt at this, although she was angry with herself for feeling so and told herself sharply that she didn't care.

Frances went home on Friday, on the five o'clock train, as usual. She and Margaret were alone that evening, Mr. and Mrs. Porter having gone out. Margaret lay on the sofa as she always did, a thin slip of a girl with blue eyes and soft fair hair. She did not look at all like Frances, and her pale, wistful face, although it bore traces of the suffering that had been her portion most of her fifteen years, was very sweet and patient.

Frances did her weekly mending in a moody silence, stabbing stockings and buttons viciously with her needle. She felt tired, and discouraged, and sulky. She *hated* Oakburn Hall, and those silly, laughing girls, who never thought of anything but their own good times. Even Pauline Wilson, in whom she had really begun to believe a little—

A knock at the hall door interrupted Frances's musings. She went to open it, still with the frown on her face. Then, as she peered out into the frosty, starlit December night, the frown gave place to blank astonishment. The tiny yard was almost filled with girls in hoods and long cloaks—the Corridor Two girls, with Pauline, and Cornelia, and Emily, and Betty in the front rank. Betty carried her violin case, and Emily had her music roll under her arm, and they all were laden with boxes and baskets. Before anyone could speak, Miss Tait stepped forward.

"Your classmates have planned a little surprise for you, Frances," she said, smiling. "They have come to repeat Betty's recital for Margaret, since you told Pauline she loved music so."

"Oh! Come in," said Frances, stupidly. She led the way silently to the little spare room off the parlour. When the girls took off their wraps, she saw that they all wore their dainty evening dresses—dresses reserved, as a usual thing, for the greatest occasions at Oakburn Hall. Somehow, this pleased this odd girl more than anything else. They had thought it worthwhile to dress up for Margaret. Margaret greeted them all joyfully when they went up. She was delighted to meet Frances's classmates, for at least

Frances had kept her bitterness to herself and had said nothing against the girls to Margaret.

They had a wonderful evening. Betty played even better than at her recital; Emily sang her sweetest songs; Cornelia's recitations were capital; and Miss Tait's nimble fingers coaxed more music out of the little old cottage organ than anyone had ever supposed was in it, even in its palmiest days. Margaret lay and listened with an enraptured face. When the programme was finished, there were tears of delight in her eyes.

"Oh, it was lovely," she said. "I never heard—never imagined such music before. I shall never forget it."

"Now, we're all hungry, and we brought our supper with us," cried Pauline, gaily. "But we must depend on you for dishes, Frances."

Frances had sat in a shadowed corner while the programme was going on, watching Margaret's face. Now she came out, smiling. Nobody had ever seen Frances Porter look like that before. But she was very quiet and said little as she brought out dishes and helped Pauline set the table. They had a merry supper, and when it was over, the girls had to hurry off to catch the last train to town. Frances bade them all goodnight and thanked them cordially. When she had shut the door behind Miss Tait, she stood and looked at herself in the little hall mirror.

"Frances Porter," she said, solemnly, "you have been a cranky, hateful, sulky, jealous, wicked little fool, and the only hope for you lies in the fact that you have sense enough left to realize it. Those girls are lovely."

On Monday evening, there was a tap at Pauline's door. In response to her invitation, Frances Porter walked in.

"I've come to thank you especially," she said, awkwardly but sincerely. "It was lovely of you to plan such a treat for Margaret. And—and—I didn't deserve that you should do it. I've been hateful to you."

"It was only just that you didn't understand," answered Pauline, gently. "But all the misunderstanding is over now, isn't it? We'll never refer to it again. Sit down and help yourself to fudge."

"So you have thawed the iceberg?" asked Cornelia later on.

"She isn't an iceberg at all," protested Pauline, warmly. "She is really a jolly girl, with lots of fun and good comradeship in her."

"Yes, she is," admitted Cornelia, "but it took you to bring it out, Polly."

TED WILLIAMS, SNEAK
(1908)

CHAPTER I.

"Hello, Milton. Coming for a swim this afternoon?" said Ted Williams gayly to the classmate he met on the Glenwood Campus one fine Saturday in October.

Milton Ross made no reply. He turned his back significantly on Ted and walked away.

Ted stared after him for a moment in amazement. Then he turned to Stanley Grant, who stood near. "What's the matter with Milt? Has he got a grouch at me?"

Stanley Grant coloured uncomfortably and looked foolish. Sundry remembrances of the many times Ted had helped him out with his Latin in his prep year came into his mind. But these were not sufficient to conquer his resentment at a more recent recollection. He, too, turned on his heel and marched away.

Ted's face crimsoned with anger. He hastened back to the residence hall without speaking to any more of the boys he met, and rushed to his room on Corridor Two. At his door he halted abruptly. Pinned to it was a broad placard with "Ted Williams, Sneak," pinned across it in huge black letters. Ted tore it down and burst into his room. His roommate, Brooks Ford, one of the senior boys (at Glenwood it was the rule that the seniors and juniors should room together), who was curled up comfortably in the sunshine on the broad window seat studying his Euclid, looked up with a frown at Ted's noisy entrance.

"Look here, Brooks, what does this mean? The fellows won't speak to me, and I find *this* pinned to my door. Sneak! I'm not a sneak. What's up? Do you know?"

Brooks shrugged his shoulders languidly. Like all the seniors, he considered the affairs of the juniors rather beneath serious notice.

"I understand your class has decided to send you to Coventry, Teddy, my boy. They blame you for peaching on them about that raid on old Vincent's orchard, and they're properly down on you. It was a shabby trick if you did it, a regular sneak's trick."

"Peaching on them?" echoed Ted in astonishment. "I never did. Who says I did? Come, now."

"So you didn't, eh? Well, I hardly thought it was like you, even if you are a junior. *That* isn't your fault, and you'll grow out of it if you live long enough."

"Look here, Brooks," said Ted impatiently. "I'm in no mood for teasing. Tell me the whole story, or what you know of it. Who says I peached? How did they know anybody peached?"

"Well, you know, somebody must have, or the doc wouldn't have got wind of it. And you don't suppose any of the seniors would take the trouble to, even if they were mean enough. Frank Long has found it all out and told it. It seems that the doctor received an anonymous note informing him that the Jolly Good Timers had perpetrated a raid on Mr. Vincent's orchard, not to mention smashing to flinders the rule that says all you children must be snug and warm in your little trundle-beds after ten o'clock. You know the result. And now Frank declares he has seen the note, and it is in your handwriting. So that's all I know about it. If you can't convince your class that you didn't tell, you're in for a freeze-out, Teddy. All the juniors are down on you. Good Timers and outsiders alike. They consider you have disgraced the class."

"How can I clear myself if they won't take my word that I didn't tell?" said Ted miserably.

Brooks shrugged again as he picked up his cap. "Find out who wrote the note and bring it home to him," he said. "The note was written. That much is certain. So there is a sneak somewhere among you juniors. And it must have been written by someone who has a grudge against you, or he wouldn't have gone to the trouble of imitating your scrawl. Your writing isn't to be equalled in Glenwood or out of it for unexpected kinks and curves, as I well know, having had to correct several of your prep exercises last year. Who's got a spite at you?"

"Ralph Sanderson is the only one I know of. He was mad because I got the Latin prize last term and because the Kappa Sigma elected me president this year. Ralph was laid up with bronchitis the night of the raid, but he knew all about it. But if he did forge that note, how can I prove it?"

"You have a bad habit of asking unanswerable questions, Teddy boy; and that's something I can't encourage in a junior," said Brooks as he went out. It would never do, Brooks thought, to take the little junior fusses seriously. Teddy Williams was a nice fellow, for a junior, and it was rather hard lines for him to be blamed for telling tales if he were innocent. Still, the juniors must manage their own affairs, thought the philosophical Brooks.

Ted threw himself on the empty window seat and gave himself over to bitter reflections. Brooks seemed to regard it as a joke, but it was no laughing matter to him to be an outcast from his peers, branded with the disgrace of tale-bearing. Ted knew he would never be forgiven for that. Yet how could he prove his innocence?

The year before, some of the preps, who were not allowed by school traditions to have Greek letter fraternities, had organized a club called the "Jolly Good Timers." As its name indicated, its sole purpose was fun; but as the fun had always been harmless and in accordance with the regulations of the school, the organization was permitted by the disdainful seniors and juniors and winked at by the faculty. This year the former preps were juniors and had their Kappa Sigma; but they kept up the Jolly Good Timers also.

Ted, however, had had his doubts about it from the opening of the term. Several new boys had joined, and the "larks" that they went in for were beginning to be rather dubious. "If we keep this sort of thing up," grumbled Ted to Stanley Grant as they sneaked in after hours from painting the janitor's two pigs with gorgeous red and yellow stripes, "the doctor will get down on us and snuff the Jolly Good Timers out."

The affair of the pigs blew over harmlessly, though the doctor frowned and the janitor growled.

At the next meeting of the club, Bert Lockhart proposed a night raid on Farmer Vincent's apple orchard. "He's got some beauties ripe, and he's meaner than second skimmings with 'em. Let's just slip out tomorrow night and help ourselves to a few."

"Won't it be rather risky?" asked Stanley Grant doubtfully. "If the doctor finds it out, he'll be furious."

"But he won't find it out," rejoined Bert easily. "Old Vincent will never suspect the Glenwood boys. He'll blame the factory crowd. They've raided his orchard several times this summer, and he is furious at them."

Astonishment and indignation had hitherto kept Ted Williams silent, but now he burst out vehemently: "Well, I call this a disgraceful idea. I for one won't take part in any such doings; and if the Good Timers are going to stoop to such things, I think it is time we disbanded."

Some of the boys looked a little ashamed, others angry.

"If you're afraid to come, you needn't," said Bert contemptuously.

"Well, I'm not afraid, but I'm not going apple-stealing to please anybody," retorted Ted hotly, and a few of the boys seemed inclined to side with him.

Nevertheless, such was Bert's influence that the raid came off on the following night. Ted did not go, but every other Good Timer was on hand, and apples were freely munched in the residence hall for a week after.

Then the thunderbolt fell from a clear sky. Farmer Vincent had not made any fuss, supposing, as Bert had foreseen, that the marauders were factory boys. But Dr. Long became mysteriously informed of it, and a strict investigation was held. The result was that fifteen juniors who had been on the raid were put on "limits" for a month. Moreover, they had to pay Farmer Vincent for the value of the stolen fruit, and the unfortunate Good Timers had a strong suspicion that the shrewd farmer had included in his bill not only the apples they had really carried off, but also all he had lost in factory raids through the summer. To crown all, the doctor, as Ted had foreseen, "snuffed out" the Jolly Good Timers altogether.

Indignation and curiosity were general. How had the doctor learned of the raid? His son Frank, who, although he was not a Good Timer, was a junior and sympathized with his friends, vowed he would find out, and did—or thought he did. An unsigned note in Ted Williams's handwriting had been sent to the doctor telling the whole story.

The news spread through the school like wildfire. The Good Timers were furious and the rest of the juniors indignant. Ted Williams had "peached"; therefore, Ted Williams must henceforth be frozen out of decent society. Glenwood had no further use for him.

CHAPTER II.

Ted, alone in his room, thought over the whole matter and arrived nowhere. What could he do? Ralph Sanderson must have forged that note. No one else, Ted felt sure, could have had any motive for doing so. He and Ralph had been bitter rivals during their prep year, and he knew Ralph had hated him for winning the Latin prize. Then Ralph had wanted the presidency of the Kappa Sigma, but Ted had been elected by an overwhelming majority, and this was an added grudge. Yet Ralph had never shown open enmity, and Ted realized that he could not even prove that Ralph *was* his enemy. Ralph had always been suave and polite to him.

Ralph Sanderson was a rather delicate boy who took little part in the school sports but was devoted to his books. He roomed by himself in the "turret room" of Residence Hall and was not particularly liked by the other boys, although nobody seemed to have any active dislike of him.

"I don't believe I can do anything to clear myself," Ted concluded, "and I'm going to have a pretty miserable time of it from this out."

Ted's foreboding was realized. He *had* a miserable time of it. None of his class would have anything to do with him. He was requested to resign the presidency of Kappa Sigma and did so in a bitterness of spirit that was not sweetened by the fact that Ralph Sanderson was promptly elected to the vacancy. At first Ted determined to tell his mother all about it when he went home for Christmas and entreat her permission to remove to another school. Then his native resolution came to his aid.

"I'll do no such thing," he vowed to himself. "I'm innocent, and I'm not going to let them drive me from Glenwood as if I were guilty. I'll go on and finish out my course as if nothing had happened."

Having no other outlet for his energies, Ted pitched into his studies with a vengeance, and with such good results that he soon outstripped all the rest in his class and learned more in a month than he would probably have done in a whole term otherwise. But nothing could make up to Ted for the loss of his chums' friendship. It was all right to be first in exams. But what good did it do you when the boys thought you were a sneak? Ted hated Ralph Sanderson more every day, for every day he felt surer that Ralph was at the bottom of it all.

One night in November all the members of the faculty save Mr. Lascelles, the French teacher, went to attend an important educational meeting in town. They would not be back until the next day. The matron of Residence Hall was also absent. It was a dark, windy night, and Ted Williams's last drowsy recollection as he dropped off to sleep was of hearing Brooks Ford say that some of the campus trees would go down before morning. The next second, as it seemed to Ted (it was really three hours later), he found himself sitting bolt upright in bed, vigorously shaken by Brooks, while the room was filled with a strange flickering glare and a pungent smell of smoke.

"Wake up," yelled Brooks, "and get out as quick as you can! The Hall's on fire! Hurry!"

There was need to hurry, as Ted realized when he sprang from his bed and threw on his clothes. The corridors were full of frightened boys, some of them panic-stricken, all bent on madly rushing out to safety. Ted was swept down the stairs with the crowd. Out on the campus, bright as day in the glare of the burning building, Mr. Lascelles joined them.

"Are you all here?" he shouted. "If you're all safe, there's nothing we can do. The Hall is doomed. It'll fall in ten minutes more."

"Where's Ralph Sanderson?" cried Bert Lockhart suddenly.

"Is Ralph Sanderson here?" shouted Mr. Lascelles. "Ralph, speak up if you are."

There was no response. The boys gazed at each other with white, horrified faces. Ralph was not there. Ralph had not escaped. Suddenly a form darted from the crowd and sped toward the steps. It was Ted Williams.

Mr. Lascelles sprang after him. "Ted, Ted, come back! You can't save him. It's too late. You'll lose your own life."

But Ted had rushed up the entrance steps and vanished inside the door. A groan went over the crowd, followed by silence. Not one of them dared to follow Ted. The sight of that flaming, smoke-wreathed building cowed even the bravest among them. To go into it seemed to go to certain death.

Ted peeled off his jacket and wound it around his head as he plunged into the hall. It was full of thick, blinding smoke that made his eyes smart and sting. Beyond it on the right, where the dining room was situated, was a mass of flames. Ted sped across the hall and up the stairs, the tongues of fire almost licking his face as he passed. The second corridor was full of smoke, and the top of the stairs was already on fire. He rushed along the corridor and burst into the turret room. Ralph lay on his bed asleep.

"Ralph! Ralph! Wake up!" Ted shrieked, shaking him.

There was no answer. Ralph was plainly stupefied by the smoke. Ted, knowing that there was not a moment to lose, seized him by the shoulders and dragged him out of bed and into the corridor. A glance told him that he could not return the way he had come. He turned to the left and started down the back staircase, which led to the janitor's apartments, dragging the still unconscious Ralph with him. Fortunately, Ralph was not heavy. Still, his dead weight was no light burden. Ted's breath came hard and fast, his eyes burned, and he felt as if his head would burst. The heat and smoke were stifling. Could he hold out? If he fell, if he paused, it was all over with him. To be sure, if he left Ralph he might escape; but the idea only flashed across his mind and was instantly rejected. It seemed a year to Ted before he got down those stairs, through the back hall, and staggered out of the side door. A moment later, he fainted from pain and exhaustion in Mr. Lascelles's arms, just as the roof of Residence Hall crashed in.

It was four days before Ted was allowed to leave his room in Dr. Long's house. In those days, order and regularity had been restored to Glenwood. Boarding houses for the boys had been found in the village, and the classes were going on as usual. Already the plans for a new residence hall were selected. The cause of the fire was a mystery, but it was supposed to have originated in a defective flue. It was so far underway by the time the janitor discovered it that nothing could be done except to get the occupants out as quickly as possible.

When Ted walked down to the campus, he found every boy in the school, with but two exceptions, assembled there. They had got wind of his coming, and as he entered the gates, the leader of the senior class, Morgan Blake, stepped out before the crowd.

"Three cheers for Ted Williams, the hero of Glenwood!" he called loudly.

The cheers were given with a right good will. Then they all crowded around Ted to shake his hands.

"Ted, we were beasts to treat you as we have done," exclaimed Bert. "We know now that you didn't write that note, because you simply couldn't have. Just forgive us, old fellow."

"It's all right," said Ted sheepishly. He had the most horrible idea that tears were on the point of coming to his eyes. Cry before the seniors? Well, he just guessed not!

At this juncture Frank Long came whistling through the gateway. He stopped when he saw the scene before him. "I guess this is just the place for my bit of news," he announced cheerfully. "I've just been in to see Ralph down at Mr. Stewart's—first time any of the boys have been let see him. He's better, but the doctor says his bronchial tubes aren't improved any by all the smoke he inhaled on the night of our little bonfire, and he is to be invalided home forthwith. Just as well, I imagine, all things considered; for, boys, Ralph wrote that note. He owned up the whole story to me. He said he had a grudge at Ted and took that way of paying him out. He's awfully sorry and repentant; and, Ted, he wanted me to ask you to forgive him."

"I'll go and tell him myself that it's all right," said Ted hastily, glad of an opportunity to escape before those disgraceful tears should fairly roll down.

"Ted Williams is a brick," said Frank as Ted dashed out of the gateway.

"Hear, hear," said the juniors unanimously.

A NARROW ESCAPE
(1909)

One Saturday evening, many years ago, when I was a lad of fourteen, living on what was known as the old Tucker homestead at Meadowby, I planned to walk over to Rennie, the next district, and spend Sunday with the family of an uncle who lived there. Accordingly, I started off after tea, telling Father and Mother not to expect me until Monday morning. My uncle's farm at Rennie was six miles away by the road, but by going "cross lots," the distance was much less.

I tramped steadily on, over breezy pasture lands and through vividly tinted maple woods, climbing fences, leaping brooks, and enjoying my walk immensely, for the evening was one of those mellow ones that come in the autumn and are full of the charm of summer and autumn combined.

A little more than halfway to Rennie was Obadiah Holmes's old barn. It was a ramshackle old affair but still useful after a fashion for storing the hay of Obadiah's back farm. It was half a mile from any inhabited dwelling and was seldom visited.

As I drew near I heard shrieks of laughter, and when I came in sight of it around the corner of the maple grove, I saw the five Holmes children having a game of Bar On. They hailed me fraternally, and insisted that I should stay a while and share in the sport.

I consented readily enough, for I was yet far from thinking myself too big to play Bar On. Besides, I liked the Holmes children. Joe, Patty, Rosella May, 'Diah, and Charlie, all tow-headed and liberally freckled, were a jolly little crew, and many a good time I had with them.

Bar On was the fashionable juvenile game in country districts at that time. It was played as follows: A goal was selected—in this case it was the door at the southeast corner of the old barn—and a goal-keeper appointed by the good-old process of "counting out," with "eeny, meeny, miny, mo," accompanied by a poke in the ribs at each word by the index finger of the counter. The goal-keeper then took his stand at the goal and shut his eyes, while the others promptly scattered and hid. When a faint, unearthly "Ready!" was piped out, the goal-keeper began to look for the hiders. If he caught a glimpse of one, he at once rushed back to the goal, struck it three times, and exclaimed "Bar on, So-and-so, one, two, three." So-and-so was then considered caught and had to come out and sit down by the goal while the hunt proceeded. If, however, So-and-so, by dint of harder running, or by virtue of not having been seen at all while the goal-keeper was hunting elsewhere, reached the goal first and hammered it with a wild whoop of "Bar free," free he was, and as such was privileged to assist those of his comrades who might yet be in durance vile by shouting "Lie low!" whenever the goal-keeper strayed too near their hiding places, lest haply they might peer out, meditating a dash for freedom, and so be seen of him.

The game was an exciting one, and very noisy. I dare say we liked it all the better on this account. Bar On, without a certain amount of yelling and screaming, would not have been Bar On at all, but only a poor pretence. The moments of tensest excitement came when a hider made a wild dash for freedom with the goal-keeper racing him. Then all those who were already out, bond or free, danced about from one leg to the other and shouted encouragement at the tops of their voices, culminating in one grand howl when the end was reached.

We had a good game, lasting about an hour. At the end of that time, the Holmeses decided that they must go home.

"We'll just have one more round for luck," said Patty, whose turn it was, as first caught in the last round, to be goal-keeper.

By this time all the hiding places were getting pretty well played out, and I looked around for a new one. It occurred to me to creep under the barn, and I ran around to the back of it.

Nobody had yet hidden under it, the general idea being that it was too low for one thing, and for another too difficult to escape from in time to make a goal. But I believed that I would try it, creeping from the back to the front, and squirming out when Patty should be at a safe distance.

The great beams underneath the barn touched the ground. Between them ran narrow passages. I selected the one that would bring me out almost at the goal, slipped down and wriggled under, unseen by any of the others, who were already in their respective ambushes.

I found progress rather slow and difficult, for I had to wriggle along on my stomach, and I had only gone about a third of the way when I heard the whoop of "Ready!" and saw Patty's red-stockinged legs flash past the opening in front of me. A few seconds later deafening yells announced that 'Diah and Joe had reached goal in safety. Now, while Patty was looking for Rosella May and Charlie, was my chance, for I knew they were hidden some distance away. I wriggled along with might and main. All at once I could go no farther. The ground seemed suddenly to rise in a small hillock, and I was firmly wedged between it and the flooring of the barn. I made a few efforts to force myself onward, and then tried to draw back. I could not move!

Just then another round of squeals announced that Rosella May was free and Charlie caught. I had opened my mouth to call for assistance when I heard Patty exclaim: "There's Jack and the cart. Hurry, and we'll get a ride home."

A scamper of feet told me that the Holmeses were racing to overtake Jack, who, as I learned later, was just then passing along a wood road at the other side of the barn clearing. I shouted to them to wait and help me out, but I could not call loudly, and the narrow passage deadened what sound I could make. In less than a minute the Holmeses were out of hearing, and I was left alone.

At first I believed I could still escape. I tried to pull back. But the effort served only to roll my jacket up in a wad on my shoulders and imprison me still more securely. Then I tried desperately to move forward. Equally in vain. Neither could I get my arms, which I had stretched out before me, back against my sides. It did not take long to convince me that no exertion of my own could free me. Besides, in my struggles I had hurt my back in some way, and every movement gave me exquisite pain.

For a time I could not even think clearly. I felt as helpless as an infant, and blinding tears rushed to my eyes. I tried to shout, but could make only a faint, gasping cry. Every few minutes I struggled fiercely, regardless of the pain it inflicted on me.

Finally, however, my panic of terror passed away and I lay quietly, trying to look my unpleasant predicament squarely in the face. Here was I pinned down under Obadiah Holmes's barn, a mile from any inhabited dwelling; and if my escape therefrom depended on my own efforts, I would remain there for all time. On the other hand, there was one chance in a hundred of anyone coming to my assistance. The Holmes children would naturally suppose that I would continue on my way to Rennie after their departure. Father and Mother would not expect me home till Monday and would not be much disturbed if I failed to appear before Tuesday. I did not believe that I could survive my imprisonment so long.

Common sense told me that, since I certainly could not free myself, I would be very foolish to exhaust my strength and further injure myself by trying to do so. My best plan was to lie quietly.

This was not easy to do. My position even when motionless was very uncomfortable. My back hurt me, and I soon became afflicted with a torturing thirst. Besides, it was now pitchy dark. At times my pain and fright overcame me, and I struggled frantically and cried hoarsely for help.

The memory of that night is still a vivid horror to me. It seemed like years. When the grey dawnlight began to creep under the barn, I was weak and spent. My throat and mouth were dry and parched, my arms were cramped, and every bone and muscle in my body ached with pain. I felt a certain stupor creeping over me, and realized that I would soon become unconscious.

All at once I heard a barn door open overhead, and the next minute footsteps were passing above me. I knew Joe Holmes's whistle.

I gathered all my remaining strength and called: "Joe! Joe!"

I heard Joe give a startled exclamation. Then he called out: "W-Who's that?"

"Fred Russell, Joe, right beneath you, under the barn. Help me, Joe!"

My voice gave out, and I could say no more. Joe rushed out of the barn and soon located me.

"You scared the wits out of me, Fred. Your voice seemed to come from the bowels of the earth. Have you been there all night? Can't you get out?"

In a few broken words I explained my situation, and Joe said: "I can't help you alone; that is certain, Fred. Some boards in the barn floor will have to be taken up. I must run home for Father. It's a piece of pure luck that I came this morning. I lost my jackknife here last night and came as soon as it was daylight to look for it."

Joe did not realize how keenly I was suffering, or he would not have wasted time in talking. But at last he started off, and I am bound to say lost no further time. Soon he was back with his father and grown-up brother Jim, who better appreciated my plight. The floor boards above me were speedily pried up, and I was lifted out more dead than alive. Then I fainted with pain and exhaustion and knew nothing more until I awoke to find myself in bed at the Holmes homestead, with good Mrs. Holmes fussing over me. Mother and Father soon arrived, and, the news having spread, neighbours kept dropping in all day to hear my story. It was three days before I could go home, and my back gave me trouble for months afterward. The doctor said I had wrenched the muscles of it terribly in my struggles.

I often played Bar On after that, but never did I crawl under a barn to hide, or into any other ambush that did not assure me a safe exit.

OUR THANKSGIVING DAY
(1909)

"Come, you and the boys, and eat Thanksgiving dinner with us at Brandon Hill," Uncle Kenneth Taylor wrote to Mother one November several years ago. Mother folded up the letter and looked at Lee and me.

"What is to be done?" she said. "Your Uncle James has asked us up to Brancepeth for Thanksgiving also. He will be offended if we don't go; and Uncle Kenneth will be hurt."

"The best plan," suggested Lee, "will be for part of us—the most important part, namely yourself, Mother Taylor—to go to Uncle James's, while Frank and I will go to Uncle Kenneth's. Of course, if you'd rather go to Brandon Hill, we'll reverse the order. But I hope you wouldn't. When I was a kiddy and therefore no respecter of persons, I delighted in a visit to Uncle James's, for it meant unlimited indulgence in candies and all sorts of goodies. I thought I was born under a lucky star to have an uncle who was a confectioner. But since I've outgrown those childish tastes"—Lee grinned, his sweet tooth is as sweet as ever to this day—"I'd ten times sooner eat my Thanksgiving dinner in Uncle Kenneth's cheerful kitchen than in Uncle James's magnificent dining room under the eyes of a scornful butler whose very expression takes away my appetite."

Mother wasn't particular where she went, so it was finally arranged as Lee had suggested. Uncle Kenneth had said he would drive in for us, but as Mother was not going, Lee and I decided to walk out and sent him word to that effect. We intended to start early on Thanksgiving morning for Brandon Hill. It was only eight miles across the country through a way we knew well through the woods. Thanksgiving fell on the twenty-sixth that year. It had been an unusually cold and surly November, with hard frost and some showers of snow. The day before Thanksgiving was dull and cold. Mother had intended to go to Brancepeth by the next morning's train but changed her mind and went by the afternoon train of that day. On our way back from seeing her off, Lee said:

"It's my opinion that if we're going to eat our Thanksgiving dinner at Brandon Hill, we'd better start tonight. The weather probs are for a storm."

Accordingly, we got our supper, locked up the house, and started. Our way to Brandon Hill lay over a backcountry of woods and hay farms, with hardly a house to be seen. Snowflakes began to fall soon after we left town, but we expected to get to Brandon Hill before it should begin to storm seriously. We tramped along briskly, enjoying our walk in spite of the dourness and cold of the early falling evening, talking as we went of our boyish plans and problems.

One of these problems was that old and exceedingly trite one, which is always figuring in stories just as it does in real life—how to get to college. Old and trite it might be, but to Lee and me it was new and burning. We were through the home high school. Mother could do nothing more for us, and in those days the opportunities for working one's way through college were not what they are now. We did not see how we were going to bring it about, and our blindness made us feel rather blue. We had both accepted clerkships in our hometown for the winter. Our wages would pay for board and clothes and thus lift some burden from Mother's shoulders. Mother had done well to keep us at school as long as she had; nobody but herself knew how she had managed it. She had, however, enough to live on in comfort herself, so we were free to go to college if we could solve the question of ways and means.

Meanwhile the wind was rising, the snow was coming thicker and faster, and we were still five miles from Brandon Hill.

"I don't like this," muttered Lee, as a stinging switch of sleet cut across our faces.

Neither did I. It was getting dark; we were in a desolate region of stumps and wastes with only a sheep track to follow.

"I don't believe we can make Uncle Kenneth's tonight," I said.

"We'll have to camp in the open then, I reckon," was Lee's grim answer. "There's no house along this trail. I'm not even very sure where we are. The only thing to do is to keep on. As long as we don't lose this track, we can get along."

We kept on, but it was hard work. The storm was now raging furiously, and it was getting dark. We were beginning to feel badly scared when Lee gave a sudden shout.

"Hurrah! I know where we are. Here's old Aunt Sally's house. We'll have to camp here for the night, and thank our lucky stars we've blundered on it. We'd never be able to make Uncle Kenneth's in this hurly-burly, with only a sheep track to follow. Come on."

"Aunt Sally's house" was built on "the old Taylor farm." Our great-aunt Sally, who had died long before we were born, had lived there. At her death, Uncle Kenneth had bought the farm from her son, who had since died also. Uncle Kenneth kept the barns in good repair, to hold the grain and hay grown on the place, but left the house pretty much to itself. It was old and small and not worth bothering with; but it was at that moment a very welcome refuge to two bewildered and belated boys.

We got in without difficulty and thankfully shut the door in the teeth of the storm. We supposed that bare shelter was all we would find, but when Lee struck a match a welcome sight revealed itself—an old, cracked, but still serviceable "Waterloo" stove, with a pile of firewood beside it. On the shelf by the stove was a tallow candle in an old tin candlestick.

In a few minutes we had a roaring fire on. Uncle Kenneth's hired men—he had no boys of his own—had been camping in the old house during haymaking and harvest, cooking their own meals and sleeping in the bedroom off the kitchen. This accounted for the stove and firewood, which had been left for use when they should be thrashing at the barn in winter.

"Whew! Doesn't look as if there was to be much of a Thanksgiving celebration for us today," said Lee. "Wish we'd put a few crackers in our pockets. I'm as hungry as a wolf!"

So was I, but there did not seem to be much prospect of satisfying our hunger. We had slept late, and it was by now nine o'clock.

"Nice jolly Thanksgiving, this!" I grumbled, as I shaved up kindling to make a fire.

"Well, we can be thankful that we have a good fire, anyhow," said Lee. "We'll not freeze; and we can hardly starve before the storm will be over. Did you ever see such a blizzard for the time of year? I can't see two yards from the window."

We put some snow in a pot to melt, for we were thirsty; and we made all the funny speeches we could about a Thanksgiving dinner of snow water. We looked upon the whole affair as a lark, for beyond the inconvenience of being mewed up for a day or so and being rather hungry, there was really nothing to be feared.

After we had breakfasted on snow water, we explored the house. Downstairs were only two rooms, the kitchen and bedroom. Off the former was the pantry, the window of which was boarded up. Lee penetrated into this with a candle and presently he whooped. I was poking about upstairs when I heard him. Running down I met Lee emerging from the pantry triumphantly.

"Frank, I've discovered a bag of beans. We'll have something for our Thanksgiving dinner after all."

We melted more snow water and put on a pot of beans to boil. Then we sat and toasted our shins before that glorious old Waterloo.

"I suppose this is Aunt Sally's old stove," said Lee. "I dare say she's made that famous candy of hers on it many a time. Wish we had some of it now!"

“Wish we had the recipe,” I said.

Lee grinned. “It would mean a thousand dollars apiece for us, if Uncle James is a man of his word,” he said.

This aforesaid Aunt Sally of ours had been noted for the manufacture of a certain very delicious kind of homemade candy that she had invented herself and the recipe of which was a carefully guarded secret. This candy had a local fame in the country; and I had heard Uncle James say he had never tasted anything so delicious in his life.

“I'd give two thousand dollars for the recipe,” he had said once.

“I don't suppose Aunt Sally ever wrote it down,” Uncle Kenneth said.

“Yes, she did. I saw it once in an old black notebook she had. I was a boy of ten and hadn't enough sense to read it or remember it. If I could put that candy on the market, it would make a hit.”

When Aunt Sally had died, her few papers and effects had been searched for the recipe, but it had never been found. Uncle James said the notebook had been very dilapidated when he saw it, and it had probably been destroyed long ago.

As soon as our beans were cooked we ate a mess of them. They had no other flavouring than their own, with a dash of some salt that we found in the pantry, but I can honestly say that never in my life did I enjoy a Thanksgiving dinner as I did those beans, eaten out of an iron pot with a chip, in an old tumbledown house with snow drifting between the chinks. Truly there is no sauce like hunger.

Then we curled ourselves up on the bed and went to sleep. We wakened at four and had another feed of beans. The storm was abating somewhat, but we knew it was no use to think of getting to Uncle Kenneth's that night.

“We'll probably be able to get out in the morning, and we have enough wood—and beans—left to do us till then,” said Lee, turning away from the window of the upstairs room whither we had gone to look over the drifts.

I was standing by the old mantelpiece. It had warped out from the wall and was very rickety. Lee, with a fiendish grin, made a dive at me. I knew what was coming—a rib-tickling, which, big boy as I was, I could never endure. I dodged Lee, tripped, and fell, catching blindly at the edge of the mantel as I went down. The whole thing tore away from the wall and fell with me.

When I picked myself up from the dust and fragments, I saw Lee pouncing on something that was lying against the wall, where the mantelpiece had been. It was a small, thin, limp, tattered black notebook. A prophetic thrill ran through me.

"Lee, is that Aunt Sally's old recipe book?"

"Looks like it," said Lee, soberly, all the nonsense knocked out of him by the glorious possibility. "Let's go down and get a light and examine it."

With trembling fingers we turned the few yellowed, faded, dusty pages, where old-fashioned recipes were written in a tremulous, uncertain hand. On the very last page there was one headed, "My Candy." Lee and I looked at each other. We saw college in each other's eyes.

Next day we got to Uncle Kenneth's and had our belated dinner. On our return to town the following day, we took the train to Brancepeth and interviewed Uncle James. The recipe we had found proved to be the identical "Aunt Sally" one, and Uncle James paid us two thousand dollars for it and thought it cheap at the price. He has made five times the amount since out of the now famous "Sally's Sweetmeat."

Lee and I got to college, so everybody was satisfied. But we have never since eaten any beans like those. They don't grow such beans nowadays, I fear.

A THORNY ROSE
(1909)

"Haven't you made enough money, Frank?" said Mrs. Romaine, in her fine, plaintive voice.

"And aren't you going to stay at home and settle down, instead of living in some dreadful, uncivilized way in some still more uncivilized place out on those prairies?"

The young man addressed coolly helped himself to an extra lump of sugar before replying. He did not look exactly as if he had been accustomed to living in an uncivilized fashion. His manners were easy, and he wore his clothes with the air of one accustomed to them. He was not especially handsome, but he had a splendid figure and a pair of sleepy-looking dark eyes that had a trick of seeing more than most people gave them credit for. His hands were a trifle browner and harder than those of the young exquisites whom Mrs. Romaine was accustomed to have drop in to afternoon tea.

There were none of them there that day. Frank Willis was the only gentleman present. His cousin, Rae, sat in the corner because she knew its crepuscular light was kind to her rather loud beauty. Olive, who was more dusky and piquant, sat on the low ottoman before the window in a carefully studied pose.

Mrs. Romaine sat opposite her nephew and held her cup long after she had finished drinking. Her hands were her pride; they were slender and white and high-bred. Mrs. Romaine knew that a pretty hand never looks prettier than when its owner is holding a fragile cup of dainty china.

Frank Willis, scanning the scene from under his dropping eyelids, acknowledged to himself that it was such as he had seldom beheld on the far Western prairies; and he meant to enjoy his surroundings to the utmost while he could.

He looked at Mrs. Romaine; he had some very vivid recollections of the sound boxes that those pretty, bejewelled white hands had bestowed on his ears more than once in his boyhood. But that was long ago, before he had grown up and made a fortune; and he had been a rather provoking youngster, no doubt.

"There is nothing to keep me East now, Aunt Lucile. I've no relatives except yourself and the girls. And I'm rather afraid I'd smother here after awhile—after breathing on the prairies so many years. This is very pleasant for a change, though."

"Why not pick out some nice girl for a wife and let her persuade you to stay at home?" suggested Mrs. Romaine.

Willis smiled again, and half glanced at the corner where Rae sat.

"I'm not much given to marrying, aunt," he said whimsically, "and as for the rest, I'm only a rough ranchman after all, and how could I ask a nice girl to go out to the prairies with me? There's no society there, you know. Who would dream of going out there with me?"

Willis was not a vain man; nor was he one of those detestable creatures who imagine that every woman who looks at them falls in love. But he knew perfectly well, as he made that innocent remark, that there were two women in the room who would go to the Arctic Zone with him if he should ask them. He had been home for only five days, but he had seen through his aunt's scheme twenty-four hours after his arrival. He did not altogether blame her. She was poor, and both Rae and Olive had been out for more years than they cared to remember. Even a Western ranch was preferable to old maidenhood in Marlboro.

Rae and Olive had not always been so complacent toward him. He remembered that, in his boyhood, he had received not a few snubs from his pert cousins; they did not think him worth cultivating then.

"By the way, Aunt Lucile," he said, after the moment of silence that had followed his last remark, "who is that young lady I met on the lawn this afternoon?"

Mrs. Romaine drew her delicate brows together in a slight frown.

"I suppose it was Rose," she said, with an undertone of patient weariness in her voice. "She has just come back today. Were you speaking to her?"

"Not I. She disappeared like a lightning flash."

"That is so like Rose. She will be so abrupt and—rude. I wanted her to come in and meet you, but she flatly refused. I do my best for her, but she is a great trial to me. I'm afraid you will find her rather disagreeable. But you must make allowances for her. She is a mere child, in spite of her height, and, really, she has had no bringing up whatever."

Mrs. Romaine sighed gently again.

"Who is Rose?" asked Frank. "Another cousin?"

"Not of yours. She is the daughter of my poor husband's sister. Her mother died when Rose was a baby, and her father brought her up. They always lived together; he never sent her to school—he had such peculiar ideas about educating girls. Rose was a sort of experiment with him. She is quite—spoiled. He died last summer, and Rose came to live with us. She had nowhere else to go. She is a strange child and very hard to manage. I have tried to do my duty by her, but I don't think she is at all grateful. It is very trying."

Mrs. Romaine sighed.

"I wonder," said Willis mentally, "just what is the reality behind all this pretense of my respected aunt's. I think I shall try to find out. I never enjoyed playing blind man's bluff—when I had to wear it. Rose—Rose—a thorny one, I should say, judging from her looks. All the more worth picking, perhaps."

Aloud he said:

"Will she condescend to recognize me as a sort of honorary relative?"

"I think it is very doubtful if she will consent to meet you at all. She is quite shy. You know she has never seen anything of society. She tries to keep out of sight—perhaps it is just as well. She is so brusque and—unconventional. You must not be surprised if she avoids you. I have very little control over her. Rae, dearest, will you please hand me my shawl? I feel a slight draft."

Willis understood, from a certain tone in his aunt's smooth voice, that she considered the subject closed. He moved over and began to talk to Rae. But he was thinking.

"That pathetic story of Aunt Lucile's isn't quite true. Aunt Lucile is Aunt Lucile yet—she never deals squarely with a fellow. I wonder when I shall see the thorny rose again."

He smiled reminiscently, recalling the girl who had flashed past him on the lawn an hour before. She was not a beauty like Rae, nor did she have Olive's style . . .

"But I feel as if I wanted to see her very soon," reflected Willis, as he swayed Rae's fan lazily before his cousin's ripely tinted face.

He still felt so later on in the twilight, when he found himself alone on the veranda and saw a slim, dark figure flit through the trees and disappear in the shrubbery at the foot of the lawn. He tossed away his cigar and sauntered down the path. Pushing his way through a tangled growth of dogwood, he came upon a little open nook where a girl was sitting in a hammock, with a book in her lap and her face turned upward to the sky.

She did not see him at first, and he lingered in the shadow for a moment to look at her. She was very slender and tall, although her short skirt detracted from her height, and the heavy braid of nut-brown hair hanging over her shoulder gave her a childish appearance. But the face beneath the rippling waves was a woman's face, and although it lacked positive beauty, it was a wonderfully attractive one. The brow was wide and low, the eyes large, dark grey, and limpid beneath the long black lashes. Her skin was a clear olive, with a rich crimson on the downy cheek. The mouth was large but ripely red, and the little head was proudly poised on the slender throat. The eyebrows were peculiarly straight and black.

"Rose is a misnomer for her," thought Willis. "She is too vivid, too dusky—yet no, she is a red rose, one of those crimson roses with almost black hearts."

He stepped forward into the light. The girl, startled, sprang to her feet and let her book slip to the ground. She seemed on the point of flight.

"Don't run," said Willis with a smile. "You've no idea what a harmless creature I am."

The girl drew herself up proudly.

"I am not going to run. It is you who are the intruder," she said scornfully.

"Can't you waive ceremony and let me know you without an introduction?" demanded Willis frankly. "I am Frank Willis, and you, I believe, are Rose Something-or-other—"

"No such thing. My name is Rosamond Lauder. Aunt Lucile calls me Rose, and I detest it."

"I like Rosamond much better, myself. We are cousins of a sort, aren't we?"

"No, we are not. You are no relation of mine at all. And I don't want to know you. I only want to be left in peace."

"You are not very flattering."

"I never mean to be. I'm only—" her eyes seemed to smile a little—"I'm only Rosamond."

"'I am that Rosamond whom men call fair,'" quoted Willis unguardedly.

The dark face crimsoned with anger.

"You are making fun of me," she cried passionately, and in another moment she would have gone had not Willis held out the book he had picked up, a well-worn volume of Scott.

"You've forgotten this."

She turned again and held out her slim brown hands for it.

"Give it to me, please. It's mine—it—was Dad's."

Her voice trembled for an instant in a quick transition of feeling. Willis coolly took the outstretched hands in his.

"You lost your father not long ago," he said gently, then repented saying it when he saw the dark grey eyes fill with tears and the red lips tremble. She looked so like a grieved child that he wanted to take her in his arms and comfort her.

"Oh, yes," she said with a little sob. "But don't speak of him now—I can't bear it."

"I am so sorry. Forgive me, please. And don't go away."

She pulled her hands rather consciously from his and dashed the tears from her eyes with a half boyish motion.

"But they will miss you—and Aunt Lucile will think—"

"Is Aunt Lucile ever guilty of thinking? I should imagine that such a proceeding was a great deal too strenuous for her."

The girl looked at him from under her wet lashes doubtfully. Then a smile broke over her face irresistibly. She shook her head.

"But I must go. In the first place, I don't want to stay. In the second, Aunt Lucile would say it was—"

"What?" as she paused.

"Very unbecoming conduct in a schoolgirl."

"I don't believe that was what you intended to say when you began."

"Perhaps not. I am learning to hold my tongue. You know I am so 'very blunt and—unconventional.'"

Her mimicry of Mrs. Romaine's plaintive voice and characteristic pause before the final word was so perfect that Willis's face twitched.

"I am sure we could be friends."

"I am sure we could be nothing of the sort. I don't want to be either. I don't like men."

"You might like me."

"It's not likely."

"Thank you."

"No charge made. Aunt would say that was slang. So it is. I can't open my lips without disgracing myself, so I mean to keep them shut. I wish you would go away. If you don't, I shall."

"Rose—Rose," called a shrill voice from the house.

The girl made a face and shrugged her shoulders.

"That means me. I daresay Aunt Lucile suspects that I'm not obeying my instructions."

"Your instructions? What—"

"Please don't ask questions. If I get a scolding it will be your fault, and I'm not patient."

She flashed a defiant look at him over her shoulder as she turned and slipped through the dogwood boughs. The branches closed behind her with a swish.

Willis opened the book he still held. Between the leaves he found some pressed purple pansies. These he coolly transferred to his pocketbook, after which he strolled back to the house.

He saw nothing of Rosamond the next day, although he heard a fresh young voice singing snatches of old ballads in the back part of the house. A sudden cessation of the music followed his aunt's visit to the kitchen. Willis, who was holding a skein of silk on the veranda for Rae, smiled significantly.

"Aunt Lucile soon choked her off," he thought. "I wonder what sort of a life the child has here. She doesn't look particularly happy. As for the 'instructions' she spoke of, I daresay I could guess their meaning if I tried."

The next afternoon Willis escorted Rae and Olive to Mrs. Fenwick's garden party. He stayed long enough to appear civil, then took a headache and excused himself to his hostess when Rae and Olive were elsewhere.

When he got back to Acacia Villa, it looked deserted. Willis reconnoitered carefully. Aunt Lucile was taking a nap. So far, the coast was clear. But where was Rosamond?

Strolling into the library, he found her poring over a book in the bay window nook; she did not see him until he pushed aside the curtains and stood before her. Then she looked up angrily.

"What brings you back this early?" she demanded without circumlocution. "I thought you were all safe at the party for two hours yet."

"It was very stupid. Don't go now—who is to entertain me if you run away?"

"I am not. You should have stayed at Mrs. Fenwick's if you wanted entertainment."

"Are you always as plain-spoken as this?"

"Yes. Dad brought me up to say what I think. I suppose it is very rude, but I can't help it."

"You think me a nuisance?"

"Well, yes, I do. Let me pass, please."

"No," declared Willis, obstinately pulling the curtain about him and standing squarely before her. "I shall do nothing of the sort. There is no reason why I should be polite to you when you won't take the trouble to be polite to me. What is it you are reading?"

"*Ivanhoe*. What did you do with my book the other night?"

"I have it safe. You are fond of reading, then?"

"Yes, of some kinds. Dad taught me that."

"Tell me about your father," said Willis with real sympathy, sitting down before her.

"There isn't much to tell," she answered half reluctantly. "Dad was—just Dad. Some people said he wasted his life. Perhaps he did. He didn't rush after money and cheat other people to get it. We were always together. I was 'Dad's boy,' and we just belonged to each other. We had nobody else—and we were so happy. We were poor, but we never minded that. We lived in an old shabby country house, with an old housekeeper to look after us. We had our books and I had my pony. I never went to school. That is one of Aunt Lucile's grievances. I've no accomplishments. I can't even behave myself properly. Dad taught me to read, and he taught me all he knew himself. Aunt Lucile says it was a dreadful way to live, but I wish I had gone on living like that. I suppose I'm rebellious—Aunt says I am. I can't help it. I don't know why I should tell you all this. I wish you had stayed at the party."

"I don't. I am very well satisfied where I am. And you are not happy here?"

"No, it is like a prison. Don't ask me any more questions. You are making me tell tales out of school. I wish you would go away and leave me in peace."

"So you said before. I don't intend to go away."

"Do you call it polite to force your company on people who don't want it?"

"Do you call it polite to let people see so openly that you don't want to be bothered with them?"

"I can't help it—it's my nature."

"Well, it's my nature to stick to a thing when I've once undertaken it. We learn that on the plains. I'm a rancher, you know, so I'm used to breaking in wild things."

The girl's eyes sparkled angrily.

"Why didn't you stay on your ranch?"

"Aunt Lucile says I came East to look for a wife."

"Oh! And have you found her?"

"Yes. I think so. But is that a polite question?"

He smiled teasingly as he saw the colour flash into her face again. She moved restlessly on the ottoman, and her black brows narrowed down into a sudden frown.

"I think you are detestable," she broke out angrily. "You are just trying to tease me and make fun of me. I suppose you will laugh at me to Aunt Lucile and Rae afterwards. I don't care if you do—I hate you."

"Thank you. May I ask, if you liked a person, would you tell him so with equal plainness?"

"I don't know—yes, I think I should. But I don't like anybody, for nobody likes me. Dad was the only one who ever cared anything for me. I'm always horrifying Aunt Lucile, but she is afraid of me for all that. She says I'm artful and designing. If she saw you here she'd be doubly sure of it. And I don't want you here, so I don't think it's fair that I should be blamed for what isn't my fault. I should think you'd go quickly after I've told you my opinion of you."

"I am going to imitate your frankness and tell you what I think of you."

"You needn't—I know already."

"No, you don't. Listen to me. You are like a thorny red rose. You are too blunt and outspoken, and you think the world and yourself are unfair foes. You give it slaps in the face and then you wonder why it doesn't use you well."

"I can't palaver over people when I don't mean it."

"That is a different thing altogether. Then you are too suspicious. You don't really dislike me half as much as you pretend you do, but you distrust me for some reason or other. Now, that isn't a sensible proceeding. You've no idea how nice I can be when I have a fair chance. However, to proceed; you are quick-tempered, impetuous, and impulsive. You hate strongly and love deeply. In short, you are just the girl—"

Willis did not complete his sentence verbally. He was suddenly overcome by a mad freak of impulse. He leaned over and kissed his black-browed vis-à-vis squarely on her red lips.

For an instant she sat as petrified. Then she sprang to her feet.

"How dare you?" she cried furiously. She dealt him a stinging slap on either cheek in quick succession, and dashed stormily past him out of the room.

Willis rubbed his tingling face ruefully. Then he picked up the rose that had dropped from her belt in her hasty exit. A thorn in it pierced his finger till the blood came, but he lifted it to his lips.

"My thorny red rose, I shall win you and wear you yet," he murmured. Then he laughed aloud. "What a fury she was in. Will she ever forgive me? What possessed me to do such a mad thing? I've lost all the ground I had gained. But that mouth of hers is irresistible."

Rae and Olive looked at him suspiciously when they came home. Privately, Rae did not believe in that headache. But she asked him very sweetly how it was.

"Better, thank you," said the hypocrite. "I think it was the sun. I hope you enjoyed yourselves."

Rae told her suspicions to her mother later on. As a result, in the week that followed, he did not see Rosamond once alone, in spite of all his efforts and ruses—perhaps all the less because of them, for Mrs. Romaine's keen eyes were wide open.

When the week was up, Willis was desperate. He resolved on a bold step. They were all bound on a picnic one morning. Willis, when he found out that Rosamond was not to be of the party, decided on his plan of action. He escorted his aunt and cousins to the train, settled them comfortably, and then got off to ask the station agent a question. The train went and left him before he had got his information.

Willis strode home exultingly and made his way straight through the dogwoods to the hammock corner. As he expected, Rosamond was there with a book.

At the sight of him she sat up and coloured violently.

"Don't be angry now," implored Willis. "I couldn't help it."

"Couldn't help what? And why didn't you go to the picnic?"

"I got left accidentally."

"I don't believe you."

"I assure you it is true—at least, about the being left. Why didn't you go to the picnic?"

"I didn't want to."

"That means that Aunt Lucile wouldn't let you."

"Well, I am much better off at home."

"So am I. Do be pleasant to me. I came back to entertain you."

"You are very kind but I'm not in need of it. I had promised myself a nice day of reading, with nothing to bother me. And now you have spoiled it—I shall have to get lunch for you."

"No, you won't. Just talk to me. Why have you kept so persistently out of my way this week?"

"Do you remember the way you acted the last time I saw you?"

"Yes. I deserved to be snubbed for that. But you know you were not really angry about that when you came to think it over, because you understood. That was not your reason for avoiding me when I sought you."

"It is all the reason I mean to give. But you know the real reason very well. I don't want to say anything about other people."

"I understand. It is just as I suspected. Well, we'll leave other people out of our thoughts and conversation. Now, what are you going to do with me? I'm here, and I'm not easily got rid of. I don't take all that trouble to be left for nothing, fair Rosamond."

The girl tapped her slender foot on the ground impatiently. Then she got up and tossed her book regretfully into the hammock.

"I shall have to do something with you. I think you are acting like an idiot and you are going to make more trouble for me. Well, I am going out to Aunt Harriet Stonewall's for a walk. If you like, you may come with me."

"I do like. But who is Aunt Harriet?"

Rosemond was tying a rather rakish sunhat on her head. She picked up her gloves with a resigned air.

"She was Dad's aunt and she lives out on the Blue Swamp Road. I go there when I get simply desperate. Things are *real* there; there isn't any sham. Aunt Harriet is old and poor and cranky, but she isn't slippery and false like some people. Besides, I can be a tomboy there if I want to be. But you'll find it poky. You'll wish you had gone to the picnic."

She led the way out of the lawn and down the village street under the elms. Neither said a word until they were well out in a deep-rutted country lane, sunshiny with buttercups. Then Willis spoke.

"One can breathe here."

The girl glanced up at him from under her low hat brim.

"Do you ever feel smothered?" she asked abruptly.

"Yes. I should have been suffocated at that picnic. Do you?"

"Often. When I have to sit in a row with Aunt Lucile and Rae and Olive and listen to their callers chattering, I feel as if I should die. I shall rise up and shriek some day. When I do talk, I am sure to put my foot in it, and when I don't, people say I'm sulky. I'm one too many in this world. That is the trouble. There is no real place for me, now that Dad is gone."

Her voice quivered away and Willis hated himself because he could not think of anything to say—at least, nothing that he would have dared to say then. Rosamond, as if ashamed of her display of emotion, turned crusty again and spoke only in monosyllables until they reached a small house half hidden among the vines and trees.

Rosamond thumped smartly at the back door. There was no response. It was the same at the front door. She tried both doors. They were locked. Rosamond wheeled about and confronted Willis in dismay.

"Aunt Harriet has gone over to Milltown. It is market day. Why didn't I think of it?"

Willis sat coolly down on the step and began to fan himself with his hat.

"What shall we do?" demanded Rosamond.

"I don't know. You got me into this scrape, and you must get me out of it."

"If you had stayed where you belonged you wouldn't have got into any scrape," retorted Rosamond thornily. "What time is it?"

"Nearly twelve. And I am hungry, Rosamond, oh, so hungry."

Rosamond, disdaining words, stalked around the corner of the house. When she returned she said abruptly, "I'll climb in by the pantry window—it isn't fastened—and open the woodshed door. It's bolted inside. I can get you something to eat then."

"Can't I climb in?"

"No, you can't. All I ask of you is to hold the barrel under the window firm for me. It wobbles."

Willis did as he was told. Rosamond squirmed through the window and disappeared. A minute later she called to him from the woodshed door.

"There is plenty to eat in the pantry. If you'll sit down in the room, I'll bring you something."

"That isn't fair," Willis objected. "I don't want you to wait on me. Just let me help you forage—I'm a good hand at it. All plainsmen are. Besides, it's ever so much jollier."

Rosamond laughed. She had a clear, pleasant laugh like a chime of bells, and she seemed to have forgotten her animosity. Willis determined to make the most of her sunny mood while it lasted.

"Come on then," she said gaily. "I can always make myself perfectly at home in Aunt Harriet's house."

She ushered him into the pantry. Search revealed a plate of caraway cookies, a box of crackers, and some cheese. Rosamond took a pitcher and went to the dairy while Willis buttered the crackers. She brought back milk and poured out a glassful for him.

"Here's to our picnic," he said, waving it gaily. "Sit down, fair Rosemond, and partake of the banquet."

"I am hungry," admitted Rosamond, making a healthy onslaught in the cookies. "But you would have had a much finer lunch at the picnic. Don't you wish you had gone?"

"Not I," said Willis, passing her a bit of cheese on his knife. "This is my ideal of a picnic—two congenial souls and bread and cheese. Those cookies are delicious. Will you ask your aunt for the recipe for me?"

When they had eaten all they possibly could, Rosamond suggested that they go fishing.

"Where?"

"Down in the pond; it's just below the field. I keep hooks and a rod here. You can cut a pole for yourself. I haven't any flies, though. We'll have to take worms, so you must dig them."

"Where are the best hunting grounds?"

“Back of the dairy. Here is a tin box to put them in. Meanwhile I’ll clean up the mess we’ve made here.”

When she rejoined him he had his pole and worms ready. He followed her down past the barn through a daisy-sprinkled lane and a ferny pasture to the pond. Rosamond led the way to a small boat moored to a willow. They got in and Willis rowed out.

“Here is the place,” said Rosamond. “Will you put on the worms, please?”

She splashed her brown hands in the water while he did so. When he was ready she took her rod and flung it skillfully.

“I shall catch nothing,” said Willis. “I haven’t fished for trout since I was a shaver.”

“Don’t talk then,” said his companion brusquely. “That is one of the cardinal rules when you are trouting.”

“But what is a fellow to do then?” complained Willis. “I’ll find it pretty dull if I’m forbidden to talk.”

“You ought to have gone to the picnic if you wanted to be entertained. I don’t mean to talk anyhow.”

Willis soon dropped his pole and leaned back in lazy contentment. He was very well satisfied to hold his tongue and do nothing but gaze at the pretty picture before him.

Rosamond sat with her profile toward him. She had taken off her hat, and her brown hair curled around her head, ruffled now and then by some stray breeze. Her cheek was flushed and her grey eyes were limpid with quiet excitement. Stray sunbeams flickered through the willow boughs above them and chased each other over her head and face, lending it all the charm of variety.

The boat floated idly on the water, and the green fields all about them tipped down to the pond. A cow came to the blue edge and looked at them with placid eyes. A squirrel chattered saucily on a willow bough, and the chirr of a locust sounded through the drowsy air.

“This is delightful,” said Willis emphatically.

Rosemond frowned.

"I had a rise just now—you've scared him off."

"Never mind. Stop fishing. You've caught enough. There is something I want to say to you. Are you in a forgiving mood just at present, Rosamond?"

"I think I am—for me. For what do you want to be forgiven?"

"My behaviour the other day. I was very much like a rude schoolboy. I know. Am I pardoned?"

Rosamond scowled.

"It was horrid of you. You wouldn't have tried to kiss Rae."

"No. I would not," vowed Willis. "Never could imagine myself wanting to. It was pure impulse in your case, I assure you. It was not premeditated."

"Well, we'll just say no more about it," was all that Rosamond would concede. "Now, you must dress my trout for me. I want to leave them for Aunt Harriet. You're not too lazy for that, I suppose?"

"I'm never lazy."

"We have been on this pond for two hours," said Rosamond severely, "and you haven't done a thing but loll back and catnap."

"I deny the catnapping. I never closed an eye. I simply looked at you the whole time. Your profile is very classic."

Rosamond blushed furiously, more at his tone than his words.

"Don't vex me again," she said shortly. "That would be a pity when I'm really feeling somewhat amiable. Row me ashore and clean these fish. It is my turn to amuse myself."

Willis prudently held his tongue and did as he was told. Rosamond left him to sit on the bank and dress her catch while she rowed herself about the pond in a skillful, easy fashion. When he had finished they went up to the house and got another lunch. They ate the rest of the cookies and demolished a dish of jelly that Rosamond discovered.

"I shall write a note for Aunt Harriet and leave it with the trout," said Rosamond, shaking back her hair. "And I shall tell her you appreciated her cookies very much."

“Can’t we wait until she comes home?” asked Willis, who was in no hurry to go.

“No, she won’t be home until dark. Besides, I want to get back before the picnickers come home, if possible. Do hurry. Are you ever going to stop eating? Do all plainsmen have such appetites?”

“No insinuations, fair Rosamond. When you come to live on the prairies yourself, you’ll learn what an appetizer the air there is.”

Rosamond deigned no reply. After securing Aunt Harriet’s little domain, they started back. Willis was inclined to lag, but Rosamond walked smartly. Her few remarks were somewhat caustic, and Willis, learning caution by experience, lapsed likewise into silence.

As they turned into the home street, Rosamond said abruptly, “You have got me into an unpleasant situation.”

“I hope not,” with anxiety.

“But you have. Aunt Lucile—” she hesitated, then went on angrily. “Aunt Lucile is always thinking things that aren’t so. She sees double. She’s always digging and probing to find out motives that don’t exist. I’m single-motived always, but she won’t believe it. I wasn’t responsible for your coming back today, but she’ll think I manoeuvred for it someway.”

“Just lay all the blame where it belongs, on me.”

“That sounds well in theory, but it won’t work in practice, with Aunt Lucile. I wish I’d never seen Acacia Villa.”

The last sentence was uttered with a passionate vehemence that startled Willis. But before he could speak, she interrupted him.

“No, I don’t want pity; it vexes me. Here we are at home. I’m going in by the dogwoods. You can go the front way. And don’t tell any fibs for my sake. Aunt Lucile won’t believe them, and it would only make matters worse.”

She was gone before he could speak.

“For a’ that and a’ that and twice as much as a’ that, I’m not sorry I ran away,” muttered the young man. “Now to face Aunt Lucile and my righteously offended cousins.”

They were sitting on the veranda as he strode up the steps whistling. Their silence was ominous. Willis had faced grizzlies and mountain cats without a tremor, but he was nervous before his injured relatives.

"Ah, you're back I see. I hope you had a good time. I got left like the ninny I was. Confound trains that leave so horribly on time."

He knew that he was not doing it well and that they were not at all deceived.

"We had a pleasant time," said Rae coldly.

"How did you amuse yourself at home, Frank?" asked Mrs. Romaine, with dangerous sweetness. She thought Rae's show of vexation poor policy. Inwardly she was furious herself, but she was resolved not to show it.

Willis remembered Rosamond's parting caution and told the truth.

"Well, I came back here and found Rosamond in the hammock. I made her entertain me, though she didn't welcome my intrusion at all. In fact, she made me feel in the way. We went for a ramble out to her aunt's place in the country and had a fishing expedition. Glad you had a good time at the picnic."

"It was very pleasant, although of course we missed you very much," murmured Mrs. Romaine. "I am glad Rosamond was home to look after you. But you must be hungry. Come and let me get you some tea."

"I know she was aching to box my ears," said Willis, when he had made his escape to his room. "I only hope my red rose will get off as well as I have done."

Whether she had or not, did not soon transpire, for at the end of three days Willis had neither heard nor seen her. He haunted every place where he was likely to meet her—the dogwood hammock, the Acacia walk, the north corner of the terrace—but in vain. He did not venture to ask openly for her, for he did not wish to arouse any fresh anger against her in his aunt and cousins.

They had forgiven him the picnic escapade, and Rae was trebly gracious to him. But on the fourth day he became desperate.

"By the way, Aunt Lucile," he said with studied carelessness, as he lounged on a rocker, "where is Rosamond? I think I haven't seen her around for a day or two."

Mrs. Romaine carefully matched the colours in her embroidery.

"Oh, Rose has gone to visit some friends of hers," she said composedly. "Some people she and her father used to know, I believe. She took it into her head to go very suddenly, and it would have been useless to oppose her. But I must admit, it was a relief to me. She is such a responsibility, with her heedless ways and disregard of all proper conventions. She will not be back for some weeks, I expect."

Willis reflected. He decided that it would be of no use to ask where Rosamond had gone or, as he believed, had been spirited to. If he compelled Mrs. Romaine to tell him, he had a shrewd suspicion that when he reached the place, he would find Rosamond gone again.

No, he would go and interview Aunt Harriet. Possibly Rosamond might have gone out to say goodbye to her. The next morning, an absurdly early hour found him again in Aunt Harriet's old-fashioned yard. He found that good lady herself diligently sweeping the garden path, with an apron tied round her head and her grey locks in a disorder the reverse of charming. Willis gravely introduced himself. Mrs. Harriet pushed up her spectacles and looked at him scrutinizingly.

"You're the young man that was here with my niece the other day?"

"I am. I hope you've forgiven us the havoc we worked in your pantry. It was all on my account. I was terribly hungry."

"It's what I should have expected of Rosamond," returned the lady grimly. "Well, what scrape has she been getting into now?"

"None that I know of. She has merely gone away for a visit. Wasn't she out to tell you so?"

"No, I didn't hear any talk of it. I haven't seen her for a fortnight."

Willis's heart sank.

"Then you don't know where she has gone?"

"I might make a guess. There is only one person that I know of that Rosamond would likely be visiting. That's her other aunt, Lydia Stormont, over at Milltown; though I don't know what'd take her there either. Ain't no love lost between them—Lydia's too much like the other one."

"Can you tell me how to find Mrs. Stormont's house if I go to Milltown?" asked Willis lamely.

"Dear me, yes. You ask some of the Milltonians for Weymouth Street, and you go down it right about to the end, where it runs out to the country, and just after you pass a brick school you'll find the house—it's a Queen Anne cottage with horse chestnuts in front of it. Say, are you Rosamond's beau?"

"Yes," said Willis unblushingly.

"Well now, I didn't know she had one. She might have told me. Well, I hope you'll find her at Milltown and tell her to behave herself. She's a good girl, is Rose, but just a mite outspoken and quick. We've all got it; it runs in the Lauder family," concluded Mrs. Stonewall complacently.

Hence it was that ten o'clock the next day found Willis stalking along an elm-shaded street in Milltown. Finally he paused before a Queen Anne cottage.

"This looks like the place," he said, cheerfully pushing the gate open. He had run away from Acacia Villa that morning on the early train, having first, such is the depravity of human nature, let his relatives to suppose that he was going on a fishing expedition.

His heart gave a throb of delight when he saw in the midst of a green wilderness to his right a slight figure picking peas. The head and face were completely enveloped in a huge sunbonnet of a startling pattern, but it was undoubtedly Rosamond. Willis leaped the garden paling and hurried across a colony of beet beds to her side. The stooping figure quickly straightened up at his approach, and a pair of startled grey eyes looked at him from the depths of the sunbonnet with a mixture of defiance and welcome.

"Rosamond," said Willis, "why did you run away?"

"I didn't. Aunt Lucile—" she began impulsively. Then she paused and a change swept over her face.

"I hadn't to ask your leave if I wanted to come to Milltown," she flashed resentfully.

"That wasn't what you began to say, Rosamond. You were going to say that Aunt Lucile sent you here to get you out of the way."

"Well, I must get the peas picked for dinner."

"Never mind the peas. I came all the way from Marlboro to tell you something, and I don't mean to be put off."

"Well, I'm listening."

She kept resolutely turned from him, and that maddening sunbonnet swallowed everything.

"I had a letter from my partner this morning with some unexpected news. Rosamond, I find that, instead of remaining here for three more months as I expected, I shall have to leave in three weeks."

The sunbonnet quivered slightly. A muffled voice in its depths remarked,

"Oh!"

"Rosamond," Willis said, coming nearer, "I want to take my bride back with me. Do you think you can get a trousseau ready in three weeks?"

He had got hold of her hands in spite of her.

"Oh, you can't care for me; I've been so horrid to you; and then Aunt Lucile—"

"Never mind Aunt Lucile. Can't you love me a little, Rosamond, when I love you so much?"

Rosamond tried to throw a note of defiance into her answer, but failed signally.

"I suppose I'll have to, for you were born to get your own way."

And then—but the sunbonnet hid it.

THE LETTER PATRICIA WROTE
(1910)

"Do I look pretty nice, Pat?" asked Sally, posing.

Patricia stopped gnawing her pen handle, laid it down carefully, and looked at Sally critically, as she was wont to look at beautiful pictures. She was curled up, Turk fashion, on the middle of the bed with a ragged portfolio in her lap and her new yellow tea gown gathered gracefully about her. Out of its billow and laces rose her thin, eager little face with the big, dark, long-lashed eyes that were looking Sally over. Patricia's only beauty was in her eyes, and she knew it. When her gaze had travelled from the tip of Sally's satin slipper to the crown of her sleek brown head, Patricia drew a long sigh and dropped her pointed chin in her hands.

"Sally Fairfax, do you know how pretty you are?"

Sally nodded. "Of course, what are looking glasses for, and men? That wasn't what I meant. Are all my ends tucked in? Is my skirt straight? And would this rose look better lower down? I'm afraid it's too high—it will make me look lopsided—but I do hate things tickling my ears."

"Sally," said Patricia again, ignoring the question, "there are times when I hate you fiercely, because you are beautiful and I am not. Just now is one of them. I would give anything in the world to be beautiful."

"Oh, I don't know," said Sally absently, craning her head over her neck to see the back of her skirt in the mirror, "beauty isn't everything. I'd be willing to give all I've got for your brains, Pat."

"No, you wouldn't. There isn't a woman in the world that wouldn't rather be beautiful than be—President. Not one! Sally, you are a little fool—you haven't an ounce of braininess to my pound—but the men would give more for that southwest dimple of yours than for all my grey matter."

"There is one who wouldn't—and the very one I am going to marry, at that!" declared Sally gloomily. "Stephen doesn't care anything about my good looks. They only make him cross because I'm frankly pleased with them. He says a woman has no business to exist unless she's clever—pictures can be bought. He's always urging me to study and improve my mind. Just as if I had any mind to improve! He knows I haven't, as well as you do. That is why I was so delighted when your aunt asked me up here for a long visit. It is jolly to be with you, Pat, of course; but I'd have come gladly even if I detested you. Anything to get away from Stephen and his everlasting theories for a breathing spell! If he knew you, Pat, he'd adore you. You're just the kind of elusive, clever, provoking creature he would worship."

"And yet, you are going to marry him!" said Patricia, frowning darkly at a photograph of Stephen on the table.

"Family arrangement, dear Pat. Stephen and I have been brought up to it. We are pretty well reconciled to the idea now. If only Stephen would give up trying to make me over, I dare say we should get on very comfortably. There are times when I think I should like Charlie Roland ever so much better—and he'd be willing to take Sally Fairfax as she is.

"Pat, you little brown monkey, why have you made me think of Stephen? It reminds me I should have written to him tonight. And now I haven't time, and he'll scold me. I can't write a decent letter anyway—my scrawls can't be a scrap of pleasure to him. But Stephen is conscientious, and he is bound I shall be conscientious, too. He writes me a great long, stupid—you'd call it clever, but it's all the same thing—epistle every week and insists that I shall do the same. I ought to have written yesterday; but I forgot all about going to the opera tonight and put it off."

"If I had a lover like Stephen Avery," said Patricia scornfully, "I'd write to him every day—I'd glory in it. Oh, Sally Fairfax, I'd love to shake you!"

"Oh, do it!—write the letter, I mean, Pat. It's an inspiration. He'll never know the difference, your handwriting is so much like mine. I've often wondered why Providence ordained it so, and now I understand. Just a note. That's all I ever send. You know all that I have been doing since Sunday."

"It would serve you right if I did," said Patricia.

"But, Pat dear, I am in earnest. You don't want me to be scolded, do you? And it would be so easy. I never put any love nonsense in them, you know. Dear me! There's the bell. Patsy, darling, bye-bye. Kiss me, and don't look so fierce. You're so horribly intense in everything! Isn't it uncomfortable? I believe I'd rather be stupid, after all."

When Sally had gone, Patricia scrambled off the bed and sat frowning before the photograph on the table. "I've always liked you," she said, shaking her finger at the likeness. "You have such a good, strong, stubborn face. You'll go on trying to make Sally over all your life and never succeed, won't you?

"I've half a mind to write that letter for Sally to you tonight, Stephen Avery—to give you something satisfying for once in your life. You would think you had wakened up Sally at last. I will, too! I'll write to you as if you were that dream lover of mine. Such letters as he has had written to him, deep down in my soul! You shall have one of them, Stephen, for the sake of that big heart of yours that dear, little, pretty, stupid Sally can't fill."

Two days afterward Stephen Avery received a plump letter addressed in the handwriting of his absent fiancée. He carried it about unread in his pocket all day; for he didn't believe in mixing love letters with business. Besides, Sally's letters kept well. In his den that night, Stephen read the letter that Patricia had written:

"Heart of my heart, I am alone tonight and I am going to write you a letter right out of my soul, out of the real me, whom nobody in the world knows, such a letter as I have never written to you before, dear love o' mine. Will you like to read it, I wonder, this page from a woman's heart? Will you only be coldly curious over it? Or perhaps only contemptuously tolerant? Or will you kiss each word as I could kiss it, just because it is to be read by your eyes?

"You will understand me because you are clever. If you were not clever, you would think all that is in this letter was just the black and white of it, and even that would puzzle you. But a woman can say anything she likes to a man like you and be sure that she will not be misunderstood.

"I am all alone—and I am not alone, because my thoughts of you are all around me like benedictions, and I sit among them enqueened because of them. Dear heart, the thought of you would make a woman better and nobler if she was in the dust of your feet. When I think of you, I am a glorious creature, loving and aspiring and reverencing with all my heart and soul and mind. I am better and higher than myself in the glamour of your love.

"The moment someone speaks of you is a golden moment to me, and I wonder what I have ever done to deserve such happiness as your love. I have done nothing—and I am nothing. It is just life's most beautiful gift to me, a gift that I take, thanking God for it and praying that it may never be taken from me, though I am not worthy of it.

"You dear one! Did I ever tell you how much I like the way your hair grows over your forehead? Almost as much as I love your crooked mouth. And that one little curl at the point always looking as if it were just going to drop down on your eyebrow but never dropping. How much I want to poke my finger through it and have it glistening there like the gold of a ring of troth! I love your hair because it is curly. But if it were straight, I should love it because it was straight. You dear one!

"Did you know that you went a'walking in the park with me yesterday? Yes, you did. We were there, together, you and me, and nobody knew it but me. It was my dear secret, and I kept it close to my heart and warmed me with it. You walked by my side under the pines, and the echo of your footsteps rang true to mine and made me dizzy with the joy of it as you tramped sturdily along. And once, when we were in a lonely road, where nobody could see, we walked hand in hand. And I told you dear, foolish things, and you listened with your dear, quizzical smile, a smile that would have made me think you were laughing at me if it hadn't been for your eyes. And we went down to the point to watch the sunset together. And you liked the music that came drifting over the harbour from a boatload of picnickers; but all the music I cared for was just in your voice saying common, sensible, everyday things. But once, just as a big white star came out over the hills across the harbour, you bent over me and said something tender that nobody else would say, as nobody else could say it; and it has made a song in my heart ever since, to which every fibre of me beats delicious time. The foolish folk around me think I was alone in the park. They don't understand; but you do.

"How I hoard up your looks and tones in my memory, as if they were jewels beyond price! When I am away from you, I count them over and revel in them. Yes, even in some cold or impatient words you once spoke. They hurt me then and they hurt me yet, but I love the pain because you inflicted it. I love better your colder, cruellest words than all the tender, loving things any other man could say. Am I spoiling you by this? I dare say. But what is the good of loving people if you don't spoil them? I like to spoil you; I shouldn't half love you if you were not spoilable.

"And you understand this too—you understand all about me, you clear-sighted one.

"And now that you have read what I have written, I leave you to read what I have not written—the dear, subtle undercurrents of thought that cannot be expressed in anything so clumsy as human speech; in the unworded messages from soul to soul across whatever may divide them.

"Heart of my Heart, I say goodnight. I go to dream of you."

"So you wish our engagement broken?" said Stephen Avery.

Sally nodded. "I know you don't mind, Stephen. Of course, all our families will have a grouse about it, but that needn't matter. If you back me up, they will soon reconcile themselves. And I'm so fond of Charlie! You'll set me free, won't you?"

"On one condition," said Stephen gravely.

"Of course," agreed Sally recklessly.

Stephen produced a letter from his pocket and held it out so that Sally might see the address and postmark. "You may marry anybody you like, if you will tell me who wrote that letter and introduce me to her," he said.

Sally had the grace to blush. "It's one of mine, isn't it," she asked guiltily.

"No, you couldn't have written that letter, Sally, any more than you could have composed a sonnet. The writing is like yours, but that is all. Own up, Sally!"

"It must be the letter I got Patricia Wyndham to write to you one night last winter when I was in a hurry. I just asked her for a joke. She never would tell me what she put in it. Pat can be so provoking by spells! What did she write, Stephen?"

"Little girls mustn't be curious," said Stephen, restoring the letter to its resting place. "Aren't you ashamed of yourself, Sally, getting another girl to write your love letters for you?"

"I did it only once," protested Sally. "And Patricia isn't like any other girl. I didn't suppose you'd ever know or care. You're not going to be nasty to her about it, are you?"

"Certainly not. But I mean to make her own up to it. Don't forget your promise, Sally."

"I'll have Pat down for my bridesmaid. But you are not to scold her, remember? It was all my doing."

When Stephen was alone he read Patricia's letter over again. When he folded it up, there was a twinkle, half of amusement, half of tenderness, in his eyes. "Little girl, you shall write me other letters like this someday!" he said determinedly.

THE HOUSE
(1932)

West Graydon people referred to it, when they remembered or mentioned it at all, as "North Pines" or "the old Conley place"; but to Alix it was always "The House"—as if there were no other house in West Graydon or in the world. No, indeed, there wasn't for Alix.

She could not remember the time when it had not held her imagination in thrall and dominated her life.

She had loved it when she was a child, living with her sister, Sadie, and their Aunt Charlotte in the little house opposite it—a lean, bare, ugly little house, so different in everything from the place across the street. The House had been very beautiful then, in still more beautiful grounds, and Alix was a born worshipper of beauty, perhaps because there was so little in her life. The House, white and stately amid its dark pines and its roses, behind the high board fence which even then was beginning to be thought old-fashioned, symbolized something for her that she could never define. She only knew she loved it as she would never love any other place.

When she was ten years old, all West Graydon was talking of the way Thekla Darrow had used Bevis Conley. Alix knew all about it when nobody suspected she knew anything or cared. She knew Bevis Conley and liked him, had liked him ever since that night two years before when she had been lost on the East Graydon road coming home from Aunt Ella's. She had been so confident that she could come home alone, and then the darkness seemed to fall so suddenly—and she didn't know which road to take at the fork—and a cold autumn wind was blowing. She was wild with terror of the falling night and the eerie wind and the huge, dark, pathless world around her. And then Bevis had come, and he had not laughed at her. He had taken her cold little hand in his warm one, and suddenly she felt safe and protected and at home. He had brought her into West Graydon, and on the way he had talked to her as nobody ever had before, as if she were grown up. He had told her he was an architect.

"All men dream," he said. "My dream is to build beautiful homes for love to dwell in. Homes to keep lovers from the biting cold and the fierce sun and the dark night and loneliness."

The words always lingered in Alix's memory. It must be a fascinating thing to build homes, to create beauty that would last for generations, beauty that would be shelter and protection and friendliness as well as beauty.

"When I grow up," she said shyly, "will you build me a house to live in?"

"That I will," Bevis had promised gravely.

In two years' time he was building a house for Thekla Darrow. For he made such changes in the old place he had always lived in that it practically amounted to building anew. Among the old pines, behind the old, vine-hung fence with its padlocked gate, The House arose in its new loveliness. Alix watched it grow with secret delight. She knew it was for Thekla, but in a sense it was for her, too, because she loved it so. Sometimes she resented the fact that Thekla was to have it. She felt sure Thekla did not—could not—never would love it as she loved it.

Perhaps that was because she did not like Thekla—Thekla, who called everybody darling but who was always saying nasty things to other girls so subtly and sweetly that she made a fool of you if you resented them. Thekla, with her red-gold hair, her brilliant white skin, her crimson mouth, her wonderful green eyes. Thekla was very beautiful, and Bevis, everyone knew, was wild about her. Aunt Charlotte and Sadie talked enough about that. Nevertheless, Alix did not like her and did not like the idea of her coming to be mistress of The House—The House that was all ready for her from cellar to attic in a fashion that made West Graydon throw up its hands in horror over Bevis Conley's extravagance. To be sure, he was doing well in his profession. But could even his income stand such lavish expenditure?

Then, a month before the day that was to have made her Bevis Conley's bride, Thekla Darrow married another man, a very rich man. And Bevis Conley had locked his house and padlocked his gate and gone to Vancouver. That was fifteen years ago, and he had never come back. Nor, so far as anybody knew, had any human being crossed the doorstep of the house he had made ready for his faithless bride. But even West Gradon people did not know everything. Alix had her own secret.

When she was fifteen she had a sudden idea. She wondered if that old key in Aunt Charlotte's bureau drawer would unlock the side door of The House. She deliberately took it and tried it. She slipped through a broken board in the fence, down the lane, and found herself in the garden—the garden that had been so lovely and was lovely still, though grown unkempt and seedy. With a wildly beating heart, Alix went past the plot of poet's narcissus on the lawn, and along an old mossy walk where the unpruned rose bushes caught at her dress, to the side door of The House, hidden from sight of anyone behind the thick pines. She had no feeling of wrongdoing. The House was hers because she loved it so. She was only entering into her own.

The key unlocked the door. Alix went in reverently, adoringly. She went all over the house. Its proportions were so right. Its rooms were so graceful. They were not just rooms, they were personalities. And filled with lovely things. But the dust lay thick over everything. The next time Alix came, she brought a duster and dusted everything—the books in the library, the dishes in the cabinet, the procession of little ivory elephants on the mantel, the gleaming mirror on the living room wall that was meant to reflect Thekla's gorgeous loveliness and now gave back only Alix's pale, flowerlike little face and great grey eyes. She went about boldly.

All her timidity and shyness vanished from her the moment she stepped over the sill. This house was hers. She had rights here.

Her whole life came to revolve around The House and the beautiful stolen hours she spent there. After dark she would open the doors and let the sweet, fresh air blow through it. She kept its vases filled with flowers. She kept the brass andirons and the silver candlesticks polished. It made her happy to do these homely services for her House. Everything she did for it was a sacrament. She loved to stand before the little round window at the curve of the stairs and watch through a gap in the pines that glimpse of a far blue mountain. She loved to sit in the library, with its arched, clematis-hung windows, reading the books or dreaming dreams. When she went into The House and shut the door, she went into a different world where the pettinesses of daily existence in the ugly Marlitt house were as if they had never been. This was her home. Here only she lived.

She never felt alone or frightened in it. The House was too much her friend. It welcomed her when she came. It longed for her when she left. And there always seemed to be some hidden meaning about it that lured her on. She was sure she would discover it some day.

She went there by twilight—by moonlight. Its rooms were so piteously lovely by moonlight. They asked her for a hundred things she could not give. All she could give was love, and she gave that in abundance.

She loved The House when she looked across at it in the early morning sunshine. She loved it on summer noons and in winter twilights. She loved it in moonlight and in rain and in falling snow. She loved it when the sunset flame kindled its western windows into a fleeting semblance of life and colour. But best of all she loved it in the darkness of night when it loomed palely clear through the gloom and beckoned to her. It was all her own then.

She resented the fact that it did not have all that other houses had. If only its windows could be lighted up! When the lights sprang up at dusk in all the other houses along the street, she resented the fact that her House had none. She hated the winter because of The House. Its heart ached with the cold then. If only fires could glow on its hearths and plumes of homely smoke drift from its chimneys! If it could only live!

Aunt Charlotte died when Alix was twenty, but she lived on with Sadie and her family. She might have gone elsewhere and earned her own living and been independent. But she found excuses for not going easily enough. Sadie, who was not strong and had four children, needed help. But her real reason was that she could not leave The House.

Once Carl Playter wanted her to marry him. She liked Carl—she even thought she might love him. It would be very nice to have a home of one's own—children. She almost decided to marry Carl. She even went to The House one night to bid it farewell. And she found she could not. The very thought was unbearable. Never to come here any more. Never to feel its welcome—to know that the dust was thick again on mirror and books and ivory elephants—to know she could have no more hours of dear, strange companionship in it. Alix laughed at herself. She told Carl she could not marry him. Sadie thought her a goose and told her she would die an old maid. Alix only smiled. They did not know.

It seemed that Sadie's prediction would come true. No more lovers came. Alix did not miss them. Year by year The House meant more to her. Year by year she knew it depended more upon her. If she went away for a visit, she was homesick until she could return to it. Nobody else might be particularly glad to see her back, but The House would. Once she was back she feasted her eyes on it until she was sated. It was seldom now that she could go to it in daylight. Sadie's children were growing up, and they had keen eyes. Only at night was it safe to slip over. Once she had dared to stay there all night and know what dawn was like in it. It hurt her. It looked so pathetic and deserted and unfriended in that chill grey light. Not even her love could warm it.

She had loved The House for fifteen years. For fifteen years it had been hers and hers only. All at once everything was changed, horribly changed. West Graydon was full of rumours. Thekla was coming home. Thekla was a wealthy widow. Bevis Conley was coming home. Thekla and Bevis were going to be married after all. They were going to live at "North Pines." Well, well, quite a fitting end to an old romance, if Bevis could forgive the trick she had played on him. He had never cared for anyone else. The Conleys were like that.

Alix felt stunned. It was unthinkable. The House could not be taken from her so. It would be too cruel, too unjust. God could not let such a thing happen. She had loved it so long when others had deserted and neglected it. She had given it her youth and the love of husband and children that might have been hers. Surely it was not going to be taken from her now. She was sick with fear and agony.

Thekla came one day. She was as beautiful as ever. Looking but little older, a slender, sinuous creature, with a blood-red flower pinned at her girdle and on her arm the slender flame of a diamond bracelet that was worth as much as The House. Bought with dead Eric Malden's money!

Lovely, exotic, charming. Beside her, Alix realized how very insignificant and unimportant she was.

Thekla wanted to look over The House. She had got a key somewhere and she contrived to give the impression, without saying so, that she had a perfect right to look over The House. She wanted Sadie to go with her. But Sadie was away, so Alix must go. At first Alix almost refused. Then she went. She knew Thekla would go anyway, and she must go with her, to protect The House from her as long as she could.

"Isn't it curious," said Thekla—Alix noticed that her voice was harder than it used to be—"I mean, coming to see a house that was made ready for me fifteen years ago? I suppose everything in it is frightfully out of date now. Fancy a rail fence like this around a house nowadays. Bevis always had an odd liking for a fence. He said it shut out the world. As if one should want to shut out the world! How out-at-elbows the place has got! The grounds so neglected . . . and so quaint and old-fashioned. But they could easily be modernized. The house itself is quite delightful . . . all it wants is a bit of remodelling here and there."

Alix, her heart bleeding drop by drop, looked at The House and saw it with Thekla's eyes. Yes, shabby and faded. The shingles on the roof were curling up. The veranda had sagged. The garden was a mass of festering weeds. But she hated Thekla for making her see it—Thekla who was going to modernize and tear up and rebuild and change and patch.

Alix had to see Thekla go into every room, laughing, exclaiming, jesting in her casual way. She paused before the tall mirror. Alix saw herself standing by Thekla and could have laughed, only she knew she was never going to laugh again. As if she could rival that brilliant creature in the heart of The House! Thekla belonged there, amid those splendours. She, Alix, was only a faded little interloper.

"You know the old story about Bevis and me, I suppose," Thekla was saying, her great eyes shimmering like green fires. "I did treat him shamefully. And I never cared for anybody else—really. But he was poor . . . he had spent everything he had on this house. And Eric was rich. Really, it would have been madness to refuse so much money, Alix. But there have been times . . . well, it's all going to come right now. Bevis has never cared for anyone but me. I'm going to make it up to him. We're both young yet. People don't grow old as quickly as they used to, except in places like West Graydon. We'll only live here in the summers, of course. Isn't it odd there is no dust? I would have supposed it would be an inch deep. But then it's so far off the street. Most of this furniture will have to be scrapped; it's hopelessly out of date. But that Tudor bedstead is quite priceless, and that old wrought-iron lantern in the hall. The cabinet of Crown Derby, too. The library is good and this mirror is charming. That east bedroom looking out on the mountain would be lovely done over in rose and grey, and the south one must be in taupe. A wall or two must be knocked out, of course."

Alix found herself speaking out. She had to speak out. She locked her hands behind her back so that Thekla should not see them trembling.

"How can you talk of changing everything, Thekla?" she exclaimed passionately. "It was made ready for you. It has waited all these years for you. Nothing should be changed—nothing!"

Thekla's desecrating laugh again echoed through the house. Her heavy eyelids, with the intriguing parallel crease in them that was considered so fascinating, flickered with amusement.

"Little sentimentalist," she drawled. "You are like Bevis in that. He used to be abominably sentimental. It bored me. I'm sure he's wiser now. What is the matter, Alix? Aren't you well?"

"No—I—I think the air is too close here," gasped Alix. She could bear no more. She must get away—at once—anywhere—out of the sight of Thekla—out of the sound of her voice. Otherwise she would strike her in the face. She knew she would. Standing there, insolent, unrepentant, claiming everything as hers by right, with her heart so cold that the red flower near it ought to die as a flower on a frosty drift. She had broken Bevis Conley's heart. She had left his house desolate. And now she was going to come back and have everything. There was no justice anywhere in the world.

Alix fairly ran down the hall and out of the door, out of The House. For the first time she was glad to be out of The House. It was desecrated. It was no longer hers. There was nothing left for her in life—nothing. Where could she go? Where could she hide herself?

Bevis Conley was coming home. He was to arrive on Wednesday night. On Tuesday night Alix stole over to bid The House farewell. After that nothing mattered. Perhaps God would be kind—even if He were not just—and let her die when she had nothing to live for.

The House looked very beautiful in the moonlight that touched it here and there through the pines with silver fingers. The old doorstep was listening for her footfall. It still welcomed her; it was still hers. But after tonight it would be hers no longer. She would never come here again. She would go out and shut the door and never reopen it. She had finished with it and the past that was linked with it.

Alix stood in the garden, rich and dim in the moonlight, and looked about her despairingly. It should not be. Thekla ought not to have The House—she had never loved it. She could never have the soul of it—she could never understand it. And she would tear it up—change it.

Alix wrung her hands together with a bitter little cry.

"Oh, dear House, you won't forget me utterly when I'm gone—all the hours we've spent together—how I've loved you! You'll always remember me a little even when Thekla has you—even though I can never come back to you again, dear, dear House."

"I'm sure it will," said a voice from the shadows beside her.

Alix looked up with a gasp. Bevis was standing there. She knew him instantly. And with the knowledge came just that same dear sense of protection and understanding that had come that night so long ago on the lonely road. In the dim, friendly light he looked no older. She forgot that it was fifteen years since he had gone away. She had no sense of strangerhood, no sense of convention.

"Oh, Bevis," she cried, "you won't let Thekla change it much, will you? Not very much. It is so perfect as it is. Don't let her change it, please."

Bevis laughed.

"I don't know what you mean, Alix. For it is Alix, I know—little grey-eyed Alix whom I found years ago in the twilight and never quite lost since. Nobody is going to change this house, least of all Thekla Malden."

"But she said—she said—"

"I understand she has been talking a great deal of nonsense," said Bevis coolly. "I don't think that I'd have chosen just this time to come home if I'd known she was to be here. But it doesn't matter much. Eric Malden's gay widow is nothing to me. Do you know why I came back, Alix? Or, rather, why I was drawn back almost against my will?"

"To see your house," laughed Alix softly. That understood itself. Of course he loved it, just as she did. But she did not resent his love. He belonged there, too.

"No, not the house. I came because your eyes called me, Alix. Those great, grey, entreating eyes of yours have haunted me all these years, after my mad infatuation for Thekla had burned itself into ashes. I thought I would come back and find out if they were still asking for something, and if it were something I could give."

"Oh!" Alix trembled. She put out her cold little hands, as she had put them out to him that evening so long ago. He enfolded them in his warm clasp.

"You seem to have been loving this house, Alix. You seem to have been coming here and caring for it. Why, I knew the house had been loved the minute I saw it."

"Oh, I've loved it so," whispered Alix.

"Then you must keep on loving it. It's your house. I may have built its body, but you've given it its soul. I wouldn't presume to claim breathing space in it, unless you'll let me. Will you give me a share in it, Alix?"

Alix wondered if anybody ever died of happiness. The House was hers—and Bevis's. It belonged to them and they to it. It would live. They would give it life. It was putting its arms around them … enclosing … enveloping.

"I've been keeping its heart beating for you, Bevis," she whispered.

ACKNOWLEDGEMENTS

Much gratitude is owed to the late Rea Wilmshurst for her dedication to finding information on hundreds of L. M. Montgomery's stories and poems. Her years of research and publications have resulted in Montgomery's work beyond the novels being read and appreciated by new generations of readers. Rea's partner, the late Dr. Andrew Silber, donated her findings to the L. M. Montgomery Institute at the University of Prince Edward Island in 2008, the outcome of which led to the publication of this and other volumes of Montgomery's stories.

Kathleen McKinnon at the Confederation Centre archives in Charlottetown, Prince Edward Island, has been of great assistance in locating and allowing access to Montgomery's original manuscripts, her scrapbooks containing mementoes, and those containing her stories and poems.

Thank you to Simon Lloyd, research librarian at the University of Prince Edward Island, for permission to photocopy Montgomery's twelve story-and-poem scrapbooks and to Dr. Philip Smith, past director of the L. M. Montgomery Institute, who generously allowed me to photocopy the Wilmshurst collection of Montgomery stories held at the Institute and to publish them in this volume. Proceeds from this volume go directly to the L. M. Montgomery Institute at the University of Prince Edward Island for the purpose of adding to and maintaining its collection of Montgomery artifacts, which are made available for Montgomery scholars and researchers all over the world to study.

To Terrilee Bulger, general manager at Nimbus, as well as editors Claire Bennet and Marianne Ward, many thanks are due for their commitment to helping L. M. Montgomery's legacy stay fresh and available to more generations of readers.

APPENDIX I

PERIODICALS IN WHICH THE STORIES WERE PUBLISHED

The place of publication of the periodical is provided in parentheses, along with the "type" of publication. If a story is in Montgomery's scrapbooks, it is noted. Stories not in the scrapbooks were discovered by Rea Wilmshurst.

The Advance (Chicago, IL; Congregational)
- "What Teddy and Gordon Saw in the Lane" (February 2, 1905; also published in *The Churchman* on December 19, 1904); in scrapbook 11

American Boy (Detroit, MI; independent)
- "A Case of Mistaken Identity" (February 1904); in scrapbook 6

American Thresherman (Madison, WI; independent)
- "Bessie's Dream" (August 1904)

Boys and Girls (Philadelphia, PA; independent)
- "A Friendship Won" (December 26, 1903; also published in *East and West*, February 26, 1910)

Boys' World (Elgin, IL, and Chicago, IL; religious)
- "The Pot of Gold at Rainbow's End" (August 25, 1906)

Chatelaine (Toronto, ON; independent)
- "The House" (May 1932)

Children's Visitor (Nashville, TN; Sunday school)
- "How Nan Went to the Party" (July 17, 1904)
- "Frank's Revenge" (May 21, 1905)
- "Discontented Dorothy" (August 6, 1905; also published in *Presbyterian Banner*, November 11, 1909)
- "Ted Williams, Sneak" (two chapters, published September 20 and 27, 1908)

The Churchman (New York, NY; Episcopal)
- "What Teddy and Gordon Saw in the Lane" (December 19, 1904; also published in *The Advance* on February 1, 1905); in scrapbook 11
- "Our Thanksgiving Day" (November 29, 1909; also published in *Hartford Courant* on November 25, 1909)

East and West (Toronto, ON; Presbyterian)
- "The Word of a Kennedy" (May 11, 1907)
- "The Winning of Frances" (April 25, 1908)
- "A Friendship Won" (February 26, 1910; also published in *Boys and Girls* on December 26, 1903)

Family Herald (Montreal, QC; independent)
- "Aunt Elmira's Thanksgiving Dinner" (October 7, 1936; first published as "Aunt Susanna's Thanksgiving Dinner" in *Housewife*, November 1907); in scrapbook 12

Forward (Philadelphia, PA; Methodist)
- "Evangeline's Father" (November 10, 1906; also published in *Wellspring* on November 10, 1906); in scrapbook 12

Hartford Courant (Hartford, CT; independent)
- "Our Thanksgiving Day" (November 25, 1909; also published in *The Churchman* on November 29, 1909)

Holland's Magazine (Dallas, TX; independent)
- "A Thorny Rose" (December 1909)

Housewife (New York, NY; independent)
- "A Platonic Experiment" (February 1904; also published in a slightly different version in *Men and Matters*, February 1900); in scrapbook 12
- "Aunt Susanna's Thanksgiving Dinner" (November 1907; published in *Family Herald* on October 7, 1926, as "Aunt Elmira's Thanksgiving Dinner"); in scrapbook 12

Men and Matters (New Orleans, LA; independent)
- "A Platonic Experiment" (February 1900; also published in a slightly different version in *Housewife* in February 1904); in scrapbook 12

Presbyterian Banner (Pittsburgh, PA; Presbyterian)
- "Discontented Dorothy" (November 11, 1909; also published in *Children's Visitor* on August 6, 1905)

Ram's Horn (New York, NY; religious)
- "The Schoolma'am's Donation Party" (October 24, 1903)

Springfield Weekly Republican (Springfield, MA; independent)
- "The Affair of the Shy Professor" (September 22, 1907, and June 27, 1936); in scrapbook 8

Sunday Magazine (New York; independent)
- "The Letter Patricia Wrote" (September 18, 1910); in scrapbook 8

The Sunday School Advocate (New York, NY, and Cincinnati, OH; Methodist Book Concern)
- "The Chiffon Dress" (June 4, 1904)

Waverly Magazine (Boston, MA; literary)
- "A Chapter of Accidents" (May 4, 1901)
- "When Hearts Are Trumps" (August 16, 1902); in scrapbook 6

Wellspring (Boston, MA; Congregationalist Sunday School and Publishing Society)
- "Evangeline's Father" (November 10, 1906); in scrapbook 12

Zion's Herald (Boston, MA; Methodist)
- "Why People Liked Amy" (May 31, 1905)
- "Dot's World" (February 28, 1906; also published in five more papers: one in 1908, two in 1909, one in 1911, and one in 1919)
- "In Place of Queen Mab" (December 4, 1907)
- "A Narrow Escape" (October 6, 1909)

APPENDIX II

COLLECTIONS OF L. M. MONTGOMERY STORIES

Two story collections were published in Montgomery's lifetime: *Chronicles of Avonlea* (L. C. Page, 1912) and *Further Chronicles of Avonlea* (L. C. Page, 1920). *The Road to Yesterday* (McGraw-Hill Ryerson) was published in 1974 and later expanded and published in 2009 by Viking Canada as *The Blythes are Quoted. The Doctor's Sweetheart and Other Stories* was published by McGraw-Hill Ryerson in 1979.

Rea Wilmshurst published eight collections of Montgomery's stories: *Akin to Anne: Tales of Other Orphans* (1988); *Along the Shore: Tales by the Sea* (1989); *Among the Shadows: Tales from the Darker Side* (1990); *After Many Days: Tales of Time Passed* (1991); *Against the Odds: Tales of Achievement* (1993); *At the Altar: Matrimonial Tales* (1994); *Across the Miles: Tales of Correspondence* (1995); and *Christmas with Anne and Other Holiday Tales* (1995), all published by McClelland & Stewart.

After Rea died in 1996, other independent Montgomery scholars published more stories. In 2018, Christy Woster and I published *After Many Years: Twenty-one "Long Lost" Stories* (Nimbus Publishing), featuring stories found by a team of scholars who continued to find more stories and poems after Rea's 1986 bibliography was published. In 2022, Dr. Benjamin Lefebvre published twenty-four Montgomery stories in *Twice Upon a Time: Selected Stories, 1898–1939* (University of Toronto Press). Also in 2022, Joanne Lebold published eighteen Montgomery stories in *Around the Hearth: Tales of Home and Family* (Nimbus Publishing).

SELECTED RESOURCES

Collins, Carolyn Strom, ed. *An Annotated Bibliography of the Stories and Poems of L. M. Montgomery*. The L. M. Montgomery Institute, 2016.

Montgomery, L. M. *After Many Years: Twenty-one "Long-Lost" Stories*. Edited by Carolyn Strom Collins and Christy Woster. Nimbus Publishing, 2018.

Rubio, Mary, and Elizabeth Waterston, eds. *The Selected Journals of L. M. Montgomery*. Vol. 1. Oxford University Press, 1985.

Russell, Ruth Weber, D. W. Russell, and Rea Wilmshurst. *Lucy Maud Montgomery: A Preliminary Bibliography*. University of Waterloo Library, 1986.

ABOUT THE AUTHOR

Lucy Maud (L. M.) Montgomery, one of Canada's best-known authors, was born in Prince Edward Island in 1874. Her career spanned fifty years and included twenty-one novels, over five hundred stories, over five hundred poems, many essays and articles, as well as volumes of journals and letters. But it is her first novel, *Anne of Green Gables* (1908), that is her best-loved work, not only in Canada but all over the world.

ABOUT THE EDITOR

Carolyn Strom Collins is the author of *The Anne of Green Gables Treasury* and other "Anne" companion books (published by Penguin Canada); she has also published companion books on *Little Women* (Viking Penguin), *The Secret Garden* (HarperCollins), and Laura Ingalls Wilder's "Little House" books (HarperCollins). Carolyn wrote two chapters for *The Lucy Maud Montgomery Album*—"Green Gables" and "The Scrapbooks"—published by Fitzhenry and Whiteside (1999), and has presented papers at many L. M. Montgomery Symposia at the University of Prince Edward Island, including pieces on the arrival of the Montgomery family in PEI (published in *Storm and Dissonance: L. M. Montgomery and Conflict*, Cambridge Scholars Publishing [2008]), the 1919 black-and-white silent movie *Anne of Green Gables*, Montgomery's stories that were based on actual events, Montgomery's publications during the Great War, Montgomery's Island scrapbooks of memorabilia, and Montgomery's poems about women.

In 2010, Carolyn helped found The Friends of the L. M. Montgomery Institute at UPEI in order to raise funds for enlarging and maintaining their Montgomery collection of publications and other materials. She also founded the L. M. Montgomery Literary Society, based in Minnesota, in 1992 with co-author Christina Wyss Eriksson. She has written many articles for the LMMLS annual newsletter, *The Shining Scroll*.

In addition to this volume of newly discovered Montgomery stories, Carolyn compiled *A Guide to L. M. Montgomery's Story and Poem Scrapbooks (1890–1940)* and edited *An Annotated Bibliography of L. M. Montgomery's Stories and Poems* (updating *Lucy Maud Montgomery: A Preliminary Bibliography*, published in 1986 by the University of Waterloo); both the *Guide* and the *Annotated Bibliography* are published by the L. M. Montgomery Institute of the University of Prince Edward Island.

She also edited *After Many Years: Twenty-one "Long-Lost" Stories by L. M. Montgomery* (Nimbus, 2017), edited *Anne of Green Gables: The Original Manuscript* (Nimbus, 2019), and edited and annotated *The Blue Castle: The Original Manuscript* (Nimbus, 2024).